THE FEAR THAT CHASES ME

K-9 SEARCH AND RESCUE BOOK 2

LINDA J. WHITE

Cover Design, June Padgett, Bright Eye Designs

First printing, June 2020

Scripture quotations are from the ESV Bible (The Holy Bible, English Standard Version) copyright 2001 by Crossway, a publishing ministry of Good News Publishing. Used by permission. All rights reserved.

White, Linda J. 1949-

The Fear That Chases Me/Linda J. White

ISBN 978-0-9912212-8-8 paperback

ISBN 978-0-9912212-9-5 ebook

❀ Created with Vellum

For Kimberly Meadows Merida,
who introduced me to Hope Reins,
and whose gentle spirit has introduced many
to the One she calls
Lord

There is no fear in love, but perfect love casts out fear.

— 1 JOHN 4:18A

1

I ANGLED myself over the bow of the jon boat and pointed at the surface of the lake we were working. "Body, Luke! Find the body!" My German shepherd leaned forward, nose working, his handsome head perfectly reflected in the glassy water, his body taut with tension. The sun glittered on the lake like gold. "Body! Find the body!"

A split second later, something popped out of the water right at Luke's nose.

My dog jumped back, his eighty-pound body jerking left toward me. I felt the boat dip and sway. I tried to catch my balance, vainly throwing up my hands, then heard Pete yell as we pitched overboard. After an inelegant splash, the chilly lake water closed over my head.

Instinctively, I kicked upward, my waterlogged boots dragging me down, my lifejacket raising me up. I burst through to the surface, gulped air, and madly looked around for Luke.

"Jess! He's fine," Pete said, laughing as he eased the boat toward me. "Look."

I shook the water from my eyes, squinted toward where he

was pointing, and saw Luke paddling to shore. Nearby, a diver surfaced, his eyes laughing behind his mask.

"How'd you stay dry?" I asked Pete.

"Practice." Pete reached his hand out for me. "C'mon, I'll help you."

Let me tell you, it is not easy to crawl back into a boat once you've fallen overboard, even if you only weigh a hundred-and-twenty pounds and you have help. The craft that appears so flat and low when you're standing on land suddenly looms like a skyscraper when you're in the water next to it.

Pete grabbed my hand, my life jacket, then my belt, and hauled me aboard like a tuna, rolling me dripping wet into the bottom of the boat.

"Thanks," I gasped, trying to reclaim my dignity. That's when I heard the clapping, cheers, and laughter of the rest of the team onshore. Apparently, I was today's entertainment.

"Congratulations, Jessica! You've been baptized," Tim Dowling said, helping drag the boat ashore. Tim, a water-search expert based in New Kent, Virginia, was about forty, sandy haired and blue-eyed, with the shimmering smile of a natural-born beach boy. "You're not the first to get dunked."

"It surprised me." Someone handed me a towel, and I dried off my face. Across the way, my wet dog stood panting at the edge of the water. Then he threw himself down on the sand and rolled over on his back, his legs kicking skyward. "Luke!"

He got up and shook, flinging wet sand on everybody around him. They were good-natured about it. Search-and-rescue people have a lot more to worry about than a little sand.

Luke and I were at Lake Anna learning to do water searches. Our team, Battlefield Search and Rescue, had been called out in the fall to look for a four-year-old missing at a campground near another lake. Luke and I responded and searched for two days. I hoped we'd find the little guy tucked into some nest of leaves he'd been smart enough to make.

But no. And because Luke and I weren't trained in water searches, the search commander sent us home. It took divers two weeks to find the boy's body. That was two weeks of agony for his parents. I felt their pain.

I vowed that when it warmed up we'd learn to do water searches, despite my aversion to finding cadavers. And here I was, shivering on this beautiful spring day, having just been dunked by my dog.

"He couldn't help it, Jess," my friend Emily said.

I raised my eyebrows.

"A fish jumped up at him. I saw it. Must've thought Luke's nose was a bug." She smiled at me.

I was going to miss these people when I moved.

That was the first time I'd actually admitted to myself that I was moving. But here's the deal...my landlord's girlfriend was moving in with him in two months and I'd agreed to be out before then. With my friend Nathan Tanner newly married and Scott Cooper all wrapped up in his FBI job again, I'd begun feeling it was time to move on. Being a single woman in a married world wasn't easy.

I'd been looking south and east toward Virginia Beach. But how could I maintain my business if I left Virginia's Piedmont area? I did private investigations for lawyers, which meant chasing cheating husbands, finding disappearing assets, and uncovering assorted (and sordid) secrets. Occasionally I got involved with outright criminal cases, and right now most of my clients were from Northern Virginia or Richmond.

The answer came to me one day while I was running. I'd gradually begin to refuse cases from Northern Virginia, increase my Richmond workload, and then begin drumming up business in Williamsburg with an eye toward Norfolk. With the Internet, that was entirely doable.

"What's the draw of the ocean?" Nate asked me when I told

him my plan. Normally mild-mannered, his eyes were practically blazing.

"I love the shore. I grew up on Long Island, remember?"

We were sitting at an outdoor café in Charlottesville with Laura, his new wife. My dog, Luke, and Nate's springer spaniel, Sprite, lay sprawled under the table.

I picked up my sandwich, a grilled "Rachel"—warm turkey, Swiss cheese, and coleslaw on rye. Nate didn't budge. He just stared at me with those searchlight blue eyes.

I guess Laura decided to mediate by changing the subject. "Except for falling out of the boat, how did the water-search training go?" she asked.

I began telling her all about it, because you know, I really didn't need Nate lecturing me about how to run my life.

"I learned a lot," I said. "I spent several days acclimating Luke to boats. Teaching him to stay still, be calm, first on land, then in a pond. And he did okay until that fish jumped out at him."

Nate still wasn't eating. In fact, he'd leaned back in his chair, studying me.

"How do they smell a body through the water?" Laura asked.

"Bodies release gases and oils that float to the surface," I explained. "But it's tricky. Currents can take the scent downstream, or once it reaches the surface, the wind may blow it another direction. It's hard to figure out where a body might be. So what we're trying to do is narrow the search field for the divers."

"You always work with divers?"

I didn't know the answer to that question. I glanced at Nate, who remained immoveable. Stony Man, like the mountain I'd climbed near Luray.

I responded despite my ignorance. "Pretty much, unless the body is caught up in a tree or on the shore. Then, obviously, you don't need divers."

"Can the divers see underwater or do they take lights down?"

"They search by feel unless the water is unusually clear." I took a big swig of sweet tea and crunched some ice. "Right, Nate?" I was determined to break his silence.

He leaned forward, resting his forearms on the table. "Yep, that's the way it's done." He tilted his chin. "Thing is, those bodies, they sometimes try to hide—behind stumps, in caves, down in pits. Some of 'em travel on, like they'd find another place calmer, better for 'em. They get in the slipstream and go down river over the rocks. They slide over a low-head dam and then find themselves in a maytag. Y'know what a maytag is, Laura?" He kept looking at me.

"A washing machine?" his wife responded.

"It's that, but it's also that place below a dam where the water falls over and starts a circulation." He gestured with his hands. "Bodies get caught in it, going up and down, up and down, rising and falling, caught in that whirlpool, that same old pattern. They cain't never get themselves out, not by themselves."

I had stopped chewing.

"Thing is, it's deceptive," he said, continuing. "The water above a low-head dam is smooth as glass. Peaceful. Looks like a good place to fish. So folks get out there and find themselves drifting toward the dam. The next thing you know, they're caught in the maytag. Helpless. When all they wanted was peace." Nate picked up his sandwich. "Cain't tell a body what to do, though." He took a big bite. "Some got to learn their same ol' pattern don't accomplish much."

I tightened my jaw against his words.

2

DESPITE OUR CONFLICT, when moving day came it was Nate who was my biggest help. He picked up the truck I'd arranged to rent and recruited Laura and Cooper. A friend of Scott's, another FBI agent named Jim, came with him. Even my landlord trudged downstairs to pitch in.

Many hands make light work, but to be honest, I felt uncomfortable with all the attention.

"I didn't know you were moving until Nate called me," Scott said. His frown conveyed a mild protest.

"Hey, grab the other end of this will you?" I said, deflecting his comment.

Scott paused, then took hold of the couch. "You still going to be doing private investigations?"

"Yes. I'm just trying to expand my client base toward Tidewater."

Across the room, Nate carried one of the boxes I'd packed. I thought he did pretty well with his artificial leg. It had been nine months since the fire that took his leg, nine months since all our lives were changed. He used a cane or crutches when he got tired, or sometimes a wheelchair at his home. Although he had not resumed actual searches, most of which were in rough terrain, he was still training director of Battlefield SAR and often acted as search commander.

Nate knew better than anyone how to logically load my stuff, how to keep the truck balanced, how to stay efficient. He took charge and we were done in less than two hours.

I had found a small, three-bedroom house on five acres between Richmond and Williamsburg to rent. Nate and the others insisted on driving down there with me and unloading my earthly possessions. As we entered the long, forest-lined drive-way, I tried not to notice how much it reminded me of Nate's place. The woods, the driveway, the little cottage-type house in a clearing on a rise, all felt like Nate's home.

To be clear, Nate and I had never been romantically involved. I thought of him as somewhere between a brother and a father— the brother I never had and the father I'd lost. Not a boyfriend. In fact, I was the one who'd reunited him with his long-lost love, Laura. Three months later, they married. I actually questioned Nate when he told me their plans. "Isn't that a little quick?"

He had grinned. "When she came back into my life, it was like we had never been apart. I lived without her all those years. I'm not wasting another minute."

The two of them were like teenagers, always holding hands, inseparable. Moving so far away, I had resigned myself to the fact we'd inevitably lose touch.

My new house had a brick walk, a porch large enough to fit a rocker, and a large, fenced area in the back. Inside there was wood laminate flooring and an open floor plan, the living room leading straight to the kitchen and dining area. One bedroom had an arched window. That would be my office. Which left the master bedroom and one guest room and a screened-in back porch.

Everybody loved the house. Honestly, it was very homey.

Once everything was inside I expected them to leave, but no, they kept going. Laura started organizing the kitchen. Jim was apparently some kind of tech expert, and he and Scott began setting up my office. That's when Nate motioned me outside.

I noticed he grabbed his cane as we left the house and was limping as he led me out and around to the side of the house with no windows. He was hurting after a long day. I also knew what he was up to—we had a conflict to clear up.

"It's a good house," he began.

Of course he would like it.

"I'm sorry I got hot. I'm just worried about you going off on your own like this."

"Why?"

"You're leaving behind the ones who care about you."

I shrugged. "I've got Luke."

Nate nodded. "Dogs are good. But you need people too. People who can help you figure things out."

How could I tell him that I felt awkward, like a third wheel, now that he had Laura? Scott and I had gone out a few times, but he canceled the last three dates because something last minute came up at work. Hey, I can take a hint! In fact, I was surprised he helped me move.

Even my landlord was shoving me out in favor of his new relationship.

I figured I was just meant to be alone, and better to be alone in a place I wasn't reminded of it all the time.

I touched Nate's arm, feigning calm resolve. "I appreciate your concern, but I need something new, Nate. A fresh start. This will be good for me. I'll join the SAR group down here. I'll make friends. I'll be fine."

He frowned, his eyes sad, but he didn't argue with me. Instead, he put his hands on my shoulders, kissed the top of my head, and then wrapped his arms around me in his signature hug. Honestly, it felt good.

I followed him back inside and thanked the others. "I can get the rest of it. You guys all need to get home."

Outside, Scott lingered while the others got in their vehicles, then he hugged me. He seemed troubled. "I'm sorry," he said.

"For what?"

"Sorry I didn't call you more often. Sorry I was so wrapped up in my work."

I didn't answer him. This was not the time to have that discussion.

He glanced around. "You gonna be okay out here all by yourself?"

"Of course!"

"You have a weapon?"

"My pistol."

"You don't want a shotgun?"

"No."

He blew out a breath and hesitated, as if he were debating whether to argue with me. Then he gave me one more quick hug and got in his car. I waved goodbye as they all drove away, a big smile plastered on my face and a lump the size of a basketball in my throat.

As the last taillights disappeared down the lane, I turned and went inside. Luke, who had been playing with Sprite while we worked, nudged my hand and then plopped down with a thump, exhausted.

Automatically, I walked into my office, stood over my computer, and booted it up. I blinked back tears as it slowly came to life. Everything was blurry. I used the bottom of my grimy T-shirt to wipe my face. I closed my eyes and took a deep breath. When I opened them again, I stared into the blackness outside that pretty, arched window. I was alone. Completely alone. I could hear the sound of panic marching toward me.

Quickly, I sat down and redirected my focus. I checked my

website, then opened up my email app. There they were—new emails for a new start.

A lawyer in Richmond working on a divorce case wanted me to do an asset search. He thought the husband was hiding something. A mother in Williamsburg wondered if I could find her daughter who had run away at age sixteen over twenty years ago. And a company in Williamsburg wanted a background check on a woman they were considering as their new CEO.

But what interested me most was in the fourth email from a man who was wondering if his middle-aged brother's suicide was really that. There was a suicide note, a pile of debt, a grieving widow, and a body with what looked like a self-inflicted gunshot wound. What made Sam Larson disbelieve the death certificate? I could hardly wait to call him.

Despite my enthusiasm for that job and my fatigue, I slept fitfully that night until Luke climbed into bed and stilled my restless legs with his body weight. The next morning, he woke me with a slurp of his big tongue.

"What?" I ruffled the thick fur on his neck. "You think it's time to get up?"

I remembered the email from Sam Larson. I swung my legs out of bed and checked my watch. It was too early to call him, so I got dressed, laced my shoes, and took Luke out for a run. We ran up the driveway to the road, then back and around the perimeter of the woods. The morning air was sweet and cool. I took a deep breath and filled my lungs. The birds chattered around me, some with beautiful songs and others kind of squawky. Even the birds reminded me I was single.

No matter. This was home, and I could make it on my own. Lots of people did.

Back inside I made coffee, poured a bowl of cereal, and sat down at the computer. I emailed the lawyer on the assets case a questionnaire, cited my fees, and sent it off. I did the same for the Williamsburg company looking for background on the potential

CEO. I rejected the case of the woman searching for her long-lost daughter. Yes, her problem plucked my heartstrings, but I knew if you don't find missing people quickly, the chances of finding them are minute. My hourly rate could bankrupt her and still yield no results.

Then I called Sam Larson. He lived in Glen Allen, just north of Richmond. We mutually decided it would be best to meet some distance away from there. I suggested the Cracker Barrel in Mechanicsville at ten.

I had no sooner hung up with Larson than my phone rang. I answered it. "Hello?"

"Miss Chamberlain? Lottie Thomas here."

Lottie Thomas. My brain searched for an ID.

"The mother of Tamara Thomas."

The missing girl. Got it. I steeled my resolve, straightening my back.

"I'd like you to reconsider—"

"Mrs. Thomas," I said, interrupting. Then I explained about my hourly rate, the probability of finding her daughter, and the process PIs go through to find someone. "If your daughter had disappeared in the last month, even the last six months, I'd certainly consider it. But twenty years. I couldn't, in all good conscience, take your money given the miniscule chance I could find her."

Silence followed. Then Mrs. Thomas spoke. Her voice was soft, southern, and country. Like Nate's. "Tammy was our only child. When she disappeared, it broke my husband. He died six months later of a massive heart attack." She paused. "Two months ago, I was diagnosed with advanced ovarian cancer. The doctors say I have, at most, six more months. This is my last chance to find my daughter, or at least find out what happened to her. Miss Chamberlain, you are my last hope. My very last hope." She paused again. "I have some savings. Who am I going to leave that to? I would like to spend that, Miss Chamberlain, on the search for my daughter...on you. Please, Miss Chamberlain. Please at least come and talk to me."

After that, how could I turn her down? I mean, there is a heart beating in my chest. I agreed I'd meet her at 1:00 p.m. at her home near Williamsburg after my meeting with Sam Larson.

3

SAM LARSON'S BROTHER, Bob, was forty-eight when he died. A home appraiser, his business was doing well, but he'd gotten suckered into a bad investment deal, one "guaranteed" to make 20 percent in the first year. "Bob was embarrassed he'd fallen for it, and his wife was livid," Sam said. "They had a vehicle repossessed and nearly lost their home. Their kids had to drop out of private school. She," by which he meant Bob's wife, "even had to sell some of her jewelry. About the only thing left was a big, fat, life-insurance policy."

"No suicide clause?" I asked.

"It was no longer in effect."

I studied the man across from me. In his early fifties, Sam was fit and trim, with a receding hairline and a five o'clock shadow. He didn't look like the type to be paranoid. "What makes you think Bob didn't kill himself?"

Sam leaned forward. "We talked a lot, even though his wife and I didn't get along. I knew what Bob thought about death. After all, he'd been through it."

I raised my eyebrows.

Sam reacted, as if realizing he'd left something out. "Bob's first wife, Jean, died of cancer five years ago. It was a long, drawn-out illness that took its toll on him, on his bank account, and on his business. He married Susan just six months later." Sam shook his head. "I told him it was too soon. But he insisted they were in love."

A shimmer went through my gut. "The kids are from his first marriage?"

"No, they're Susan's."

"Bob had no kids of his own."

"That's right."

"Who's the beneficiary on his life-insurance policy?"

"I suspect Susan is now. Of course, it had been Jean."

"And you're the successor beneficiary?"

He bristled. "Look, it's not about that." He took a moment to calm down. "I probably am. I don't know. And I don't care." He shook his head. "What I do care about is justice. And the truth."

I stared into his eyes, reading his sincerity. "I believe you. Has the insurance company paid out?"

He shook his head. "They're stalling."

Good. That would give me some leverage. "What happened to Susan's prior marriages? Was she divorced?"

My question stopped Sam short. "I don't know."

I decided not to say anymore. "Did you bring the documents we talked about?"

Sam reached into his attaché case and pulled out Bob's death certificate, the medical examiner's report, and the police report. "They're my only copies."

"All right." I pulled out my phone and began scanning them.

He passed some other printouts over to me. "Those are some of Bob's neighbors, a couple of realtors I know he worked with, some friends, our relatives—my sister and some cousins and my aunt—and the church he and Jean used to go to."

"He stopped going?"

"I don't think Susan's into religion. Although that's where he met her."

How odd. Had she been at church trolling for a sucker? I kept scanning.

When I was done, we left the restaurant. "I'll get back to you, soon," I said, as I shook his hand. Then Sam climbed into his Toyota Camry and left.

I could hardly wait to get going on his case. But it was nearly eleven-thirty, and I'd promised Mrs. Lottie Thomas I'd come by about one o'clock and talk about her daughter.

Miss Lottie lived in a brick rambler on a quarter-acre lot in a community that looked like it was built in the sixties. The yard looked neatly trimmed, and the back was fenced in with chain link. If I had to guess, I'd bet she'd lived there her whole adult life.

I knocked on the door and she answered, a tiny, wispy-haired woman dressed in a housecoat. A small, short-haired terrier with a gray muzzle barked as she opened the storm door.

"You must be Miss Chamberlain," she said in a voice that was surprisingly strong. She looked down at her dog. "Tiger, hush!"

"Yes, ma'am." I stepped inside the house, right into the living room, dominated by a large-screen TV. Next to it, a large picture of a dark-haired, dark-eyed girl hung on the wall. A pretty girl with a nice smile.

Miss Lottie saw me looking at it. "That's her. That's Tamara. That was the last picture we had taken of her."

Two identical recliners, side by side with a lamp table in between, sat across from the TV. One of the recliners, I knew, was now perpetually empty, and I wondered what it was like to lose a mate you'd had for years. Was it worse than losing your father? Worse than never being married? How did Miss Lottie make it all on her own?

Shaking off my thoughts, I moved over to the portrait, took out my cell phone, and took a picture of it.

"Can I get you some iced tea?" Miss Lottie asked.

"I really don't have time," I said.

"Oh, it's already made. Have a seat." She gestured toward the recliner on the right. I was still standing, trying to figure out how to escape, when she returned and handed me the glass of tea and a napkin. Then she put out a coaster and sat down in her chair.

What could I do? I sat down and sipped the drink. Of course it was sweet tea. Although there were a lot of what Nate would call "come-heres" in the state, a true Virginian would make sweet tea. I could feel myself being sucked in.

I needed to distance myself. "Miss Lottie," I began, "I'm afraid it's just been too long since your daughter disappeared for me to be able to help you."

She smiled and looked at me with soft gray eyes. Her skin was thinning, and the rims of her eyes were almost translucent. I wondered for a moment how old she was and how she'd face cancer on her own.

My upfront disclaimer did not deter her. "My daughter," she said in her soft southern voice, "was a sweet girl. But she had a stubborn streak. We had rules, you know, about dating and boys and drinking and smoking. We went to church, taught her right from wrong, but she had to try things. I guess she had to figure out who she was apart from us."

Her little dog jumped into her lap. She absentmindedly stroked him as she spoke. "My husband, he had a soft heart. He couldn't bear to punish her, told me just to be patient with her. He was too soft in my opinion, and in the end, that soft heart of his just got broke in two."

I opened my mouth, about to interject, but she just kept talking.

"One night, it was a Sunday, September the ninth, we said goodnight to her and went to bed. She was always staying up late, studying, talking to friends, the phone cradled on her shoulder. It wasn't unusual for us to leave her alone downstairs. This time, though, when we came down in the morning, she wasn't there. She wasn't downstairs, she wasn't in her room, she wasn't anywhere.

"First I was angry. Frank, that's my husband, he told me to calm down. She'd show up sooner or later. Then he kissed me and went off to work. I couldn't help it. I fretted all day. I fretted as I did my laundry, fretted as I cleaned, fretted until school opened. I called them and found she hadn't shown up for classes. And then I got mad.

"I called her friends. I called their mothers. I called the library and the restaurant where she liked to hang out. Finally, I called Frank on his lunch break. 'Frank,' I said, 'it's time to call the police.' 'Oh, Lottie,' he said, 'give her a little room. She'll come back.'"

Lottie looked at me, her mouth a straight line. "Do you think, Miss Chamberlain, that seventeen years, eight months, and twelve days is enough *room*?"

I took a sip of sweet tea. "Did you call the police anyway?"

"That night when Frank got home, I made him call. I forced him to report her missing. The sheriff's deputy came and took down information. A detective talked to us, then called around to a bunch of her friends and interviewed her teachers and her field-hockey coach. And that was about the end of it."

"Did they track her cell phone, or download her contacts?"

Miss Lottie frowned at me. "Honey, this was 2001. Nobody had cell phones. No teenagers, anyway."

"She disappeared on September 9, 2001?" My heart beat hard.

"Yes. And you know what happened on September 11. You think anybody paid attention to a runaway teen after that?"

I swallowed and took a deep breath.

I considered interviewing the most important skill in my quiver, and to be honest, I'm good at it. Yet here was Miss Lottie, taking me places I never meant to go, wrapping my heart in her silken threads.

I had to escape. I shifted in my chair, about to get up.

Miss Lottie reached over and laid her hand over mine. "Since that day, you are the only one who has tried to help me at all. The only one. I'd been praying for someone to help me find Tamara ever since I found out about the cancer, and I believe God sent you to me."

Oh, good grief. I took a deep breath. I was pretty sure I was no one's answer to prayer.

I was about to tell her I had to go but that seemed cruel, even to me. So against my better judgment, I began asking questions about her daughter—details, like height, weight, interests, skills, the names of her friends, the names of her teachers. She excused herself, left the room, and came back with a file full of lists of important facts and contact information, some of it updated, on Tamara's friends and other people who knew her. She smiled and handed it over to me.

I thumbed through that file. I really needed to get out of there. Then she dropped a bombshell. "Now you should know, Tamara, she was adopted."

I startled. That fact seemed too important to save for last.

"Frank and me, we went all the way to Europe to get her, to Romania. We had tried for years to have a baby of our own, but I never did get pregnant. So we saved and saved and I started working at Walmart for extra money. Finally, we had enough, and we got Tamara."

"How old was she?"

"Three, and she'd been in the orphanage since she was born. I sometimes wonder if that's why she had such a hard time figuring out who she was. But thank the Lord, I knew who *I* was —I was a mother and I loved that little girl just as if I'd had her. And Frank did too. Much as it hurt at the end."

I drove away from Miss Lottie's house cursing myself for not staying on top of that interview, for letting her lure me into something I knew would be a fruitless pursuit. Later that day, Nate called, and when I told him about it, instead of sympathizing, he said, "She's in your life for a reason."

"Seriously? Is that true for every person I meet? The guy at the gas station? The checker at the grocery store?"

My sharp tongue hadn't softened at all.

4

It rained that night, hard, and by the next morning a heavy fog had set in. The trees, oaks, poplars, dogwoods, and Virginia pines were shrouded in gray. I couldn't even see where the driveway broke into the clearing. A line from a Carl Sandburg poem I'd read in high school jumped into my head. "The fog comes in on little cat feet." Perfect description.

I stepped outside to let Luke out. Raindrops dripped off the branches of the trees. The wind was absolutely still, but a scampering squirrel set off a downpour as tree branches shook with his energy. The beauty of the day calmed my soul.

I'd set up a series of interviews that day regarding Shaleen Boyer, the potential CEO. She was a Virginia native, a graduate of the prestigious McIntire School of Commerce at UVA. I had a lot of contacts from which to choose.

The night before I had run my usual searches on the Internet. Bankruptcy filings, marriage and divorce records, criminal complaints. So far, Shaleen looked squeaky clean.

I'd done the same thing on Bob Larson, but that was a different story. I found his bankruptcy, the repo of his car, his lousy credit rating. What's more, I'd found dirt on his second wife. She'd been married at eighteen, divorced at twenty, remarried at twenty-three, had two sons, and then that husband had died of anaphylactic shock. He'd ingested something to which he was highly allergic.

Was Susan a black widow? Had she killed that second husband? Had she killed Sam for his life insurance?

I decided to start by interviewing the detective who'd worked Sam's death.

DETECTIVE HAP CARROLL agreed to see me, but clearly, he was annoyed. "Of course, I looked at the wife. It was an unattended death. But she had an alibi."

"What was that?"

"She was at their church at some meeting." He opened the file on his desk and looked at a paper inside. "At a women's ministry meeting planning an upcoming luncheon."

"What was the name of that church?" He told me, and I continued. "And she found the body when she got back?"

"That's right. She said she screamed her head off." Carroll tapped his pen on his desk. "Look, I've known her for years. Her father was a cop in Newport News. She didn't do nothing."

He knew her? I filed that fact and rose to leave. Carroll did too. He was not much taller than I am, but his gut spilled over his belt like the Niagara River over the Falls. I wondered what the sheriff's department rules on fitness were.

I can be so judgmental.

I thanked him and left.

My interviews on the potential CEO went well. Shaleen Boyer got high marks for integrity, work ethics, and compatibility from all those I'd interviewed. I suspect if there were an evening-gown component, she'd score highly on that too. Some people have it all together.

After documenting all the interviews, I figured I'd make one more Internet check and then I'd be ready to report back to that company, close her case, and collect my fee.

I got caught up in a traffic jam on Interstate 64 and began running late. I needed to get home, let Luke out, change, exercise him some, and then leave again. Our first meetup with the new SAR group I hoped to join was tonight.

Hampton Search & Rescue covered the whole Hampton Roads area—Williamsburg, down to Norfolk and Virginia Beach, and then across the Chesapeake Bay Bridge Tunnel to Virginia's Eastern Shore. The reality was, of course, that any SAR group in Virginia could get called out to assist on any search, but that was their primary territory.

I'd never gone out on a search with them, but Tim Dowling, the guy who saw me dumped overboard ignominiously at Lake Anna, was part of the group. Training director, just like Nate.

We were meeting at a park about twenty minutes from my house. After I exercised Luke, I put on my blue cargo pants and a long-sleeved shirt. I laced up my boots and grabbed my SAR gear. Luke, of course, went crazy when he saw that. As I walked out the door with him, I considered leaving my place unlocked like most people do in the country. Who, after all, would think they could venture down that long driveway undetected?

But at the last minute, I locked it. I put Luke in his crate in the Jeep, closed the liftgate, and drove off.

The SAR meetup was in a county park. The directions said meet at Pavilion B, a covered picnic structure. I spotted it easily by the number of SUVs, liftgates up, parked nearby.

Tim Dowling walked over to greet me as soon as I got out of my car. "Good to see you, Jess. Come on over and I'll introduce you."

"What's the schedule?"

"We'll do some obedience, and then we'll talk."

"Great!" I let Luke out, leashed him up, and followed Tim up the rise to the pavilion. He introduced me to the nine handlers clustered there and invited me to tell the folks a little about myself.

My mind instantly seized up. What was I supposed to tell them? That I'd left a job out of guilt and shame and adopted Luke because I'd felt responsible for his owner's death? That Luke and SAR were the best things that had ever happened to me? That through them I'd met Nate and he had introduced me to something so beautiful and true it had begun to heal me? But that, inexplicably, I'd run away again?

My throat clenched. I swallowed hard. "Hi, I'm Jess and this is Luke. He's almost four and is cross-trained for HRD and live finds. I'm hoping we can get water-search certified. I've just moved to the area, about fifteen minutes from here. I have about five acres, and a lot of it is wooded. Maybe we can do some training out there sometime." I tossed the conversational ball back to Tim.

"Sounds interesting," he said, and my heart stopped racing as the spotlight moved away.

That first meetup was fun. I liked the dogs—four Labradors, two Aussies, a border collie, a Malinois, and a couple of shepherds. Tim had a solid-black, female shepherd. The other handlers seemed nice and the dogs were well-behaved. At the meeting, I found they had scheduled a water-search training day for the coming Saturday.

Afterward, I drove away feeling encouraged, so encouraged I decided I had the energy to finish up the Shaleen Boyer case. I searched the Internet once more, concluded Miss Boyer was a saint, wrote up my report, and emailed it in along with my invoice.

Case closed. On to the next one.

A GRAY DAWN greeted me the next day, clouds hanging like thick cotton over the trees. I got up, made a cup of coffee, and checked my email. Two more cases had come in the day before, both from women suspecting their husbands of cheating. I emailed my usual questionnaire back to each of them. Marriage was just like my coffee, I concluded—dark and bitter.

Immediately, an image of Nate and Laura jumped into my head. So far they were two lovebirds, each trying to outdo the other in kindness. How long would that last?

After catching up on email and what news I could stomach, I slipped into some shorts and a T-shirt, laced on my running shoes, and Luke and I went for a run. Up the driveway and back, around the cleared area, then up the driveway again. When we finished, I showered and changed into semi-professional looking clothes. I pulled my long, sandy-colored hair into a low ponytail, fed Luke, and left.

My mission today was to look further into the death of Bob Larson. Rather than walk straight at the target, though, I thought I'd nose around places where Susan had lived. Then I'd go by the church and, if I had time, check Bob's former coworkers. Was Bob concerned at all about his wife? After that, I'd be ready to talk to Susan's current neighbors and then, finally, Susan.

Somebody was bound to talk.

Before her marriage to Bob, Susan lived in West Point, Virginia, where her second husband, Tyler Burns, was an insurance agent. I had gotten the police report on his death. Mr. Burns was tragically allergic to shellfish. I say "tragically" because the man lived all his life in Tidewater Virginia, home to oysters, clams, and the sweet and succulent Chesapeake Bay blue crabs. Missing out on all that delicious dining, well, that was a tragedy in my book.

The night he died, he'd had dinner with his wife at Tommy's, a down-home restaurant in an old house on the main drag. Tommy, the owner, knew about Tyler's allergy, according to the police report, and was always careful to make sure the surf 'n turf and crab-cake dinners stayed well away from Tyler's. But Tommy was at home sick that day. Was it possible Tyler's plate was accidentally contaminated with seafood by the substitute chef?

Furthermore, I wondered why Tyler wasn't carrying an epinephrine syringe, the antidote to allergic reactions.

The police didn't ask that question but a local reporter did, and I found the answer in his story online. Tyler normally did carry epinephrine, but the night he died he'd changed his sports coat at the last minute before leaving home, and the pen had been left in the first coat.

That's what his grieving widow Susan said.

How'd she get him to do that, I wondered?

5

THE TOWN of West Point sits at the confluence of the Pamunkey and Mattaponi rivers. Joined together, they become the York River, a major shipping channel flowing into the Chesapeake Bay. As I drove over the impressive Coleman Bridge, I could imagine how beautiful the place must be on a bright, sunny day.

This was not that day. Instead, gray clouds merged with gray water until the whole world seemed ready to cry. I headed for the only places I could think of that might be gossipy—the local visitors' center, the library, and McDonald's. (Note to self: Try to take cases that involve towns with legitimate local coffee shops.)

Since it was still a little early and my other targeted places weren't open, I pulled into McDonald's. Sliding into my relaxed, chatty persona, I ordered a bacon, egg, and cheese biscuit and a large coffee.

"How y'all doin' today?" I asked the order taker.

"I'd be better if I weren't openin' three days in a row," she said. "You want cream and sugar, honey?"

"Yes, lots."

In the nearly empty dining area, I took a seat near a group of senior citizens and perked up my ears. I mean, you never know what you're going to pick up. After twenty minutes, I knew more about what fish folks were catching and the possibilities of a good crab harvest this year than I cared to know. I decided to be more direct.

"Hey," I said, approaching the table where three men sat. "Any of y'all know where a guy named Tyler Burns lived? I've got an address but I can't find it. I've been working on my family genealogy and found out he was a cousin." I was getting pretty good at putting on a southern accent.

The three men—grizzled, gray, and paunchy—looked at each other, then looked at me. "Sit down," one of them said, gesturing toward an empty chair.

"Which side? Your momma's or your daddy's?" one guy asked.

I thought quickly. "Momma's. By the way, I'm Jen Baker." I shook hands with each of them.

"Where you from?" asked a man wearing a red ball cap with the curly "W" of the Washington Nationals.

"Fairfax." I might as well have said "New York." Fairfax was a different world to these guys. I quickly added, "Love the Nats, by the way. I think they're going to go all the way this year. Again."

The man in the hat nodded.

The man on his right, a gray-whiskered guy dressed in a tan, long-sleeved work shirt, said, "You 'llergic to shellfish?"

I acted surprised. "In fact, I am!"

A general grumbling followed. "What?" I asked.

"It's what killed him." The Nats fan leaned back and hiked up his pants. "Everybody know'd he was 'llergic to shellfish. Somehow, he got some anyway."

The other two snorted, and I knew I was on to something. "Oh, that's sad!"

"If ya ask me, it was more than sad. It was crim'nal."

They clammed up after that, but I played naïve and smiled and said I was glad to meet someone who knew my cousin. They told me to be careful where I ate, then I left, pleased with the twenty minutes I'd invested in the place.

I didn't get much out of the rest of my time in West Point, but as I drove back over the Coleman Bridge, I knew I had enough to continue to pursue Sam Larson's suspicions that his brother's death was not a suicide.

But killing someone who was highly allergic to seafood was one thing. Making a shooting appear to be self-inflicted was quite something else.

On the other hand, walking into a room where there's a note and a body with a gun near his hand and a bullet in his brain would tend to make a sloppy detective quit looking for another cause, wouldn't it?

A thought occurred to me that made me pull right over and check the police report on Bob Larson's death. Had anyone swabbed Susan Larson's hands at the crime scene to see if there was gunshot residue on them? I read the report thoroughly. I saw no note of that—no note of anything about her except her alibi, which I was about to check out.

The pastor of the Larsons' small independent church had nothing to say about Susan or Bob beyond vanilla platitudes. He didn't know anything about the meeting that was Susan's alibi. But then, that was "women's ministry" stuff, and he dismissed it with a wave.

Was he covering up, or did he just have a bland personality? After a half hour, I could tell our conversation was going nowhere, so I thanked him, handed him my business card, and turned to leave. That's when I noticed he'd left the door to his office cracked open. His secretary sat right outside.

As I left, I paused at her desk and looked at her, hoping she'd read my eyes. "Do you have someplace you like to go for lunch?"

She paused, apparently absorbing the subtext. "Why, yes." Brenda Bellamy wrote something on a scrap of paper and handed it to me.

"Thanks!" Outside, in my car, I read the name and address of The Cooked Goose. She'd meet me there in fifteen minutes.

"I never trusted her," Brenda said as she slid into the booth across from me. A woman in her fifties with wavy, dark hair, she was obviously ready to talk. "She'd come in to get 'counseling' from Pastor Jim, and every time she did, I'd make dang sure that door stayed cracked open. Then I'd call Corinne, his wife."

"How'd she react? His wife?"

"Oh, she'd ask him about it straight out. Jim's a good guy, but any guy can be manipulated if they stop thinking with their brain. Corinne was determined to protect him and his ministry, not to mention their marriage."

The waitress came and we ordered, a salad for Brenda and a big, juicy burger for me.

"What made you suspicious of her?" I asked after the waitress had left.

"Oh, I can tell when a woman's trolling. And that woman was just looking for a guy to hook."

"What about her husband?"

"Bob?" Brenda shook her head. "That poor man. He was overwhelmed from the day he met her." She leaned forward. "I don't believe he killed himself."

I hid my reaction. "Why do you say that?"

"I've known Bob for twenty years. Saw him walk with his wife through cancer. Saw him struggle with grief after she died. He was a good guy, but shy and kind of nerdy. Easy pickin's for a designing woman. And Susan? She moved right in. His wife's body wasn't even cold before she was at his house, 'helping' him, cooking dinner, and who knows what else."

"With her kids?"

"With and without. Sittin' with him in church. They were a couple right away." She paused. "You know, men don't do well alone. Women looking for a meal ticket know that. Bob never had a chance."

Well, then, I thought, as I left the restaurant twenty minutes later, I guess I am onto something. But why didn't the police investigation pick up on this stuff?

Maybe the detective just talked to the pastor. Maybe he didn't have the imagination to see beyond Susan Larson's tears. I didn't know.

I decided to push a little. I called Detective Hap Carroll. I asked him if anyone had swabbed Susan Larson's hands to check for gunshot residue when they responded to her 911 call. There was a long pause.

"I'm sure it was done," he said finally. "Probably forgot to put it in the report. Look, I told you, we cleared her."

I thanked him for his time.

The next day, I woke up to an email from Miss Lottie. *Praying for you today, honey!*

I had not done one single thing on her case.

I quickly rationalized it. I was making great progress on the Larson case. I planned to spend the day interviewing others who knew Bob and former neighbors of Susan. After that, I'd be ready to interview Susan. I hadn't quite figured out how to approach her. But regardless, the Larson case was hot and Miss Lottie's was not.

I took Luke for a run, did some SAR training with him, and then worked in my office for a little while. I had emails to respond to, new potential clients, and I had financial stuff to do. Then I headed out to the interviews I'd scheduled.

The day went well. When I canvassed Susan's former neighbors, the men all thought well of her, but the women were suspicious. Interesting!

I really wanted to meet Susan. As I drove, I devised a plausible reason for contacting her. But should I call the potential black widow first, or just drop in on her?

I decided on the latter. After all, she wasn't compelled to talk to me. She'd probably be suspicious. If I were her, I wouldn't talk to me at all.

A school bus caught my eye. I checked my watch. Would she be waiting at home for her kids to get off the bus right now? If I hurried, could I catch her off guard?

I pulled over, plugged her address into my nav app, and wound through neighborhood streets to her house, a 1990s-style split level with an attached garage and what looked like a big backyard. Rehearsing the half-truths I'd devised in my head, I walked up to her front door, and rang the bell. I heard the sound of a heavy engine. Sure enough, the school bus was coming down the street.

The door opened and there she was. Susan Larson in the flesh. Pretty, blonde, and slim, with an edge like a machete. I smiled and held out my business card. "Mrs. Larson, I'm Jessica Chamberlain. I'm sorry to hear about your husband. The insurance company needs..."

I never finished that sentence. She snatched the card, ripped it in half, dropped it, and hissed, "I know exactly why you're here. Been talking to my friends? Nosing around where you got no right to be? Get off my property. Now!"

"I just..."

She reached to the left. When her hand reemerged, I saw the edge of a barrel of a shotgun. "Git!"

I held up my hands. "Okay, okay. I'm leaving." I backed off. I turned toward my Jeep, half-expecting Susan to fire a shot over my head. The school bus stopped out front and two little boys got off. They stared at me as they ran past. When I glanced back, Susan still stood in her doorway, glaring at me.

I played and replayed that scene as I drove home. Was I stupid to approach Susan directly? Had I blown the case already?

It was dinnertime, but I had no appetite for food, I changed my clothes, fed Luke and walked around my yard with him.

Thankfully, I'd been invited to join some of the SAR people for some informal obedience work that evening.

SAR changed my focus and drove Susan Larson out of my head, temporarily anyway. One of the Aussie handlers was having trouble with her dog taking off into the woods and ignoring her commands to come. I thought I could help.

I had a thirty-foot leash in my Jeep. I remembered how I'd dealt with my first dog, Finn, who had that problem when he was young. I gave her some principles. Never call him if you think he won't come, then make the recall the most fun event ever, and so on. She made some progress, I loaned her the leash, and all in all, it was a fun night.

Leaving the park where we'd met, Susan Larson resurfaced in my thoughts. Her behavior at the house had deepened my suspicions. But how could she have made a homicide look like a suicide? And how could the sheriff's department have failed to see that possibility?

Impulsively, I decided to drive by her house on my way home. I could take advantage of the dark and just see what I could see. And I could scope out the neighborhood. Maybe something would trigger an answer to my questions and give me a lead to my next step.

Luke laid down with a huff in his crate, tired out. I figured he wouldn't mind a little extra car time.

I had my notes with me and my camera with the long lens. It was an SLR, and the telephoto lens was capable of capturing scenes in low light. I'd found it quite handy and kept it on the floor in front of the passenger seat covered with an old T-shirt.

I first drove by the church and then the elementary school, noting the distances between the two. I drove by the neighborhood grocery, the bank, and memorized the general layout of the streets.

Then I drove by Susan Larson's house. A late-model Chevy pickup sat in the driveway. It hadn't been there that afternoon.

I made one pass by the house, then circled around the block and parked three doors down on the opposite side of the street. I chose a place where the streetlight was out. I was curious. Whose truck was in Susan's driveway?

The houses were set apart by about fifty feet and there were no sidewalks. It was dark and quiet, just the kind of place you'd want to raise a family. I sat there thinking about Susan, her kids, and Bob Larson. Were they a happy family or did Susan set him up?

All I needed was one piece of incriminating information. Then Sam Larson's lawyer could pursue it.

Lightning flashed in the distance. Maybe that rain was coming after all. I slouched down in my seat like a Sam Spade wannabe. Suddenly, Susan's front door opened. Was the truck owner about to emerge?

Automatically, I reached for my camera. A man walked out of the door. Who was he? A friend? A brother?

No, it was a man whose belly fell over his belt like Niagara over the Falls.

Detective Hap Carroll walked to the truck in the driveway and slid in. Susan Larson, dressed in a robe, waved from the front door.

My camera whirred. My heart pounded. The investigating detective was at the widow's house at ten o'clock at night. I had my piece of information.

6

I was charged with adrenaline as I left Susan Larson's neighborhood that night. I mean, seriously? She seduces the detective investigating her husband's death? Do men ever think beyond their zippers?

Maybe I needed to take lessons from her. Here she was, drawing man after man into her bed, and here I was, thirty-two and single and likely to remain that way.

Maybe I needed a sexy bathrobe like hers. Or a bleach job. Or maybe she had an essential oil that attracted men.

If she did, maybe I should buy a gallon. Make my mother happy.

Quips kept spilling out of my brain. I was in such a good mood.

The rain that had held off all day began to fall. I flipped on my wipers as I turned out of Susan's neighborhood and onto the two-lane road that would lead me back to my neck of the woods. Soon the windows of my Jeep were streaked with rain pelting down hard. My wipers could barely keep up. I forced myself to focus on the dark, twisty road ahead.

It didn't help that some idiot in a truck tailgated me. His

pickup was tall, and the headlights reflected in my mirrors, blinding me. The interior of my car was lit up like it was daylight. So annoying. I started looking for a place to pull off so he could go around. It was hard enough to see without those headlights glaring in my eyes.

I couldn't find a place for the life of me. Not even a driveway. What's worse, the road had no shoulder, just a deep drainage ditch running along the edge. I was already driving fifty-five. What more did he want? It was raining for crying out loud.

Suddenly, the angle of his lights shifted. *He's going to pass me on the double-yellow line. And with a curve coming up.* How stupid could he be?

As his lights shifted to my left, I expected him to accelerate around me, but he didn't. He matched my speed. Suddenly, I felt pressure on the back-left panel of my car.

What the...? My Jeep's back end moved to the right. Instinctively, I hit my brakes. The truck continued to push.

My car spun on the wet road. Gripping the wheel, I tried to maintain control. Luke stood up in his crate, barking. Disoriented by the truck's lights and the spin, I felt the Jeep leave the road and then, as the truck accelerated away, we slid into a ditch and hit something solid. *Bang!* The airbags exploded.

I lost consciousness momentarily, although I never admitted that. When I came to, I was choking on airbag dust. The Jeep leaned hard to the right. I could hear Luke coughing and choking, then he started to bark frantically. I began to panic. Was my dog hurt? I turned the engine off, then tried to push my door open, but it was jammed.

I released my seat belt and crawled into the back seat. Luke's crate was pushed hard against the passenger side window. The wire door was broken and as Luke tried to push his way out, he had gotten caught.

"Wait, Luke! Wait! Hold on, buddy," I said, trying to calm him down. I tried using my key fob to release the back liftgate. It opened about four inches, then stopped. The back doors were jammed too. I looked around for something, anything, to break the glass. "Hang on, Luke! I'm going to get us out of here."

Suddenly, I saw a light. A man peered through my window. "You okay?"

I blinked at the light. "I can't get out!"

"Move away."

I turned my back and closed my eyes. I heard a tremendous crash and felt fresh air flow in. I looked and saw my rescuer clearing the rest of the window glass off the frame.

"Can you get through that?"

As I crawled out of the window, I heard sirens. "My dog!" I gasped as he helped me to solid ground.

Everything felt otherworldly. I moved to the back of the Jeep. It lay in a ditch, slammed up against a tree. The rain poured down in buckets. I tried to force the liftgate up higher, but it wouldn't budge. My hand wasn't working right. Meanwhile, Luke was yowling, making a noise I'd never heard.

"Here," the man said, and he grabbed the liftgate so we could both pull up on it.

Another man's voice said, "Let me get that."

I turned and saw a state trooper on my left, his hat covered in plastic. "My dog!" I couldn't complete that thought. The two men muscled open the liftgate. When I saw blood, I nearly passed out.

A fire truck and an ambulance arrived, their lights flashing and radios blaring. Panic gripped me. I fumbled at the crate door.

"Does he bite?" the trooper asked.

"No."

"Let me get him."

I stepped aside as the trooper lifted him out of the Jeep and carried him out of the ditch. I grabbed Luke's leash and tried to follow, but I slipped.

"Here." My original rescuer offered me his hand.

Luke sat, panting. Blood dripped from a cut on his shoulder.

A broken metal bar on the crate had sliced him open. Then I saw other wounds on his neck. I clipped on his leash. "It's okay, buddy." I looked up at the trooper. "I need to get him to a vet."

A woman, an EMT, bent down. "You're hurt. You need to go to the hospital."

"No."

"You have a gash on your head."

"No!"

The trooper touched my shoulder. "I'm a K-9 officer. Let me take care of your dog and you go get checked out."

"I can't leave him!"

"Look at your hand," he said firmly.

I looked. The airbag must have slammed my hand into something. It was swelling, badly. I panicked. I hadn't even noticed. Suddenly, I felt dizzy.

"You need to be checked, honey," the EMT said.

My cell phone in my back pocket buzzed. I took it out and answered it.

"How's it goin', Jess?"

Nate. My throat completely closed. I could not get one word out. I simply handed the phone to the officer. Trooper C.E. McCoy told him everything.

Ninety minutes later, I lay on a gurney in the ER, diagnosed with a concussion, a sprained wrist, bruises, and contusions. Evidently, I'd hit my head on the driver's side window, and the airbag caused my other injuries.

"No, sir," I told the second trooper, who'd come to take my report. "I did not just lose control. This was no accident. He meant to do it."

Trooper T.R. Rothsfeld hesitated. I could tell he didn't believe me. "Who might want to hurt you?"

I told him about my job. I told him what I was investigating. Then, making sure we were alone, I lowered my voice and told him about what I'd just seen, what I'd taken a picture of, about Detective Hap Carroll walking out of Susan Larson's house.

He looked at me skeptically.

"I think it was him. He pulled a PIT maneuver on my Jeep. That's why I spun out."

"Okay."

He definitely didn't believe me. At least he wrote it down. But I admit, I was near tears when a familiar face appeared behind him.

Laura. Laura Tanner. Nate's Laura. I bit my lip to keep from crying.

"Oh, I'm sorry to interrupt," she said to the trooper, who'd turned to look at her.

"We're done, ma'am." He looked back to me. "I'll be in touch."

I nodded. He left. Then Laura came to me, wrapped me in her arms, and that's when my tears turned loose.

"I'm so worried about Luke!" I said.

"I know, honey. Nate's gone to take care of him. Don't worry. He'll be fine."

Nate. Bailing me out again. It was embarrassing.

———

AT TWO IN THE MORNING, the hospital finally decided to release me. My wrist was in a brace. They told me to schedule a follow-up with my doctor (as if I had one). I couldn't drive until I did, and I needed someone with me for the next twenty-four hours. *Yada, yada.*

We called Nate and got an update on Luke. The emergency vet had patched up a couple of wounds. Nate would stay with him until my dog could leave.

Laura drove me home. The rain had stopped, but thunder still rumbled in the east. As we drove down my driveway, reality hit me. I had been attacked, my dog hurt, my car probably totaled.

Talk about a hostile work environment.

As we walked into my house, I realized I hadn't taken the time to set up the guest room. I didn't have a bed or anything.

I turned to Laura. "Look, I'm sorry. I just realized I haven't had a chance to put together another bedroom. I'll change the sheets on my bed—"

She waved off that idea. "No. You need your rest. I can sleep right here in the recliner or on the couch. I'll be fine."

I started to protest but realized it was useless. Nodding, I walked down the hall, took a hot shower, and climbed into bed.

But I couldn't sleep. I laid there in the dark, tears dripping down my face, images flashing in my mind. Those lights, the rain, the darkness, and then that terrible spinning sensation. It was an instant replay of another traumatic night in my past, one I was just getting over.

7

Nate brought Luke home around seven the next morning. I had finally fallen asleep around four, but as soon as I heard his tires on the gravel driveway, my eyes flew open.

Luke limped a little, but when he saw me, he dissolved into wags and slurpy kisses. I got down on the floor and hugged him, taking care to avoid his wounds, tears of both relief and stress falling freely. "Hey buddy, hey buddy! Are you okay?"

Sprite, Nate's black and white springer spaniel, was with them, and she added her own little stubby tail greeting.

Then Luke pulled one of his tricks, as if to show me he was fine. He carefully grabbed the toe of my sock with his teeth, and tugged and tugged until he'd yanked it off my foot. He danced around the room, throwing it up in the air and catching it, teasing me with his prize, until Sprite grabbed the other end and the two dogs played tug-of-war.

We laughed.

"Dogs rebound pretty good," Nate said. Fatigue creased his face.

"I'm sorry you had to come all this way," I said. "Thank you for taking care of Luke."

He shrugged. "I wanted to. Now, tell me what happened."

"Wait," Laura said, holding up her hand. "Do you need a break from your leg?"

"Yeah."

"Let's do that first."

I took Luke and Sprite outside while Laura helped Nate get his prosthetic leg off. The early morning air was fresh and clean. The rain from last night lay heavily on the grass and promised to add to the humidity later in the day. It glistened in the morning sunlight. Despite all my worries and the stress and pain, I took in a deep breath. *His mercies are new every morning.* Just being around Nate made me think of stuff like that.

Laura came out and retrieved Nate's crutches from his car. "The leg is great," she explained, "but he does get tired and sometimes sore."

I followed her back in. Nate lay stretched out on the couch. Sprite curled up in the place his lower left leg should have been. I must have stared because Nate grinned at me. "Pretty handy, that extra room."

I closed my eyes and shook my head. Maybe he had recovered from that terrible fire, but I hadn't.

"Now, tell me how you ended up in a ditch," Nate said, drawing me back.

Before I could answer, I heard a car on the driveway. Luke jumped up, barking. I went to the door and looked out. Who comes visiting before 8:00 a.m.? I turned to Nate, frowning. "Scott?"

"I may have called him last night."

I sighed deeply, a mixture of embarrassment and annoyance coloring my reaction. I opened the door, my hand on Luke's collar.

Scott jogged up the steps.

"Hey," I said, keeping my voice neutral. "Come on in."

"Jess! How are you? Are you all right?"

"A little banged up, that's all." I held up my wrist, which was in a soft cast. "Why'd you come all the way down here?" He lived at least two hours away.

"What happened?"

I moved to fetch a chair out of my office, but Scott stopped me. He sat down on the floor, so I resumed my place and Luke flopped down next to me.

I went through the whole story, beginning with the case I was working, my hunches about Susan Larson, and then what happened that night.

"You're sure it was intentional?" Scott asked.

"It felt like a PIT maneuver." My hand continued to stroke my dog even as a tremor ran through me.

"A what?" Laura asked.

Scott explained it. "Pursuit Intervention Technique. It's a move cops are taught to stop a suspect fleeing in a vehicle. If they push the back left quarter-panel of the car, the wheels break loose from the road. Inevitably, the suspect hits the brakes—that's just instinctive—and the car starts to spin. Usually other cops will then block the suspect in."

"So," Laura said, "you think it was someone in law enforcement?"

"Who else would know how to pull it off?" I took a deep breath. "It felt intentional, so yes, I think it was law enforcement. I think it was the detective who closed the case as a suicide. He must have seen me across the street from Larson's house. He watched me leave the subdivision and then followed me."

Nate remained quiet. Scott's frown suggested he doubted my story. I felt frustration building in my bones.

Then Scott spoke. "Who else knows about your theory?"

"I told the trooper at the hospital last night." I grabbed my phone and retrieved his name. "T. R. Rothsfeld. I made sure no one else was around to hear me."

Scott nodded. "It's a serious charge."

"I know!"

"But it wouldn't be the first time a cop had crossed the line."

I blinked. "Thank you."

Then Nate piped up. "You have pictures? Where's your camera?"

My camera! "In the car. Front passenger seat, on the floor." My stomach twisted. The camera contained the evidence I needed.

I rose to my feet and faced Scott. "I need to get my stuff from my car."

"You're not supposed to drive," Laura reminded me.

"I'll take you," Scott said.

"But I don't know where..." I was starting to panic.

Scott remained calm. "You have the trooper's contact information?"

I nodded.

"I'll call him."

Normally, I would have bristled at that, but today I felt fragile, and I didn't fight him.

Ten minutes later he had the name and address of the lot where the car had been towed. It didn't open until nine, so Laura volunteered to make us all breakfast. Fortunately, I had eggs and ham and orange juice in the refrigerator.

While she cooked, I slipped into my favorite jeans and a fresh shirt, no small task with my wounded hand. By the time I reemerged, the food was ready and Nate was sound asleep.

"He's more tired than he is hungry," Laura said softly.

We ate out on the back deck in the screened-in portion. I could barely swallow past the knot in my throat. The food was delicious, but my nerves were shot.

After breakfast, Scott and I headed for the towing company's lot. A big, burly, tatted-up dude showed us the car. In the daylight, it looked even worse than I had imagined. It was totaled for sure.

I tugged at the door, but it wouldn't budge, and I was wondering if I'd have to crawl back through the window when the owner produced a crowbar and forced the door open enough for me to squeeze through. I climbed in and retrieved my wallet and reached down for my camera.

I couldn't feel it. I ran my hand over the whole floorboard of the passenger side. The camera wasn't there.

The car hadn't rolled, had it? I reached back in my memory, only half-trusting it. But I was convinced, the car hadn't rolled and the door had not opened enough for the camera to fall out.

Now my stomach was really tied in a knot. I pulled my iPhone out of my back pocket and clicked on the flashlight. I used it to search every square inch of that car. In the driver's side foot well, under the seats, in the back. I even crawled into the cargo area.

I stepped out of the car and looked at Scott. "It's gone." My voice was barely above a whisper.

The muscles in Scott's jaw flexed. "Describe it."

I did, and he left to find the tow-truck driver. I closed my eyes and leaned against my Jeep, running my hand over a portion of the body that hadn't sustained any damage. I loved my car, but it was clear, the Jeep was dead. Totaled. Gone.

That hurt.

I heard Scott's footsteps crunching the gravel.

"You okay?"

I nodded and opened my eyes. "What'd you find out?"

"He's coming."

The driver appeared, clipboard in hand, a frown on his face. "State police did an inventory. It does show a camera, but ain't nobody been near that car far as I know." He looked at me.

Scott frowned. He looked past me to my car. He touched a dark spot on the left rear quarter panel. "Does this look like a paint remnant?"

The tow-truck driver looked at it. "Could be."

Was it proof I'd been run off the road?

Scott raised his eyes to mine. "I'll call Rothsfeld and make sure he gets a sample of this. You want to go back to the accident scene? Maybe the camera fell out as the car was being towed.."

I said yes, but I knew it wouldn't be there. The camera was missing. The only proof I had of professional misconduct in the Bob Larson case was gone.

I wasn't just back to square one, I had slid clear off the game board.

The bad guys were winning.

8

BY THE TIME we got back to my house an hour later, my shoes were muddy and my brain muddled. I couldn't think. I could only feel, and what I felt was pain. I ached all over—my chest from where the airbag slammed into me, my wrist, my head. I felt like I'd been run over by a herd of wild horses, and right now the last one was still kicking me.

Worse than the physical pain was the emotional. I'd been attacked. I'd lost my sense of security—and my proof. Who would believe me now?

So many feelings poured over me, feelings from past events I thought I'd dealt with. Shame, fear, anxiety, frustration, anger. Failure.

I must have been unsteady on my feet, because Scott took my elbow walking up the stairs. To be honest, I dreaded going inside, having to interact with Nate and Laura. I just wanted to curl up in bed for the rest of my life.

Nate, of course, got that. He took one look at me as I came in the door and his eyes narrowed.

"It was gone," I said, emotion clogging my throat.

He stood up on his one leg. "C'mere," he said, and he hugged me.

Scott told me I should report the missing camera. Then he started talking, something about pawn shops and eBay. I couldn't listen. I just soaked in the strength of Nate's hug.

"You need to rest," Nate said, his voice barely above a whisper.

"Yes."

Laura helped me into bed. Vaguely, I remember Luke padding in and jumping up on it, curling up next to my legs, his warm body a comfort to me.

I slept well into the afternoon. I expected my friends to leave, but no, they stuck by me. Periodically, one of them would wake me, because with head injuries, you're supposed to do that, but my exhaustion was like a weighted blanket. Every time they woke me, I fell right back to sleep.

Finally, I awakened on my own. The sun had begun its descent in the west. Luke had moved to the floor but was lying right next to my bed. I reached down and stroked his fur. He turned his head around and licked me.

I dragged myself out of bed and let Luke out. Nate and Laura sat in camp chairs on my screened-in back deck.

"What can I get you?" Laura asked, jumping to her feet.

I rubbed my stomach. I was hungry, no doubt, but what I really wanted was coffee. I told her, and she said she'd make some.

"Where's Scott?" I asked Nate.

"He had to go to work."

Of course. Always work. I sat down in the third chair.

"He's comin' back tomorrow," Nate continued.

"Why?"

"He said he had something for you."

Laura emerged from the kitchen with a cup of coffee. "Black, right?"

"Yes. Thank you." My hand shook as I took the mug from her. I wondered if she'd noticed. I turned my focus to Luke and Sprite, happily playing on the deck. I wish I could be that resilient. Wave after wave of traumatic images passed through my mind. The rain. The lights. The feeling of my car being pushed. Spinning out of control. Luke's cries.

I sipped my coffee. It burned my tongue. That's when I realized they were talking to me. "What? I'm sorry. I didn't hear what you said."

Nate repeated his statement. "We were saying one of us can stay as long as you need someone here."

"I'm fine. You all have been great. But you have jobs and lives. You should go home. I'll be fine."

Nate shifted in his chair, a wry smile on his face. "If we leave, how do you get to the doctor? The store? And wherever else you have to go?"

He had a point. I had no vehicle. "I'll rent a car." I took another sip of coffee, my hand shaking worse. At least they couldn't see my head pounding.

Laura reached over and covered Nate's hand with her own. "One of us should stay." I opened my mouth to protest but she looked at me with a surprisingly assertive gaze. "You don't need to deal with this on your own. Look at all you did for Nate. Now it's our turn to help you."

End of discussion.

The two of them decided Laura would be the one to remain behind. She cleared it with her boss, and within half an hour, Nate was ready to head for home.

"Finally," he said, smiling at his wife, "I get the whole bed to myself."

The look in his eye and the length of their embrace told an entirely different story. I watched them, their affection so apparent, their bond so strong, and I wondered, how does the universe decide who deserves that kind of love?

Nate turned to me and gave me his characteristic kiss on the top of my head and then wrapped his arms around me. He loved me, too, in a different way—like a brother.

Laura and I walked outside and watched Nate and Sprite hop into his Tahoe. "Will he be all right by himself?" I asked as they drove away.

"He'll use the wheelchair a lot, but he'll be fine."

————

THE NEXT FEW days were crazy, dealing with insurance, finding a doctor who would clear me to drive, talking to Sam Larson's lawyer, reporting the theft of my camera. That last item was dicey. I really did not want Detective Hap Carroll to find out I knew it was missing.

Scott came to see me the day after Nate left and brought along his techie friend Jim. "I have something for you," he said.

"What?"

He began opening boxes and held up a camera. "Security cameras. Jim picked out everything you'll need."

I blinked. It was actually a good idea. I was out here all alone. I had thought of buying some myself. Accepting the cameras from Scott was just ... embarrassing.

Or maybe the problem was pride.

I swallowed it. "Thank you. Very thoughtful of you."

Scott smiled. "Good. We'll get started."

By the end of the day, Jim had installed motion-detector floodlights and cameras on the front and back of the house. If anyone approached, the cameras would trigger an alert on my cell phone.

"Unfortunately, that doesn't work when you're away from home—your Internet access is too unreliable out here. But as long as you're in the house, it'll let you know someone's here," explained Jim.

"Thank you," I said. Curious, I added, "What do you do for the FBI?"

An odd silence followed. The two men looked at each other.

Jim grinned. "Let's just say I've installed a lot of these things."

I felt my face redden. Of course. I should have known. Wire-taps. Bugging the bad guys. I smiled. "I hope the FBI enjoys all the conversations I have with my dog."

"Speaking of which," Scott said, switching gears, "let us show you how it works. Can I take the dog out?"

"Sure."

He called Luke. I was a little disappointed my dog went with him that readily. They disappeared out the front door. A few minutes later, my phone signaled me. I stared at the screen.

"See?" Jim said. "They're on the front porch." Then he turned to my computer. "And here is the backup. It's in this folder, time-stamped and everything."

I had to admit, the equipment would make me feel a lot more secure. "How can I thank you?"

"Just be safe."

I felt anything but safe. I felt vulnerable, hypervigilant, in a constant state of alarm. I envied Luke. He seemed completely back to normal. And although I wouldn't admit it, I was glad Laura was still here.

After the guys left, I dug out my old gun bag. I'd been casual lately about carrying my weapon. That had to change. I made sure my permit was in my wallet. I looked out my back window and imagined where I might set up a shooting range. Because my right hand was injured, I put the gun bag on my left hip and prac-ticed drawing with my left hand. That felt awkward, so I tried a holster. Much better.

Laura looked up from the book she was reading and watched me. I tried to look confident. I was not. In fact, I nearly jumped out of my skin when I heard a vehicle on my gravel driveway. I looked outside, my hand on my gun.

A state police car pulled up. Trooper C.E. McCoy stepped out. Scott had called him for me. I quickly put the gun and holster on the table.

"I have a loaded gun in plain sight on the table inside," I said, as I opened the door. You can't be too careful with law enforcement. I knew that from experience.

McCoy looked at me with gray eyes bordered by tiny wrinkles. His face was chiseled, his jawline angular. He nodded. "Okay."

I opened the door, inviting him in. I introduced Laura and gestured for him to take the green camp chair in the living room, the one nearest the gun, so he'd feel like it was in his control.

He asked me some questions, and I told him about the camera, my suspicions, and my concerns.

"I really don't want Carroll knowing I know it's missing. And I don't know if Rothsfeld is his buddy, if he's the one who revealed where my car was." I braced myself for a dismissive response.

But McCoy took me seriously. "I understand. I'll be discreet."

We talked for about fifteen minutes, and when he left, Laura said, "He seems like a good guy."

"Let's hope."

———

SLOWLY, over the next few days, my life came back together. Laura drove me to a doctor. I had my head examined and was cleared to drive. Then she took me to a car rental place, and I got a sedan to use while I figured out how to replace the Jeep. On the fourth day, after a trip to the grocery store, I was ready to send Laura home.

"Are you sure you'll be okay?"

Of course, I would. My body still hurt from the accident. My head ached nearly all the time. My nerves were shot. I jumped every time my phone buzzed. But I'd be okay. Nate had called

Laura every morning and every evening and sometimes in between. The two lovebirds needed to be back in the same nest.

The night Laura left, I barely slept.

9

Scott Cooper stood in line, restlessly tapping the pack of D-cell batteries in his right hand against the palm of his left. He'd thought stopping by the store on his lunch hour would be faster than going after work, but no. Only two checkout lines were open, and the elderly lady in front of him was taking forever to fish thirty-two cents out of her wallet.

He'd had an early morning meeting with the assistant US attorney on a case of his that was about to go to trial. Scott liked the investigation part of his job, and testifying was always interesting, but this part—the final back-and-forth between the lawyers on both sides—proved tedious every time.

Scott checked his watch. He was due in his boss's office in twenty-five minutes. Thankfully, he was just ten minutes from the FBI resident agency, but if this lady didn't hurry...

He shifted his gaze toward the door. Sunlight streamed in, creating bright patterns on the wall and floor. The high today would be close to eighty, about right for the end of May.

He was about to look away when he saw a young man dressed in black, wearing a long trench coat, walk through the door. He felt an instant pop of adrenaline. The kid was dressed wrong.

Scott narrowed his eyes. When the kid's arms came up and Scott saw the gun he was holding, he dropped the batteries, pushed past the shoppers behind him, and ran toward the threat.

The rest of the store seemed to fade away. All Scott could see was the kid. All he could hear was the pop—pop—pop—pop of the kid's gun, and the screams.

"Drop the gun!" Scott yelled, drawing his weapon. He aimed straight at the kid. "Drop it!"

The shooter turned toward him, his face pale. Later Scott would remember his eyes looked empty, dead. "Drop it!"

The kid swung his gun toward Scott And Scott fired. One-two-three-four-five-six shots from his Bureau-issued Glock. The kid fell. Scott ran to him, heart pounding. He used his foot to move the kid's gun out of reach. Then he cuffed him, although he could tell the shooter was dead.

Scott holstered his weapon, then looked around. He saw several people on the floor. Just four feet from the shooter lay a little girl. Scott stepped over to her, knelt down, turned her over, and saw the blood on her dress and the pulsing wound in her chest. He pressed his palm against it, trying to stop or at least slow down the bleeding. She looked at him, her big blue eyes wide with shock.

"We're going to help you, honey. Hang on." Scott put his left hand under her head, cradling it. Where were her parents? "Hold on, hold on." But as he pressed his hand on her chest, her breathing faltered. "Stay with me, honey!"

She took one last, gasping breath, and the light in her eyes went out. Scott blinked. The magnitude of that moment made his heart shudder.

Quickly he laid the girl flat on the floor, pressed his hands to her chest, and began CPR. *Find the rhythm, find it!*

Sirens, shouts, weeping. Someone touched his arm. Scott barely noticed.

"We'll take it, sir."

The hand gripped him and Scott realized it was a medic. He stood and moved away.

"You the one who got him?" a uniformed cop asked.

He wiped his bloody hands on his slacks. "Yeah. Scott Cooper, FBI." He pulled out his credentials and badge, his hands shaking.

"Sarge! I got the guy who took him out."

Five minutes later, he stood in the store manager's office, trying to calm down, trying to remain professional. Six shot. Two dead. That was the body count. Plus the shooter. Three dead.

It could have been so much worse, they said. Thank God he was in the store, they said.

Scott wasn't sure about all that. All he could see in his mind's eye was that little girl's big blue eyes.

The door opened. His new boss, Javier Portillo, walked in. Scott faced him.

"Good job, Scott."

He nodded in response. He couldn't trust his voice. That little girl ...

"They want your gun. I brought you a backup."

Scott handed over his weapon. It had to be tested and the bullets compared against the ones removed from the gunman and the victims. But right now, the last thing in the world Scott wanted to be was unarmed. His body was on full alert, ready for another threat.

Thankfully, his boss was smart enough to know that. Portillo handed him another Glock, and Scott slid it into his holster and felt the weight of it on his hip.

"I'll come with you to the police station."

Scott nodded. "Did you tell the boss?"

"Yes. He's on it. You want me to call your lawyer?"

Scott looked down. His slacks and jacket were bloody, but he wouldn't have a chance to change them anytime soon. He'd have to go down to police headquarters and give a statement. Even though his actions were completely justified, applauded by the people on the scene, the lawyer would ensure things didn't turn around on him, that his rights were protected. Because these days, you never knew.

He pulled out his credentials case, removed the lawyer's business card, and handed it to Portillo. "Yes, sir."

"You all right?"

"Yeah."

"Okay, I'll call this guy, then we'll go."

A few minutes later, Portillo led him out through the store and past the crowd gathered outside. Scott kept a firm grip on his emotions, avoiding eye contact and staring at his boss's back. But as he was getting into Portillo's Bucar, he saw the medical examiner's office rolling out a gurney holding a very small body bag. Scott looked away quickly, his stomach roiling.

Please don't let it be my bullet that killed her.

10

THAT MORNING I had a meeting with Sam Larson and his lawyer. Sam was excited I'd started to confirm his suspicions. But the lawyer wanted me to back off.

"I'll take it from here," he said. "I know the DA."

I protested. I wanted to see the case through. But the lawyer thought it was time for the authorities to get involved.

"Am I in danger?" Sam asked, glancing from his lawyer to me.

I shrugged. "I never mentioned your name to anyone. Never said who'd hired me. But who knows? I never expected to get run off the road. And you're the one with the most to gain if Susan Larson is found to be guilty."

"That isn't why I started this!"

"I know. But they won't care."

Twenty minutes later, I walked out, unlocked the door of my rental car, and climbed in. Staring at the building I'd just left, I tried to let go of the case. That was hard. Not only had I cracked it, the perps had come after me. I wanted to end it. I wanted revenge.

I started the rental car, a cheap little Ford economy model, and pulled out of the parking space. Everything in me wanted to nail Susan Larson for Bob's murder. And could I get Detective Hap Carroll on public corruption? Wasn't public corruption an FBI-type case? Maybe I should call Scott.

I actually reached for my phone, then thought better of it. Public corruption that the FBI would get involved in would be something more widespread than one sloppy detective, right?

Right. I'd have to let it go.

Irritated, I flipped on the radio to distract myself. It was set on an all-news station.

Great. Another mass shooting. What was wrong with people?

I turned up the volume. A store in Manassas. Three dead, including the shooter. Six injured. Off-duty FBI agent stopped it.

Good for him. Or her. *Wonder if Scott knows the agent?*

Again, I started to reach for the phone, then checked myself. In a mass shooting case with an agent involved, it was probably all hands on deck. Everybody had something to investigate. Scott would be busy.

Meanwhile, the door had closed on my most interesting case. What would I do now?

I sighed. Back to philandering husbands. A background check or two. And Miss Lottie's case.

Miss Lottie. My career was scraping the bottom of the barrel.

When I got home, I took Luke for a walk. He clearly wanted to run, but my body wasn't ready for that yet. Back inside, instead of looking at my cases on the computer, I started shopping for cars. What could I find that would hold Luke and his crate and all my SAR gear, and that I could afford?

An hour later, I closed the computer, discouraged. I certainly couldn't afford anything new. And I couldn't focus enough to sort through all the used ones.

My phone rang. It was Miss Lottie. I almost pushed the ignore button. Instead, I answered. "Hello?"

Miss Lottie asked me if I was okay. "The Lord has been pressing your name on me."

That was weird. I told her I had a little car accident. That shocked her, but I told her I was okay, and yes, my dog was okay too. And then, because I felt guilty about doing nothing on her case, I asked about her daughter's high school friends.

"I saw one of them a week ago, all grown up now with children of her own. I looked at her and thought, 'That could be my Tamara.'"

"Did you get her number?"

A long silence followed.

"Miss Lottie?"

"I couldn't even speak to her," she said, her voice cracking. "I just couldn't." She blew her nose softly. "I'm sorry."

She was sorry? I'm the one who'd completely ignored her case. "It's okay. I understand," I assured her. She gave me the friend's name—at least her maiden name—the location of the store, and, although it was a long shot, I promised Miss Lottie I'd try to find the young woman.

She thanked me profusely and then said, "How can I pray for you?"

I felt my jaw tighten. *How could she pray for me? I don't need...* "I need another car," I blurted out. "A used one. Big enough for my dog, a German shepherd." *What made me say that?*

"I'll pray for one!" And she did, right there on the phone, asking that the Lord meet my need.

Weird. Not even Nate had prayed for me over the phone.

Luke had come in and was lying down at my feet. He looked up as I clicked off my phone. "People are strange," I said to him, and he thumped his tail.

Exhaustion from my lousy night's sleep suddenly swept over me. Was it okay to take a nap? I never did that. But maybe I should listen to my body.

I went back in the bedroom, took off my business suit, slipped into shorts and a T-shirt, and climbed into bed. Luke came in and sniffed me, as if to figure out if I needed him to snuggle or if lying nearby was enough. He decided to flop down on the floor, stretching out right next to my bed. I dropped my arm over the side and ran my fingers through his coat. What a blessing this dog was to me!

When did I start using the word "blessing"?

Sleep fell hard over me. I didn't wake up for two hours, and even then I was lazy getting out of bed. I was brushing my teeth to wake myself up when my phone buzzed. I looked at the text.

A callout! A child was missing from a school field trip to Yorktown.

I quickly assessed my readiness. My body still ached, my head hurt occasionally, I didn't have an appropriate vehicle, and Luke had no crate.

Yes, I could definitely do it. No problem.

I texted back that I'd respond, ETA on the scene thirty minutes.

I double-checked Luke's wounds. They were healing nicely and Luke was running around without any sign of impairment. Good to go. I grinned at him. "Wanna go search?"

He exploded with joy. What a knucklehead. He ran into the living room and grabbed the first thing he could find, a tennis ball. Then he dropped that and grabbed my sock. He put both in his mouth and came racing back to me.

"All right, all right!" I said, laughing.

Twenty-nine minutes later, I pulled up to the command post in Yorktown. On the drive over I had decided what I would and would not put Luke through. No water searches (we weren't certified yet anyway) and if I saw any signs of fatigue or pain, I would pull him out.

I had no rules for myself. I was adrenalized. Pain? What pain? I'd wear the brace to protect my wrist, but otherwise, I was ready to go.

Tim was in charge of the search. He watched me exit the car and raised his eyebrows. I busied myself with Luke.

Four teams had responded. Tim called us over for a briefing.

Steven Chambers, age eight, had gotten separated from his group on a school field trip. The adult chaperone, who had twelve kids to watch, was busy helping a little girl who was throwing up. Stevie's designated buddy couldn't take his eyes off the girl. He didn't see Stevie leave the group. They'd checked the bus and the buildings and still couldn't find him.

The area we had to search included the historic area and its open fields, woods, and water—lots of water, including the York River and a "pitch-and-tar" swamp. We'd get volunteer walkers to help us. Some would be law enforcement officers, some not. I raised my hand and asked if I could avoid water search areas.

"We're not certified yet," I explained, although really I wanted to keep Luke out of the water with not-quite-healed wounds.

"No problem," Tim said.

When he handed out the topographic maps, Luke and I were assigned to a wooded area. "It's hard to avoid water," Tim said, "but this section has less of it than any of the others."

I glanced at the map. There were some hills and gullies but no mountains. This was Tidewater Virginia after all. I saw some marshy areas, but mostly what we'd be searching was woods like we were used to. That encouraged me.

I buckled on my gaiters and put on Luke's SAR vest. Then I shrugged on my pack, my still-sore body protesting.

Tim walked over, handed me a picture of Stevie, and gestured toward the man with him. "This is Jason Broward. He's going to be your walker."

Six feet tall, brown hair, brown eyes, slim and fit. Good looking, I might add. I shook Jason's hand. "I'm Jess, and this is Luke."

"Okay if I pet him?"

"You were smart to ask. But yes, you can pet him."

Jason had on jeans, a white golf shirt, and Teva low-rise boots that looked like he was used to hiking in rough terrain. "You work here?" I asked him.

He finished petting Luke and said, "Yeah, I'm a park service interpreter. I had just spoken to these kids a short time before we got word one of them was missing." He wiped his hand on his jeans. "You want to run through what I'm supposed to do?"

"Do you know anything about search and rescue?"

He shook his head. "But I've done orienteering. I was a scout."

"Okay, then. That helps." I held the topographic map so he could see it and pointed. "We've been given this area to search. Luke is trained as an air-scent dog. He will run out ahead of us and find any human in that area. If he finds someone, he'll run back to me and tug on this rope on my belt and then we'll follow him to the person."

"What's my job?"

"I'm going to be paying attention mostly to the dog. You know how to work a GPS, right?"

"Yes."

"Okay, you're going to mark our start point, any turns we make, and the location of any human-related item we find." I pulled the second GPS out of my pocket, clicked it on, and handed it to him.

Luke whined. He was ready to go.

"It's up to you to make sure we don't get lost and that we don't overlook any evidence along the way. Okay?"

He nodded. "I'm ready."

I took a little bottle of baby powder out of my pack and puffed it in the air.

"What's that for?"

"To determine the wind direction. I want to set a course that will have my dog working downwind of our ultimate target."

"Okay."

I drew a few faint lines on the plastic cover over the topo map. "The wind is coming from this way. We'll start here." I dotted the spot. "Our ultimate target is here, and so we'll make this the initial target. We'll search back-and-forth against the wind."

"It's kind of like tacking in a sailboat."

I nodded. "If Luke catches the scent, then we follow him straight to the human." I positioned Luke near the edge of the woods and turned to Jason. "Our starting point."

"Got it." He noted the spot on the GPS.

"Okay, Luke, are you ready? Are you ready?" He was more than ready. He wagged his tail, his muscles tensed up and ready for my signal. I unclipped his leash, extended my arm in the direction I wanted him to run. "Go, Luke! Seek!"

He took off, his beautiful gold-and-black coat shimmering in the sun.

"Wow," Jason said.

"Keep up!" I said to him as I raced after my dog. My body aches no longer seemed relevant. This was what I loved, working with my dog to find lost people.

Jason had a million questions, which he threw at me as we worked our way through the forest. Why didn't Luke work on leash? Was he better than a bloodhound? How did I train him? What happens if he finds the wrong person? Could he work in the snow? Does rain wash scent away? Why did I get into this?

I explained the difference between an air-scent dog (searching for any human) and a trailing dog (following a particular scent). I told him no breed can beat a bloodhound in tracking a specific scent, but Luke was a great general search dog. I explained how I trained him, and how I'd reward him if he found another human, then restart him in another direction.

When I'd answered the other questions, I stopped for a second, looked at Jason, and said, "Why do I do this? I love working with my dog. I love the bond we have. I love being out in the woods with him. I love finding lost people." I shrugged. "I love everything about it."

He nodded. "Fair enough."

We searched for an hour, then took a water break, and started back toward our base. Halfway there, I heard an air horn sound. I grabbed my radio, talked to Tim, then turned to Jason. "They found him."

"Yes!"

"Luke! Luke!" I called my dog back. "He's fine. They found him curled up asleep on the school bus."

"Wow. I thought they checked the bus," Jason said.

"They did. Maybe he wandered a while before going back to it."

Luke came bounding back to me, and I patted him. Smiling, I looked at Jason. "Are you up for a game?"

"Sure. What?"

"Would you go ahead of us and hide somewhere? And let Luke find you?"

"Sure!"

"Go out about ten minutes, back toward our start, and then we'll come looking for you."

I distracted Luke, playing with him with a tug toy, while Jason disappeared into the woods. As we played, I couldn't help but admire Luke—his strength, his ability to play hard without hurting me, his shiny coat, his gorgeous brown eyes. I guess I'm a dog snob. I love having a smart, beautiful dog.

I checked my watch. "Okay, enough!" I said, ending the game. "How about a drink?" I pulled his collapsible water bowl out of my pack and filled it. Luke drank noisily, and I stroked his back as he did. "You are a good, good boy," I said, and his tail wagged in response.

Time to go. I put away his water bowl, told Luke to "heel," extended my arm, and said, "Seek! Seek, Luke!"

He was off like a shot, ranging forward, nose working, looking for the scent. I hurried to keep up with him. He disappeared ahead, and then, a few minutes later, he reappeared, racing toward me, and tugged on the rope on my belt. He'd found a human! He was so excited.

"Good dog! Good boy." I followed my dog. He ran through the

woods and up to a big cedar tree, jumped up, and started barking. "Whatcha got, buddy? What'd you find?" I looked up and laughed. Jason was about six feet up in the tree.

"Good, Luke! Good boy. You won the game!" I took out the Kong toy Luke loved and threw it for him.

Jason climbed down. "I thought I'd fool him!"

"But you didn't."

"Nope. He came right to me. Smart dog."

"He's got a good nose." I threw the Kong again, smiling with pride.

We made our way back to the command post. I thanked Jason for helping me.

"It was fun!" he said.

"Well, the important thing is, the kid is safe." I removed Luke's vest and leashed him up. As I took off my pack, I noticed how much my body ached. No matter. It was worth it.

"Hey, uh..."

I looked up. Jason had come back.

"Are you with anyone?"

What? It took me a minute to comprehend his question. "Do I have a boyfriend?"

He nodded.

"No."

"Do you mind if I call you?"

I thought for a minute. He was a guy. With a job. Not bad looking. And Luke didn't seem to mind him. I shrugged. "We could do coffee or something."

He handed me his phone, and I entered my name and number in his contacts list. "I'll call you," he said. "Soon."

"Okay." I watched him walk away, down toward the administrative building. What had I just done? I hadn't been out on a date since...well, since Scott had last asked me out. Months ago.

I shook off the feeling and was about to put Luke in the rental car when Tim came over. "What in the world are you driving?" he asked.

"Had a little accident." I put my pack in the trunk, then turned to face him. "Somebody ran me off the road."

"Seriously?"

I nodded.

"Is it in the shop?"

"Totaled." I felt my mood slip as I once again faced reality.

"What are you going to do?"

"I'll have to buy something. For now," I gestured for Luke to climb in the back seat, "this'll have to do."

Tim shook his head. "That thing's pathetic."

11

THE SUN WAS SLIDING toward the horizon as I drove home. I noticed a kernel of fear sprouting in my belly. I really didn't want to be on the road at night. I wanted to hurry home, back to my nest. I was also hungry and didn't feel like cooking. In fact, though SAR had distracted me temporarily, my emotions now came washing back over me like an angry creek, churning and uprooting the rocks in my soul.

I needed to get home. I opted for fast food and bought an extra hamburger for Luke. As I hit the road for the last ten minutes of my drive, I felt angry with myself for being scared. Chances were whoever knocked me off the road would leave me alone now. He was just trying to scare me. I needed to relax.

In for four, hold for seven, out for eight. I practiced the breathing Nate had taught me, trying to let go of my anxiety. But anxiety is like a cat, stalking you, springing at you when you least expect it.

I looked in my rearview mirror at Luke. "Cats can be sneaky." I heard his tail thump. I assumed that meant he agreed.

I turned on the radio to distract myself and heard more about the shooting in Manassas. The shooter was sixteen, a loner, according to his classmates at the local high school, and he'd recently gotten into a nihilistic online group.

Sure. If life is meaningless, why not just increase the chaos? Randomly kill people. If there is no God, and no accountability, do whatever you please.

The news story went on to describe the five-year-old girl. She'd been sick that day, so her mom had taken her to the doctor, and they were at the store picking up a prescription. And just like that, she died.

I'd argued with Nate about that kind of thing many, many times. Where was God? Why'd she die? She had her whole life ahead of her! She was an innocent child.

In my head I could hear my arguments, which I had flung at Nate like grenades, one after the other. And I could see him patiently listening. After a while, he'd say something like, "Now we see in a mirror dimly," or "Where were you when God created the foundations of the earth?" I used to think they were platitudes. Only much later did I find out they were Scripture verses, verses that meant something to him. They still didn't mean much to me.

I flipped the radio to a music station to quiet the voices in my head.

I turned into my driveway. The lane going through the woods looked gloomy. I found myself on high alert, Little Red Riding Hood venturing through the forest for the first time after her encounter with the wolf. I parked next to the house, turned off the ignition, and let Luke out. Surely, he'd let me know if someone was around. I grabbed my dinner and my pack and scampered up the front steps. I unlocked the door, then waited while Luke emptied his bladder. When we were safe inside. I threw the deadbolt, put down my pack, and collapsed onto the couch.

Was I always going to be this skittish?

Five minutes later my phone rang and I jumped. I looked at the caller ID, then I answered it. "Hey, Tim, what's up?"

"I didn't want to say anything at the park, but I know of a car you might want to look at."

"Tell me about it."

"We have a former member, Fred Knowles, whose dog got too old. He's decided to give up search and rescue. He doesn't want to start over with another dog. He has a Jeep Wrangler SKU that he's modified for SAR. I called him to see if he's interested in selling, and he is."

A Wrangler. They were the rough-and-tumble Jeeps. And if I remembered correctly, the SKU was long, almost like a square station wagon. "It's big enough for a big dog?"

"Yep. He had a shepherd too."

My interest rose. "What year is it?"

"It's a '15. Has about forty-five thousand miles on it. Still in good shape. Gas mileage stinks, but it's good what he's done with it. He's taken the back seat out and put in storage. Plenty of room for a crate. You ought to look at it."

I felt my gut tighten. I knew how much I could afford to spend. "How much is he asking?"

"You'd have to talk to him about that. He said it's worth about $26K."

"I don't think I can go that high."

"Talk to him about it. He may come down. After all, how many people want a Jeep with no back seat?"

Why not at least look at it? Maybe I'd get an idea for modifying a cheaper Jeep. Or maybe I wouldn't like the Wrangler at all.

Tim and I arranged to meet up the next day, which was Saturday. Tim's friend said he'd be home all day.

I thought of calling Nate to see if he'd look at it with me. Then I rejected that idea. Time to stop depending on him.

I MET Tim at a shopping center, where he parked his car and rode with me to his friend's house. I'd brought Luke with me. For some reason, I wanted him along.

I don't believe in love at first sight, but I came close to it with that Jeep. White with a black interior, the Wrangler gleamed in the sun. It had hard and soft covers for the convertible back end, and a spare tire mounted on the back. You could take off the doors. It had big, wide-set tires. *Try to knock that off the road!* It looked rugged—one step short of a Hummer, at least in my eyes.

I put Luke on a down-stay and began asking Fred Knowles questions as we went over the car. He had modified the back, taking out the back seat so he could install one or two crates and have room for storage. I saw where his pack went, his cooler. He had hooks for leashes and harnesses, a place for a good-sized first-aid kit, and a VHF radio mounted under the glove box.

I asked him to pop the hood, and I looked over the engine like I knew what I was looking at. I took the oil cap off and inspected it, the one thing my stepfather had taught me to look for in used cars. Clean meant the oil was changed regularly.

Fred kept glancing at Luke while we talked. "He's well-behaved."

"Want to say hi?"

"Sure!"

I called Luke over and Fred took to him immediately. He rubbed his ears and jostled him around. Luke loved it. Meanwhile, I kept looking at the Jeep and wondering if I could afford it. I played my cards close to my chest. "Can I take it for a test drive?"

"You bet!"

I left Luke with Tim and climbed in the Jeep. Fred came along. The ride was rough and noisy. I loved it.

"My wife doesn't find it comfortable," Fred said over the noise. "That's why I'm selling it. Are you just getting into SAR?"

I explained about adopting Luke and needing something to do with him and then getting into SAR. I didn't tell him about finding the lost boy in Westmoreland State Park before Christmas, or working with the FBI to find and arrest a serial killer. I did mention Nate, and it turned out he knew him.

Then I told him about the guy running me off the road and totaling my Cherokee, injuring both Luke and me. "That's why I need a new car. But you know, insurance never gives you what your car was worth to you."

"No, they get you on that."

I didn't say how much I loved the Wrangler. Back at his house, as he resumed playing with my dog, I approached the price issue. "How much are you asking?"

"Kelly Blue Book is about twenty-six," he said.

I took a deep, calculated breath and frowned.

"Well," he said, after a pause, "if you promise not to tell my wife," he grinned and glanced at Tim, "I'll sell it to you for less." He laughed. "She hates it anyway. She'll be glad it's gone."

"How much less?"

"Twenty-four."

I grimaced. "I really can't go above twenty-two."

"Okay."

And just like that, we had a deal.

I wrote out a thousand-dollar check as a deposit and handed it to him. "Tell you what," he said, "I'll throw in something." He disappeared into his garage and came back out with a Luke-sized crate that was so sturdy it looked like it could be dropped from an airplane. He placed it in the back of the Jeep and invited me to let Luke try it.

I did. My dog readily jumped up and settled down immediately. I gripped the bars of the crate and tried shaking them. Perfect. No more injuries from cheap crates.

"I doubt that I'll ever have another dog, at least not a shepherd. I'd like you to have that. Keep this big guy safe."

I thanked Fred profusely. This was really more than I could have asked for.

We shook on it, and I said I'd be back with full payment on Monday after the banks opened.

"He cut you a break," Tim said as we drove back to where he'd left his car.

"Yes, he did."

"I think he likes your dog."

I laughed. "No doubt."

"If you need a ride to pick it up on Monday, I might be able to do it. I'll have to ask my wife."

We got to talking about other things. Tim was a professional firefighter for the city of Richmond. He worked twenty-four-hour shifts. His wife was a teacher.

"It works out," he said, shrugging, "but we don't have a lot of time together."

"No kids?"

"No kids," he responded. Then he asked me what I did.

"I'm a private investigator," I said. "I chase down missing assets, cheating husbands, the occasional unfaithful wife, and sometimes runaway teens."

I don't know why I added that last bit. Miss Lottie's daughter was the only one of those cases I'd ever had, and I'd done virtually nothing on it.

Maybe it was my guilty conscience, but when I got home, I settled down to really look at Miss Lottie's case. I owed her that much.

Miss Lottie had given me the names of about eight of her daughter's friends, including the one she'd seen in the store. I used Google and found three of them. Two were still in the area, and I decided to try contacting them. That would show her I at least tried to find her daughter.

While I was on my computer, I also looked up ovarian cancer. Miss Lottie had a Stage IV diagnosis, and from what I read, that was a death sentence.

My sympathy stirred for her, but so did my aversion. I remembered Nate helping a woman with cancer. Beth's husband had left her shortly after her diagnosis. Nate stepped up, taking her to appointments, grocery shopping for her, and eventually arranging hospice care. He was even with her when she died.

Not me. No way could I do that. I would never make First-Class Saint.

I made my calls and managed to set up appointments with two of Tamara's friends, one for Tuesday and one for Wednesday. Cool. I'd have my new Jeep by then.

My cell phone rang, but I didn't recognize the number. I let it go to voicemail. When I listened to the message, it was Jason asking me out. I decided to let that slide for a while. I don't know, it felt weird.

Nate had called me, too, twice, but I hadn't answered. I didn't want him thinking he had to check up on me all the time. I was fine!

I turned to my other cases, both men whose wives suspected affairs. I stalked them both online. It was amazing how much you could find on social media. The guys were usually discreet, but if I could identify the women involved, I could usually find something to give me a lead. It was like the women lived in a fantasy world, thinking this guy was really theirs and they could flaunt it.

So, for example, they might put up a picture of dinner at a favorite restaurant with "my special guy." Even though they might keep his face out of the picture, I'd still get a lead out of that. In one instance, a woman took a picture in a hotel bar, not realizing the guy was perfectly reflected in a mirror. She made it too easy for me. I took several screen shots, printed them, and the aggrieved wife had her proof.

What amazed me, though, was how many wives forgave their

husbands even after I handed them the evidence of their misbehavior. With some, it was not the first affair, yet they couldn't pull the divorce trigger.

Why? What kept women in unhealthy marriages? It was a subject that intrigued me. At the same time, I felt like an outsider, someone whose knowledge of matrimony was limited to what I could see through brightly lit windows while walking suburban streets at night. I'd never been married. What did I know about the dynamics of that bond?

I'd come close once with a guy named Mitch. We'd met when I was a police detective and he was a cop. When I left the force, I left him too. I don't think my mother ever forgave me.

12

SCOTT LIVED on adrenaline for thirty hours, until about five o'clock on Saturday, when an avalanche of emotions swept over him, threatening to drown him. He kept replaying the shooting in his head, seeing the gun, seeing the kid, hearing his own shouts and then the gunfire, then seeing the girl. Experiencing little shots of adrenaline followed by horror.

The girl. It would be Monday before they got back the ballistics, Monday before he knew whether or not he'd killed a five-year-old. He'd given the suit she'd bled all over to the evidence response team. He'd showered and scrubbed his hands, but he still didn't feel clean. He hadn't slept all night, despite the alcohol he'd downed in an attempt to calm down.

In the law enforcement community, even in the press, he was a hero. Why didn't he feel like one?

He wasn't supposed to be identified to the media except as a "veteran FBI agent who was off-duty at the time," but someone slipped and revealed his name. Now it was all over the national news. His boss had called, advising him to avoid the coverage.

He'd just hung up from talking to his daughter, Mandy. She was fourteen going on twenty and lived in California with his ex-

wife and her current live-in boyfriend, who was apparently viru-
lently anti-cop. Mandy had seen the news and was full of questions. Why did he have to shoot the boy? Was he shooting to kill?
Why so many bullets? Did he shoot the girl, too? And then back
to the boy—"He was my age, Dad. My age. You couldn't just shoot
him in the leg?"

He'd found himself trying to explain the Bureau's deadly
force policy to a teenager who wasn't buying it.

"What am I supposed to tell my friends?" she'd said. "If that
kid was black I'd never live it down!"

She didn't know him, Scott realized. They'd been away from
each other too long. She didn't understand who he was.

Her reaction led to a whole other chain of thoughts after he
hung up. Should he move to California to be near her? Fight for
more custody? Wait it out? Call her more often? Try Skype?

That phone conversation had thrust him further down into
the emotional pit, and now he'd have to figure out how to climb
out of it. Scott checked his watch. He was due back at the office
Sunday afternoon at one. More debriefing. He desperately
needed sleep, but how could he turn off his brain?

He changed into running shorts, then thought better of it. He
didn't feel comfortable out in public without a gun. Nor did he
want to go to the gym. Everyone there knew he was FBI, and
frankly, he didn't want to have any more questions thrown at him.

But he had to do something. So he drove to the FBI Academy
and ran the roads and trails there. Eight miles. Then he spent an
hour in the Academy gym.

On the way home, he stopped at a local sub shop, ordered a
large steak and cheese with everything, and picked up a six-pack
of beer.

By the time he unlocked his front door, it was ten o'clock.
He turned on Netflix and watched *Longmire* while he downed
three beers along with the sub. Finally, near 2:00 a.m., he
nodded off. His sleep was restless, full of dreams, and when he

woke up the next morning he felt stiff, like he'd been working all night.

Again, he went through the motions. Breakfast. Coffee. Shower. His townhouse was quiet, which was normally the way he liked it, but today, the silence just amplified the noises in his head. The gunshots. The screams. The sound of his own heart drumming as he held that little girl.

He flipped on the TV to drown out the internal noise. He shouldn't have. The Sunday morning news show was profiling the girl, displaying images of her smiling face, holding a puppy, playing with her little brother, on her first day of school, and then the camera moved onto her devastated parents, while the voice of the newscaster droned on.

Alicia. Alicia Morgan. Now the little girl had a name.

Scott barely breathed. His chest felt tight, like steel bands were compressing it. His head began to spin. He fired his weapon and Alicia Morgan died. Age five.

He stabbed at the remote, dropped it, found it, grabbed it, and pressed the power button. Then he threw it across the room, cursing. "Why'd you let this happen?"

Was he at fault? Had he shot that girl? Was his aim off? Had he messed up? He'd definitely shot the boy. Multiple times. Was he the person Mandy thought he was?

Loneliness swept over him in a wave, the kind of deep loneliness he'd felt only once before when his sister was murdered. He thought about calling Nate, but it was Sunday morning and no doubt he'd be at church. Then he thought about Jess. After all she'd been through, he imagined she'd understand. He could talk to her.

He picked up his phone, but his fingers froze.

———

NATE GENERALLY AVOIDED WATCHING TV, especially the news. It

was not until after church, when he and Laura were driving home and had the radio on in the car, that he first heard Scott's name associated with the shooting in Manassas.

"That's got to be hard," Laura said, as the report went on to mention the five-year-old girl.

Nate's jaw muscles felt piano-wire tight. "I'll call him soon as we get home."

But there was no answer on Scott's cell, and Nate had to leave a voice mail message. And there was also no answer when he tried again at four o'clock.

"He wouldn't be at work, would he?" Laura asked. "It's Sunday."

"Somethin' like this going on, no tellin' what he has to do," Nate said. "Jess ain't pickin' up neither. I left her two messages."

Laura rubbed his shoulders. "In God's time."

He looked at her. "I'm the one's usually saying that kind of thing." He shook his head. "It sure is weird having it come right back at me."

———

Scott drove to the office. He had paperwork to fill out, a mountain of it, and a shooting incident review board process to go through. His boss met him there.

"We've got no additional information," Portillo said, in answer to Scott's question. "How are you doing?"

"I'm fine." Scott didn't know Javier Portillo well enough yet to go beyond that. He shrugged like the weight on his shoulders wasn't a ton.

"You played the way you practiced," his boss suggested.

Scott nodded. "Yes." So why did he feel so jumpy? What was wrong with him?

"Why don't you get started with the reports?" Portillo gestured toward Scott's laptop. "And you have a three o'clock meeting with the shrink."

"Already?" Scott's heart beat hard. The FBI had two contract psychologists who worked post shooting-incident cases. Agents thought that one of them was pretty good, and the other was a disaster.

"Got to do it."

"Who is it?"

Portillo frowned, a question on his face.

"Who's the shrink?" Scott asked again.

Portillo looked down at the email he'd received. "Name's Schneider."

Scott cursed. The bad one. "I don't want to see him."

"Got to. Sorry, man. You don't get to choose."

They may be able to make me see him, Scott fumed, *but they can't make me open up. No way.*

Still, even Scott realized that stuffing his emotions was exhausting. By the time they released him at the Bureau, it was seven o'clock. He was hungry and tired and just wanted to go home.

He was halfway there when his phone rang. It was his neighbor, really the only person in his neighborhood he knew. Scott listened, continuing to navigate the route home, his blood-pressure rising.

"You have got to be kidding!" he said. "Call the cops, and don't say you've talked to me."

Shaking, Scott thumbed his boss's number. "It's the press," he said, barely containing his anger. "They're at my house with cameras, trucks, everything. Clogging the whole street." He paused. "I am not going to subject myself to that."

His boss suggested he check on a room at the Academy. The dorms there housed agents-in-training as well as National Academy students.

"This better blow over soon," Scott replied, "and if I catch the guy who released my name..."

He clicked off the phone and started to turn around to head back to the Academy. Then he thought better of it. Instead, he drove south—south to where the roads turned into two lanes and the streetlights ended. South to where pickups outnumbered cars. South to where he could be alone on a dark and twisty road.

He thought he knew where he was going. Instead, he found himself turning into a long driveway. He made his way slowly between the trees, gravel crunching under his tires, through the low spot at the bottom, and then up the little hill.

The lights were still on in the log home, glowing warm and inviting. Scott parked, turned off his engine, and took a deep breath, wondering how he ended up at this place. He opened his door and got out. Above him the crystalline black sky was studded with stars. A plane made its way across the night, too high for him to hear, its lights blinking rhythmically. Scott stood for a minute, soaking in the beauty of it, the vastness of the universe. Then he heard a noise.

The door to the house opened. Nate emerged. Sprite raced down the stairs barking. Scott bent down to pet her, then walked toward Nate, waiting at the top.

"I'm glad you came," Nate said, his handshake evolving into a man-hug. "I'm real glad you came."

"I was headed for the bar," Scott confessed.

"I know you were. But you came here."

Scott followed Nate into the house, his gut shaky. It would have been easier to go to the bar, to just drink his thoughts away, but something had drawn him here. He trusted Nate.

"Scott!" Laura said. "Welcome."

"I'm sorry to just show up. I know it's late."

"We're glad you're here. What can I get you to eat?"

Over bacon and eggs they talked. Nothing, though, about the shooting. They weren't pushing him, and Scott appreciated that.

Instead, they talked about planting the garden, and about Laura's job, and about the argument they'd had because Laura wanted another dog and Nate wasn't sure it was a good idea. They laughed and teased each other. It all felt normal, and normal felt pretty good to Scott right then.

About an hour later at ten o'clock, Laura excused herself and went to bed. She'd invited Scott to spend the night, and at first he'd declined, but then the warmth of the home got to him. He had a ready bag in the Bucar, a couple of changes of clothes, shaving stuff, toiletries, and so he changed his mind.

While he retrieved the bag, Nate put on some soft music and took off his leg. He was sitting in his wheelchair in the living room near the couch, a fragrant candle flickering on the end table, when Scott walked back in.

"The guest room is down the hall, first room on the right," Nate said, gesturing.

Scott put his bag in the room, took off his jacket, walked back out, and sat down on the couch. Sprite jumped up next to him, which surprised him, but he soon found himself petting her.

"When you built this house," he asked, "why'd you make it wheelchair-accessible?" He'd noticed the wide hallway and doorways.

"I was thinking about buddies from the Marines. Maybe one of them would need a place to stay for a while. A lot of them were amputees."

"But you didn't build a ramp outside."

Nate laughed. "I ain't saying I was altogether logical about it." He shook his head and grew serious. "What happened?"

The story tumbled out...the alarm as Scott saw the kid entering the store, the sound of the gun, the screams, and then his training engaging. "I had to stop him. I yelled 'drop the gun!' but he didn't, and he turned toward me and I discharged my weapon. I shot him, six times. And somehow...somehow the little girl got shot too."

He stopped there, his throat closing. Sprite adjusted her position, resting her head on his thigh.

"By you?"

Scott kept his eyes on Sprite. "I don't know."

"That's the hard part, ain't it?" Nate said softly.

"The kid was one thing. He called the play. But the little girl..."

"I seen it myself in Afghanistan. Hard thing, that, knowing some innocent child got killed."

"How did you deal with it?" Scott asked.

It was more a rhetorical question than anything, but Nate responded. "I carried those memories around for years, until I began to see I had no control over it. None."

"Unless you pulled the trigger."

"Even then." Nate changed his position in the chair. He reached over and picked up the empty pipe sitting on the end table and stuck it in his mouth. "I'd never purposely kill an innocent child. And I know neither would you."

Scott could see the scars on his arms, burn scars from wounds suffered in Afghanistan. He saw Nate's anchor tattoo as well, though he couldn't remember what it stood for. He did remember —how could he ever forget!—the night Nate lost his leg as together they chased down a serial killer. Nate had walked the walk.

"What are you going to do," Nate asked, "if it was your bullet?"

Nausea swept over him. Scott shrugged.

"When do you find out?"

"Tomorrow...maybe."

Sprite snuggled closer. Her motion apparently did not get by Nate. "I can't never hide things from my dog. She keeps me honest, she does."

Scott kept petting the dog. The silence grew between them, the candle sending its soft scent through the room, the quiet music in the background. Finally, he said, "I don't know how I'll live with myself if I killed her." He looked away quickly. He tried to talk, choked up, took a deep breath, and tried again. "I didn't join the Bureau to kill innocent kids."

"I don't imagine that you did."

"It's a mess, once you fire your gun. A mountain of paperwork. The shooting incident review board. Mandatory counseling. And always the possibility of disciplinary action. Criminal complaints. Civil suits."

"You had to expect that when you joined."

"Sure I did. And I don't regret shooting that kid. Not for a minute. I'm sorry he died, but he called the play."

"And you probably saved a boatload of people."

Scott shrugged. "Hard to know."

"It's just the girl's got to you."

He looked up at Nate.

Nate didn't say anything for a while. Then he spoke. "What'd you want to be when you grew up, before your sister got killed?"

That question took Scott by surprise. "A rodeo cowboy." He laughed softly. "Bull riding. Working with the horses. That was my dream job." He ran his hand through his hair. "After that, I was thinking about medicine. I wanted to be a vet."

"And your sister's murder changed all that."

"Changed everything. Changed my dreams, changed my parents, changed my friends. Everything. I became focused on one thing—getting justice for Janey." It was the first time he'd said her name out loud in a long time. Janey.

Scott cleared his throat. "As hard as I try, I can't fix my sister's murder. Not my sister's murder, not my divorce, not my daughter's attitude, and not this little girl's death. None of it!" The tension that started in his back crept up to his neck until he felt like he had a dragon on his back and it was gripping his neck with its claws.

"It all piles up."

He shook his head, unable to speak.

———

"HOW WAS SCOTT WHEN HE LEFT?" Laura asked as she sat down for breakfast with Nate early the next morning.

"He was pretty broke up last night," Nate said. "We talked 'til past two."

"Did he leave then or did he sleep here?"

"Slept here. Said he was going to set an alarm for five, try to get home before the news people came back so he could get a shower and some fresh clothes 'fore he went to work." Then Nate reached over and took Laura's hand. "The Lord addressed something with me last night after Scott and I finished talking."

Laura raised her eyebrows. "What?"

He squeezed her hand. "The reason I didn't want to get another dog is, well, I'm the dog man, you know? That's been who I am these last twenty years, maybe more, stretchin' back to when I was a kid. I'm afraid." He choked up a little. "I'm afraid that, with this leg gone, I...I cain't do it again, I cain't be the dog man."

"Oh, Nate!"

"It's true. Scott, he's been thinking law enforcement so long, he doesn't know who he'd be without it. Me, it's the dog stuff. And I'm afraid, I *was* afraid, a new dog would be a reminder every day that I ain't who I was. But the Lord, he reminded me last night who I am. His child. Beloved. Forgiven. Accepted. Just as I am." Nate grabbed a tissue off the table and blew his nose. "I'm sorry for being self-centered and cowardly. We can get another dog if you want to. And if I cain't do it, well, I just cain't."

Laura got up and embraced him as he sat. "Oh, Nate. The reason I want another dog is, well, Sprite's getting up there. And I can't imagine you without a dog." She kissed him. "You will always be the dog man. Always. No matter how many legs you have." She sat back down and took his hand in hers. "The new dog will be yours to pick out and yours to train. You may have to do it differently, but Nate, you *will* be able to do it."

"But not for SAR." His stomach twisted.

"Yes, for SAR. I have an idea."

Nate raised his eyebrows.

13

By midday Monday, I'd been to the bank and had a certified check in hand. After cleaning dog hair out of the rental, I'd returned it, and now I was waiting for my ride to pick me up so I could collect the Jeep.

My ride was Jason. He'd wanted a date. This was it.

He didn't seem to mind when I'd returned his call and suggested this plan. He was late by ten minutes, but I decided not to count that against him. We drove to Fred Knowles's house and in short order I had my Jeep Wrangler. Sweet!

By pre-arrangement, his part of the date came next. I followed him to a restaurant down near Williamsburg. Over a lunch of crab bisque and salad, I found out Jason had applied to join the US Park Police.

"I've jumped through all the hoops," he said, "and passed all the tests. I'm just waiting for them to finish my background investigation and for a spot to open up at Club Fed."

Club Fed was the federal officer training facility at Glynco, Georgia. I knew that much at least.

I felt a twinge of jealousy. Scott had tried to recruit me for the FBI after we'd worked together. My years with Fairfax County police, my athleticism, and my master's degree would make me a shoo-in, he'd said. But I had chosen not to apply, and here I was, still scraping together a living as a private investigator, working without a badge or any authority whatsoever while someone was trying to kill me.

Why had I turned down Scott's offer? Part of it was an aversion to joining that male-dominated culture. Again. Been there, done that.

Another part was that I'd tried to picture myself at the Bureau, working long hours, leaving Luke home alone, and well, I just didn't want to do it. I wanted a life that included more than a job. I might not have a family, but I had Luke.

The third part was harder to admit, even to myself. I liked Scott. He was a man's man with a vulnerable side. It hurt when he got so wrapped up in his job that he stopped calling. And I knew it would always be that way with him. I had to protect myself.

As a result, I wanted nothing to do with the FBI. Now, listening to Jason and his dreams, I could see he could be headed down the same road as Scott.

Jason kept talking. He'd joined the Army right out of high school, worked as an MP, got deployed to Korea, returned home, and used the GI Bill to get his degree.

"It's all going just as I'd planned," he said, confidence gushing out.

Well, good luck with that. My mind instantly flashed through the twists and turns my life had taken.

When we'd finished our meals, I put my napkin on the table. "Thanks, Jason, for taking me out to get my car."

He looked surprised but took the hint and signaled for the check.

"I'll get mine," I said, pulling out a credit card.

That confused him, but I needed to draw a line. No more law-enforcement relationships. I saw him grimace, then concede. He had more in mind. I didn't.

Five minutes later I was out of there. First, I went to the DMV to register the car and get tags. Then I took the Jeep home, let Luke out, and began installing our SAR gear in our new ride. All the time I was working, I had two thoughts running through my head. I couldn't wait to show Nate my car and I wondered what else I could get on Susan Larson.

I'm sorry, I was not letting that go. I'd have to be careful, of course, but I was convinced Detective Hap Carroll had come after me. And Susan Larson was the cause. I might not be able to nail Carroll so easily, but I was sure I could get something on her.

I kept thinking about how to do that. Identify any friends she had? Find out where she worked? Stalk her on Facebook?

I finished with the Jeep and called Luke. We went inside, and he flopped down in the living room. I retreated to my office and booted up my computer. I had two new job offers, both background checks. I shot back my questionnaire to each of them, then reviewed my other cases.

Of the cheating husbands, I'd only caught one with a woman. I'd do some surveillance on him once the new camera I'd ordered from New York came. I was convinced the other one was not cheating. But I'd follow him, too, as soon as I had my new equipment.

Which reminded me of my old camera. The way I saw it, Trooper Rothsfeld could have told Detective Carroll about finding it in the wrecked Jeep. Or, if Carroll saw me taking pictures, he could have asked Rothsfeld to look for it. Either way, one of them could have retrieved it.

Or, the tow-truck driver or another employee of that company could have simply stolen it to sell.

I'd checked Craigslist and Facebook Marketplace multiple times, and eBay as well. Nothing so far. Which made me lean toward Carroll, who I figured was now laying low until I tired of looking for my property. If that was the case, he'd have taken the SD card out anyway by the time I found it.

So frustrating.

The next day I had my first of two appointments with Tamara Thomas's high-school friend. It was irritating, wasting time on this, but I'd promised.

Julie Long was thirty-six, the same age as Tamara would be, assuming she was still alive. I'd arranged to meet her at a coffee shop near her office. I ponied up for the drinks, then we sat down at a table near the back.

"It wasn't much of a shock when she ran away," Julie said. "She always had a restlessness about her. It was like...like her center didn't hold."

I raised my eyebrows.

She regrouped. "You know how fitness trainers push people nowadays to strengthen their cores because a strong core holds everything else in place?"

"Yes."

"Well, it's like Tammy had no emotional core, no center of gravity, and therefore no stability. She was supposedly my friend, but I never felt really close to her, you know? We didn't share secrets, or talk for a long time on the phone."

"Who was her boyfriend?" I always found it better to let people believe I knew more than I did.

Julie reacted. "Boyfriend? I don't think she had a boyfriend, not at school anyway." She sipped her macchiato. "I do remember this...right before she disappeared, she suddenly seemed happy, and I wondered whether there was someone in her life, someone she wasn't telling us about."

"Us?"

"The four of us who hung out together. Me, Shelley Sawyer, Bobbie Ridgeway, and Tammy."

Bobbie Ridgeway Markham was tomorrow's appointment. "Are you still in touch with Shelley and Bobbie?

"Bobbie yes, Shelley no. She got into drugs, and we parted company. My dad was a cop. He would have killed me."

I laughed softly. "I get that. My dad was a cop too." I shot the next question at her before we could continue down that path. "What kinds of things did the four of you do when you were hanging out?"

"Oh you know, we'd lie out in the sun and try to get tan. Listen to music. Talk about boys. We'd talk about girls too. We were so catty!" She laughed. "Tammy was always on the edge of things, never in the middle, even in our group."

She was describing another of my childhood traumas. I never could get into sitting around in a circle talking at recess, making fun of other girls and cataloging the attributes of the boys. I'd rather play softball with the guys, though most of them hated my intrusion into "their" game. I was either the subject of ridicule by the girls or rejection by the boys. No wonder I'd loved my dog.

"When did you first meet Tammy? How old were you?" I asked.

"My family moved here when I was twelve. We met in middle school. We were all boy crazy back then. Tamara seemed exotic with her dark hair and dark eyes. Quiet too. She usually didn't give the teachers any trouble, but she had a stubborn streak. If she didn't want to do something, she didn't do it. Her grades weren't great."

"When she disappeared, what did you think had happened?"

"I figured she ran away. But I didn't know who she'd go with or to."

"And where is Shelley today?"

Julie shrugged. "Like I said, I lost track."

"How about Shelley's parents?"

"As far as I know," said Julie, "they still live in the same house. I don't remember the address, but it's on the same street I lived on —Silver Street. My address was 4872. Shelley was four or five doors down in a brown house with brown shutters." She shrugged. "Very weird."

"How so?"

"We always said it was like living in a UPS truck. Brown on brown."

Like she said, girls are catty.

———

MY APPOINTMENT the next day with Bobbie went down a similar path. She didn't know of any boyfriend in Tammy's life. They'd drifted apart by tenth grade, the year Tammy disappeared. She was sorry she couldn't help more.

After Bobbie, I decided to see if I could find Shelley's parents. Maybe I'd get lucky. Maybe they'd be home and could clear up this mystery, and I could tell Miss Lottie everything I'd found out and be done with it.

I drove over to that neighborhood. I found 4872 Silver Street, then looked four or five houses each direction. Sure enough, at 4882 stood a brown house with brown shutters. The front bushes were overgrown, the yard shabby. I walked up to the door and rang the bell, then knocked when I didn't get an answer. After no response, I trudged back to my Jeep, determined to call them once I'd developed a phone number for that address.

As I started the engine, I realized I was three streets over from Miss Lottie's house. The least I could do was show her my new Jeep, the one she'd prayed for.

Of course, I drove over there and knocked on the door and almost passed out when she answered it. She was so gray—her hair, her face, everything.

"Oh, honey! Come in!" She stepped back to admit me.

"I, uh, can't stay. I just wanted to show you ... " I gestured back toward the Wrangler.

"Your car! Oh, what a blessing! God is good." She clasped her hands together.

It was a car. Just a car. Obviously, she was dealing with something far more serious than my little car problem.

Suddenly, Miss Lottie sagged against the doorframe. "Are you all right?" I asked, alarmed.

"I'm sorry. I'm just feelin' poorly."

I grabbed her elbow, put my arm around her waist, and helped her into the house, into her recliner in the living room. "What can I get you?"

"Maybe a little water."

Her voice was so faint. I hurried into the kitchen, poured a glass of water, and took it back out to her. Miss Lottie's little dog, who hadn't even barked when I came in, followed me, like he was worried, too, and thought maybe I'd fix her.

Meanwhile, my heart was drumming and I felt slightly sick. "What's going on?" I asked her. "Why do you feel bad?"

Miss Lottie took a sip of water. "I had my chemo yesterday." She looked at me with those gray eyes. "I wasn't going to do it, but now that you're helpin' me, well, honey, I just decided to buy a little more time. Maybe the Lord will let me see my Tamara."

Guilt bordering on despair flooded me. A: I hadn't done much of anything to find Tamara. B: I didn't think I would ever find her. And here Miss Lottie was, choosing the rigors of chemo in hopes I'd succeed.

"Miss Lottie, do you have any relatives, anybody who can come and stay with you?"

She laughed softly. "Honey, I'm all alone 'cept for the Lord and Tiger. I got my church family. They fetched me to and from chemo. I got a niece in California, but she's busy with her own life. So no, I got no one else."

Oh my gosh! It was one thing for me to have nobody. I was young and strong. I could make it on my own. But Miss Lottie!

"I'll stay here for a while," I heard myself saying, "to make sure you're okay." I don't know where that came from.

"I know you have to work. Somebody's bringing dinner by after a while." She patted my hand. "I'll be fine."

I did stay, though, for half an hour more. She talked a little, but mostly we just sat and I held her hand, unable to leave her but terrified she would die right there. Finally, she opened her eyes and patted my hand. "Honey, you go on home now. I'm going to take a little nap. Just leave the door unlocked. My friends will be here soon."

I left, wondering if I'd ever see her again.

14

I MANAGED to put Miss Lottie out of my mind the rest of the week, but I didn't forget Susan Larson. I stalked her on social media, went by her house twice, and even staked out the grocery store near her home. I drew a line at watching her kids' elementary school. That seemed creepy.

My new camera arrived by UPS, and I immediately started working on the possible straying husband cases. One guy was for sure innocent. He was seeing a psychologist and apparently hadn't told his wife. The other? I didn't know. I saw him with some woman close to his age, but he never took her hand, or kissed her, or did anything that suggested they were having an affair. One day, I got a great picture of them at an outdoor café. When I sent it to his wife, she immediately recognized the woman. She was his sister.

That wife paid me promptly, in cash, and begged me not to tell her husband of her suspicions.

I had a SAR practice that would take up all day Sunday, so I decided to drive my new Wrangler up to Nate's on Saturday and surprise him. I figured if I left by six-thirty in the morning, I would catch him and Laura before they went out anywhere. I was taking a chance, I knew, but somehow I think I was hoping that his enthusiasm for my new car would temper his annoyance that I'd never called him back.

I left as planned, drove the ninety minutes with Luke safely installed in his new crate, and pulled up in Nate's driveway.

Eight o'clock in the morning and there was already another car there. Worse, it looked like Scott's. And there was no way I could turn around and leave without someone noticing.

Great. I let Luke out of the car. I heard the door open and looked up. Laura came out on the porch.

"Hey, there! Very nice, Jess! I like it!"

I trudged up the steps, "trudge" being the right word for it. Laura was smiling, but the worst was yet to come. The two guys, Nate, whose calls I had let pass, and Scott, were inside.

To my surprise, when I made it to the porch, Laura pulled the inside door most of the way shut and touched my arm, causing me to stop.

"You should know," she said softly, "Scott's pretty broken up. It was his bullet that killed that girl."

His bullet? A girl? What was going on? What had I missed? Too proud to admit I was out of the loop, I simply nodded. My gut felt like a wet rag twisting inside me. Laura pushed open the door, and Luke and I walked in.

Nate sat in the wheelchair next to the fireplace. He looked up, and his eyes narrowed. I didn't want to read what was in them.

Scott sat on the couch, his back to me. He turned, and if Scott could ever look scruffy, he definitely looked scruffy. He had a day-old beard, his eyes were red like he hadn't slept, and his shirt was askew. Either he'd been drinking a lot or something. Crying? I couldn't even imagine Scott crying.

"How's it goin', Jess?" Nate said.

"I'm sorry. I came at a bad time." Shame and guilt poured over my soul like hot tar. These people had helped me move, rescued me when someone tried to kill me, and I couldn't even return their phone calls? What was wrong with me?

I tried to recover. I walked over to Nate and gave him our normal hug. When I straightened up and turned around, Scott was walking out of the room. Shocked, I turned and sat down on the hearth, near Nate.

"I'm sorry," I whispered.

Nate shifted in his chair. "He ain't ready to talk. He's takin' it hard."

"What happened?"

He told me the whole story, that it was Scott in the store when the shooting happened, and Scott who took down the shooter, and Scott's bullet that ended up in the little girl who died.

"Forensics showed the shooter's DNA on it from a piece of flesh and blood."

I raised my eyebrows, processing what he said.

"It appears Scott's aim was true. The bullet entered the shooter, then ricocheted off a bone or something and went into the little girl. Hit an artery. She bled out."

"So Scott didn't shoot her."

"Not directly. But that don't mean nothin' to Scott. He pulled the trigger and the girl died. He's all broke up about it." He reached over and patted my hand. "Don't take it personal, him walkin' out like that. He's just tore up."

And so Scott had come to the Tanner House of Healing like I had, and I suspect so many others had as well. I rose. "I'll go. Please tell him I'm sorry. And I'm sorry, Nate, for popping in on you like this."

Nate nodded. "You're welcome anytime, you know that." Grace. Nate's specialty.

"She bought a new car," Laura said.

"Well then, afore you go, let's have a look at it."

———

I DROVE HOME HALF an hour later, deflated, angry with myself, vowing to do better, to be a better friend. But I had a nagging feeling that probably wouldn't happen. Something inside me needed to change, something I couldn't see.

The thought crossed my mind I should make an appointment with my counselor, but no—I had moved too far away from Sarah Pennington for that to be practical. And I really didn't want to have to start with someone new. I'd have to figure this out on my own.

Nate had admired my Jeep Wrangler appropriately. He loved the custom fittings and the leather interior. When I opened the rear door, Luke jumped straight up into his crate. I took that as my cue to leave. I closed everything up and hugged Nate goodbye. The hug was a little longer on my part because I felt bad. When I finally let go, he looked at me with those blue eyes.

"Don't be a stranger, now. We could use a little brightenin' up around here now and then."

Brightening up? Me?

———

THE SAR PRACTICE the next day took my mind off things. We worked all day in a wooded area, each of the handlers taking turns hiding so the dogs could find us. Luke did great, completing two complicated tests. Then I let him rest while I helped a young woman with a puppy, a Border collie named Pip.

Starting a dog, especially a puppy, is fun. Luke was two when we started, but I'd had an Australian shepherd as a kid that I trained in agility, and the basic principles are the same.

In SAR, the idea is to teach them from the get-go that "seek" or "go find" is the most fun game ever. You want to develop drive in dogs, so you start them out seeking the person they love most in the world—their owner.

"What command are you going to use?" I asked Cindy, Pip's owner. After all, there were options.

"Find," she replied. She was in her twenties, a virtual assistant who worked from home, and this was their very first attempt at SAR.

"On leash or off?" I asked.

"Off leash." Cindy had been working with Pip in obedience.

I explained how the exercise would play out, then I held Pip while Cindy ran away, flapping her arms dramatically and making happy noises. Pip strained against my grip. The second Cindy ducked behind a bush, I let Pip go, saying "Find! Find, Pip, find!"

The little black-and-white dog took off, racing toward Cindy, who rewarded him generously. I joined them, and we made a big, happy party out of it.

A few more times and that was it for the day. But Pip did well. "He's a natural," I assured Cindy, as if I were an old pro. I was actually only a mid-level SAR handler. Yes, I'd been successful in some complicated real-life situations, but most of them were working as a team with Nate, and you couldn't get a better mentor.

Just thinking about my day with the SAR team as I drove home that night made me think about Nate and Scott. I'd been where Scott was now, consumed with guilt over something that was not my fault, grieving a death that seemed like it came from my hands.

And I remembered what helped me get over it. Nate slowly and gently taught me about grace and God's love, while I, in my stubbornness, resisted him.

I imagined Nate would be doing that same thing now with Scott, because, well, that's who Nate is.

———

THE NEXT FEW weeks I kept busy. I wanted to up my running game, now that I'd recovered from my accident. Luke needed the exercise and so did I. Second, I had several new cases come in, including a background check from down in Hampton, which was my furthest job south so far. Third, I intended to check in on Miss Lottie and Scott.

Fourth, I had a little extracurricular activity planned—continuing my surveillance on Susan Larson and Hap Carroll. Both of them. Separately or together. Because someone had tried to kill me, and I was not letting that go.

I tried to stay disciplined. Every morning, even when it rained, Luke and I ran, two miles at first, then three, then four (the distance I wanted to become my standard) with a longer run thrown in once or twice a week. I was used to competing in mountain-trail races, and everything down here was near flat. Easy running. Too easy. I didn't want to lose my fitness.

After our run, I'd shower while Luke cooled down, then I'd feed him before working on my paid jobs. I had to support myself. Nobody else was going to.

But I confess it was really hard when I was finished doing background checks or stalking straying husbands, not to check out Susan Larson's Facebook page. Why do so many people leave them public? Just asking for stalkers. Or I'd do a little online sleuthing of Hap Carroll's life. As a detective, he laid pretty low, which is what I would expect, but I'd identified his wife and found a bunch of stuff that she'd posted. So far, I'd found out his home address, the names of his children, and the kind of personally owned vehicle he drove, which just happened to be a truck.

15

SCOTT STEPPED out of his car and stretched. The late-June sun felt hot, especially after the chill of his car's air-conditioning. A cloudless blue sky stretched like a bright blue tarp overhead, undisturbed by wrinkles or flaws. He took a deep breath and inhaled the fresh country air.

He'd grown up in Colorado, and the air in Virginia in the summer felt perpetually sticky to him. Still, he liked being out in the country.

In the weeks since the shooting, he'd felt like he was suffocating. He was either answering questions from someone investigating the incident or working on something no one gave a rip about. His assignments, he knew, were designed to keep him off the street. He hadn't been cleared for regular duty yet, which meant he hadn't been able to hide his mental state from the Bureau up-and-ups. And that bothered him.

As did the nightmares. And the queasy way he felt half the time. And the anxiety that would sweep over him like a flash flood and be gone just as fast.

Right after the shooting, he'd come close to quitting. But then he thought about his daughter. She was just fourteen, which meant he had eight more years of financial obligation, at least. High school, then college. He had to keep his income, no matter how distasteful his job had become.

And what else could he do besides law enforcement? It was too late to start medical school.

Visits with the Bureau psychologist remained mandatory, although he had been able to switch to the "good one." That guy was okay to talk to, but Scott still hadn't really opened up. Why would he want to? So he could have a flag on his file?

That didn't make sense. Nothing made sense.

Nate had called and said he had a two-man job to do and asked if Scott could help him. "It'll get you sweaty, so bring a change of clothes and your work gloves. And you might as well plan to stay the night," Nate had said. "I intend to work late."

So Scott had come. What else did he have to do on a weekend?

As Scott pulled up, he noticed two things—a new building going up behind Nate's house and a bunch of fence posts lying on the ground, forming an L-shape in a large portion of the grassy area of Nate's front yard.

He grabbed a backpack and his work gloves out of his Nissan Rogue and walked up to the front door. He could hear Sprite barking inside. He knocked, and Nate opened it.

"Hey, man!" Nate said, giving Scott his customary man-hug. "Thank you for coming."

"Hey," Scott responded. "What's going on?"

"Put your stuff in the guest room and I'll show you."

Scott threw his pack on the floor, and they walked outside, with Sprite following them. "What's this?" He gestured toward the building.

"A stable."

"For a horse?"

"Yep."

"When'd you get a horse?"

"Came with the woman. Part of the negotiations. Sort of a country prenup. We just put off bringing her here 'til Laura figured I was recovered."

"Are you building it yourself?"

"No. Laura sold her house and put money into this. You and me, our job is fencin' the pasture."

Scott tried to wrap his head around that idea. "Wow, okay. You draw up plans?"

Nate pulled a folded piece of paper out of his pocket. Scott studied it, impressed with the detail and the size of the fenced area.

"She's taking everything but my garden," Nate said, laughing. "But that's okay. I cut enough grass on the job. That hoss can help out here."

"This is for one horse?" Scott said.

"That woman, she's talking about two. Reminding me that horses are herd animals."

Scott nodded. "She's right."

"I reminded her I cut grass for a living."

"Horses are expensive."

"She has got this hair-brained notion of me doin' search-and-rescue on horseback."

"What a great idea!"

"Sounds crazy to me."

"If you're thinking about two horses, you might want to consider curving the corners."

"Why's that?"

"If you have more than one horse, it blocks the dominant horse from having a place to bully the other one."

"You know about horses?"

"My dad's brother had a ranch in Colorado. I spent a lot of time there." He paused. "Me and my sister," Scott said, bracing for the inevitable stab of sorrow. He looked up at the job ahead of them. "We're setting the posts?"

"Right."

"You're using boards?"

"No, it's a plastic-coated high-tensile with electric on top. Comes in a roll."

Scott raised his eyebrows.

"There's more opinions about horse fencing than ideas on where Cain got a wife." Nate shook his head. "She finally chose this stuff. Looks like board and you don't have to paint it. Is it the best thing to use? I have no idea. Guess we'll find out."

"Okay, then. You got a posthole digger?"

"Rented a two-man, gasoline-powered job."

"I've used one of those before."

"Good," Nate said. "Let's get goin' then."

Wrestling with that two-man posthole digger soon had sweat running down both of their backs. They were digging down about three feet to drop in an eight-foot fence post, which would give them a five-foot fence. Up on the hill, they ran into a rock now and then, which they had to dig out with a pickaxe and shovel. Down the hill, next to the tree line, they had roots to contend with.

Scott lost himself in the job. The smell of the gasoline, the vibration of the digger, the sweat drenching his shirt drowned out his problems. Neither he nor Nate talked much—they couldn't over the noise of the digger. When they finished one hole, they said just enough to go on to the next one.

Scott figured he was five years younger, four inches taller, and thirty or forty pounds heavier than Nate, plus he had two legs, but he couldn't outwork the dog man. By noon they both had their shirts off. By one o'clock, Scott was glad Nate suggested they break for lunch.

They hosed off out back and then Nate brought some pre-made sandwiches and lemonade out on the front porch.

"Where's Laura today?" Scott asked.

"Let me say grace and I'll tell ya," Nate said. He blessed the food and said amen. "She's up with the horse, preparing her to move, practicing with the trailer and all."

"She rides English?"

"Oh no, Western all the way. Did barrel racing when she was younger. You two will get along great."

"Wow." Scott took a bite of his sandwich. "What kind of horse does she have?"

"Quarter Hoss. Chestnut. 'Bout six years old. Well broke."

"That's cool. That's what my uncle had. Quarter Horses."

"Laura, she's about that hoss like I am with dogs. She'd starve before she gave up that mare. I'm lucky I had a place big enough for the hoss. Don't know if she would've married me. You'll have to come by when Laura brings her home. She's gonna want to show her off."

16

ONE LATE JUNE DAY, I hit pay dirt on a trip down Susan Larson's street. She was just pulling out of her driveway.

I followed her, discreetly, to a nearby strip mall and watched her walk into a fitness center. She was a gym rat! By the way she was dressed, I wondered if she was trolling again.

I checked the time and entered it into a little logbook I'd been keeping, along with the date and day of the week. Then I left and spent a few hours looking into leads on other cases.

I started driving by the gym, and within three weeks, I had identified Susan Larson's pattern and spotted someone else I recognized going into the same gym.

Hap Carroll.

No, seriously.

A thought flashed into my mind. *He works out?*

Two days later, on my next surveillance outing, I was sitting in my Jeep in the parking lot taking notes when a woman emerged from the gym. She looked vaguely familiar. She was crying.

My mind shifted off of Susan, who was inside the gym, and Hap. The crying woman was in her forties. Short, maybe five foot two, she carried her extra weight like an inner tube, around the middle. I watched her walk away from the gym, cross the street, trip over a curb, and then collapse.

She'd disappeared behind the parked cars. Alarmed, I got out and jogged over toward her. "Ma'am, are you all right?" I asked, finding her sobbing on the ground next to a minivan.

She shook her head.

"Are you hurt? Can you get up?" I held out my hand. She took it, and I helped her to her feet. She seemed so unsteady. "Let's just sit for a minute," I said, and I guided her over to a nearby bench. I kept my hand around her waist because she seemed so weak. I helped her sit, then squatted down in front of her. I positioned myself so I could see the front door of the gym. I sure didn't want to be surprised by either Susan or Hap. "What's going on?"

While the woman glanced around nervously, my mind imagined answers to my question. I expected a cancer diagnosis. Or a miscarriage. Or maybe her best friend's death. But instead, she said, "I just had a big fight with my husband." She fixed her red-rimmed blue eyes on me, and as she did, her face began to align itself with the faces in my memory. "Are you married?" she asked.

"No."

"Lucky you."

She began sobbing again, and the face came into focus and I realized who she was: a sobbing Mrs. Hap Carroll. I couldn't believe it. My mind raced.

"I'm sorry you're having problems. My name's...Lorie," I said, quickly coming up with a pseudonym. "How can I help?" My heart beat like a sparrow's.

She spilled her guts all over me, all over the ground—sorrow after sorrow streaming out of her. She'd had a fight with her husband. He'd been acting strange lately, working late, walking out of the room to take phone calls, keeping erratic hours.

"He's a detective. I get that he needs privacy. I understand the abnormal hours. But..." she broke down, "...but we've been married eighteen years and this is different."

I squeezed her hand. "I'm sorry. What do you think is going on?"

She looked at me and sobbed, "I think he's having an affair."

"Oh, no! What makes you think that?"

"I've...I've smelled perfume on him." Her pain made my gut twist.

"How long has this been going on?"

"I don't know—two months, maybe?" Mrs. Carroll's swollen face, her tear-streaked cheeks, implored me to do something. "Hap isn't, well, he's not exactly David Beckham." She reached for a paper towel and wiped her nose. Then she looked at me defiantly. "But he's *my* husband!" She doubled up her fist and hit her thigh. "I decided to fight for him. Beat this other woman at her own game. Today, I came down here, joined the gym, and I'm going to start working out. I'm going to try to be the woman he needs. The problem is...I have a feeling I can't be!"

How could I tell her she was right? I'd seen enough of cheaters to know they could be married to the sexiest woman alive and they'd still be going after the filly in the next field.

A fresh breeze lifted her auburn hair. "Do you have children?" I asked.

"Two. A boy fourteen and a girl eleven."

"Do you work?"

She shook her head.

Get a job, lady. Get. A. Job.

But realistically, I knew it wasn't that easy. It takes a lot to keep a family going, and I could understand her staying home. Especially since I suspected ol' Hap wasn't exactly the most attentive husband and father.

My mind raced. This lady needed help. My eyes fell on the gold chain around her neck and its cross pendant. "Do you go to church?" Nate would be proud of me.

She nodded.

"Go to your pastor. Tell him what's going on."

"Okay."

But then I qualified my advice. "If he says something like, 'just forgive him,' or 'be a better wife,' or 'spice things up,' ignore him. Find a counselor. If he says, 'I'll talk to him,' or 'I'll help you two get counseling,' then do what he says."

I may not have ever been married, and I may not be much of a churchgoer, but I'd been around the horn enough to know what kind of bad advice was floating around out there. It seemed to me a lot of women think it's their job to carry the emotional weight of the marriage, to put up with anything from a guy. It was a huge issue for me, one which prompted heated discussions with Nate about patriarchy and Christianity.

But after endlessly challenging Nate and scrupulously double-checking his answers defending true Christianity, I knew now that the idea that it was all on the women wasn't right. *Husbands, love your wives as Christ loved the church*, he'd read straight from his Bible to me one night when we were battling it out.

"If I recall," he'd said, "Christ *died* for his church."

It struck me that Laura was one lucky woman.

I moved to the bench and hugged Mrs. Carroll gently. Her sobs had reduced to sniffles. "What's your name?"

"Tanya."

"Okay, Tanya, do you think you can get yourself home?"

She glanced at her watch. "I need to. My daughter will be home soon." She stood up, as did I. "Thank you. I'm glad you were here. Are you a counselor or something?"

"No. I've just...been around."

She hugged me. "I'm calling my pastor as soon as I get home."

"Let me walk you to your car."

She guided me to a blue Ford Focus, got in, and gave me a little wave. "Thank you. You are a blessing."

Me? My head swimming with thoughts, I snapped a quick picture of her license plate, then walked back to my own car. So,

Hap Carroll was having an affair. With Susan Larson. What was he thinking?

I started my Jeep, but then sat there thinking. I was angry. Angry at Hap Carroll, angry at Susan Larson, angry at the pain Tanya was going through. It was so unjust. I especially hated the fact she thought she could change it by being thinner!

Then a horrible thought struck me. I wondered if Tanya would end up divorced—or worse? Dead, like Bob Larson. Would Hap or Susan be that stupid?

But then, he *had* run me off the road.

I had to do something. My mind started creating options. I could track down Tanya and admit to her all that I knew and advise her to get a lawyer. Or I could report Hap Carroll to his boss. I could call Trooper McCoy and fill him in. I could tell Bob Larson's lawyer. I could confront Hap—or Susan—directly.

That would be crazy. Hap had tried to kill me. Susan had offed her husband. That was way too dangerous!

I had just soundly rejected that thought when I looked up, and who should come walking out of the gym but Hap? Right behind him was Susan.

Impulse drove me out of that car. Impulse and anger. I grabbed a bag from the front seat and, crouching low, I quickly moved two car rows over so it looked like I was coming from another car. Then I walked back toward the gym, rummaging in my bag.

I nearly ran into Hap. Two feet from him, I stopped, acted surprised, then said, "Detective!"

His eyes narrowed. Susan, about five feet behind him, suddenly veered off to the right.

"Hello," Carroll said.

"I'm surprised to see you here," I said. He looked at me like I was crazy. "I think I just met your wife. Tanya, is it?"

His face reddened. Unable to control his alarm, his eyes darted left and right.

"Oh, she's gone. She left a while ago. Had to be home for your daughter," I said, slathering on the guilt. "She was here, in the parking lot, crying her eyes out. I hope everything's okay." I shot him a piercing look. "See you around, Detective." I resumed walking toward the gym.

"Hey," he called after me. "Hey! You still on that case?"

I stopped, turned, and lobbed a grenade. "Nope. I'm sure you're covering all the bases."

I laughed at my own middle-school joke all the way into the building.

That night, I called Nate and told him what I'd done. A long silence followed. "What?" I said, demanding a response.

"Strikes me you're askin' for trouble."

I climbed onto my high horse. "We can't let them get away with this! Not what they did to Bob, and not what they tried to do to me."

"Who's 'we'?"

I hesitated. "Well, me anyway."

Nate made a soft clicking sound. "You watch your back, girl. That's all I'm sayin'."

That night, as I was trying to fall asleep, his comments bothered me. Still, I kept thinking about Sam Larson's brother and Tanya Carroll, and doggone it, *somebody* had to do *something*.

I had taken action. So sue me.

17

SOMETIMES WHEN I'VE done something boneheaded, I've tried to make up for it by doing something right–something I really don't want to do. It's like the game the father of a friend of mine told me about when I was a kid. He was a sailor. He said sailors have an imaginary black box. When they do something good but not immediately necessary for their boat (like changing the oil early), they think of it as making a deposit in the black box. These deposits became "insurance" so when they do something stupid, like forget to untie a line, it isn't catastrophic.

When I told Nate about that, he rolled his eyes. "Sounds like karma."

Sometimes Nate takes things much too seriously. Most of the time.

After a restless sleep, I decided maybe confronting Hap Carroll had been a bad idea. I needed to make a deposit in my black box. So after running with Luke and checking my work email, I debated with myself. Should I call Miss Lottie or Scott?

I didn't want to call either of them, Miss Lottie because of the hopelessness of her life and her case, and Scott because, well, I didn't know what to say. I had not been a very good friend. But then, he had hurt me by not calling me.

I decided to call Miss Lottie. But first, I had to do *something* on her case. That something turned out to be contacting Shelley Sawyer's parents. Her mother, actually, because her father had died. I arranged to meet her later that morning, then I called Miss Lottie.

When she answered the phone her voice was so weak I could barely hear her.

"How are you feeling?" I asked.

"Oh, I'm gettin' along. I've missed you, honey, but I know you're working hard."

I told her about my appointment with Shelley Sawyer's mother, and she was thrilled. Then I turned the subject to her. "What are the doctors saying, Miss Lottie?"

"Well, I don't know. I've had a little trouble gettin' in to see them."

"Too sick?"

"No, had trouble gettin' rides."

Oh, good grief. On top of everything else. And somehow I suspected there was no point in explaining Uber. "When's your next appointment?"

"I'm s'posed to go this afternoon...at one. I just don't have a way to get there."

I'd just made an eleven-thirty appointment three streets over from Miss Lottie. How could I sidestep this need of hers? "I'll take you," I said, hoping she couldn't hear the reluctance in my voice. I had things to do.

"Oh, honey, thank you! You are so sweet."

I wasn't, really. I was just filling the black box, one good deed at a time.

After I hung up with her, I changed into nicer clothes, let

Luke out one more time, and then drove over to their neighborhood. I pulled up in front of the brown box house at 11:28 a.m. Mrs. Sawyer met me at the door.

Mrs. Sawyer, it turned out, knew little about Tamara Thomas. "Dark-haired. Pretty. Foreign girl," she said. "Don't know what happened to her."

Her own daughter, Shelley, was in prison. She'd run afoul of the drug laws too many times. "I did my best," Mrs. Sawyer said, "but my daughter just couldn't get off the drugs. At least she's in prison now, where there aren't any."

I almost laughed. Prisons were full of drugs.

———

AFTER THAT DEPRESSING VISIT, Miss Lottie was a breath of fresh air. She looked a little better than the last time I'd seen her. Maybe she'd finished the chemo? I didn't know. But it was her attitude that provided the freshness. Her gray eyes lit up when she opened the door. She was all dressed up with a handbag on her arm and her cane in her other hand. I couldn't help but hug her.

"Oh, I get to ride in your new car," she said, her voice filled with delight.

"Yes, ma'am."

Sharp-eyed, as soon as she got in, she started asking questions about it. Why was the back seat missing? What was that box for? Was this a different kind of radio?

She had me talking about search-and-rescue all the way over to her doctor's office. It positively lifted my spirits.

I helped her into the doctor's office, then sat in the waiting room thumbing through magazines featuring upbeat stories of cancer survivors. I read a couple, but I just didn't get it. Sure these people could be upbeat—they were winning the fight. But what about those losing the battle? What about the ones doing the chemo, doing the radiation, having the operations and the scans and all the rest, who were nonetheless dying? Miserably.

I slapped the magazine down on the end table a little too hard. The other two people in the waiting room looked up at me.

Sorry, I just didn't get it. Just like I didn't get all those Bible verses that talked about "rejoicing always" and being "anxious for nothing" and all the rest. I mean, c'mon!

I sighed. Where was Nate when I was ready for a good argument?

Miss Lottie emerged from the door a few minutes after that. I shook off my scowl, stood, and walked over to her. "Ready to go?"

"Oh, yes, dear," she said.

"Is this your daughter?" asked the receptionist, smiling at Miss Lottie.

I felt my face flush.

"Oh, no," said Miss Lottie kindly. She patted my hand, which was on her arm. "She's a friend. A very sweet young woman."

I knew I was anything but. But I had a black box entry to complete, so I walked Miss Lottie out to my car, helped her in, and headed for home. For good measure, I asked her if she needed anything while we were out, and she admitted she needed a little food. I pulled into the grocery store, helped her shop, and stood patiently while she paid for it.

When we got to her house, I helped her inside, carried the groceries in, and was shocked to find her refrigerator almost empty and her shelves as well. Had she been eating at all?

I fixed a little meal for her, a quick favorite of my own invention. A pound of ground beef (browned), a can of cream of chicken soup, and some frozen mixed vegetables. Heat and serve over rice or noodles. Fake Stroganoff had carried me through many a chilly night. I fixed her a bowl with some noodles, put the rest in the fridge, poured her a glass of water, and carried it out to her.

"Here you go," I said, putting it on the end table. Tiger, who had been on the couch next to her, stood and sniffed the air. "You need to eat a little. Keep your strength up."

"Oh, honey, thank you," Miss Lottie replied. "I promise, I will. I just need to close my eyes for a second."

"Okay, I have to go, but I'll call you."

"Oh, sweetie! I forgot. I found something for you. It's back there, on Tamara's bed." Miss Lottie gestured toward the bedrooms.

I walked back, flipped on the light, and there, on the bed was a photo album. Picking it up, I leafed through it as I returned to the living room. The album was full of pictures of Tamara as a child.

"I found it just the other day. I thought it might help you," Miss Lottie said.

"Thank you," I said. "I'll look through it." I left, and shoved the album under the front seat of the Jeep. I'd look at it when I had time.

———

THAT EVENING I CALLED NATE, complaining, as I always did, about how unfair life was, and where was God, and how could he allow Miss Lottie to suffer there all alone. And Nate listened patiently, as he always did, despite the fact we'd been over this ground many, many times and even though he knew in his heart I had not yet cracked open that Bible to find answers for myself.

"So do you know what I did?" I said, challenging him as God's personal representative.

"No, Jess. What?"

"I set a reminder on my phone to check with her every week. I'll see what groceries she needs, and what appointments she has, and what bills are coming due. That's how you take care of an elderly widow!"

I made it sound like I was kinder, more compassionate, more *godly* than God. It was one of those times when, looking back, I am surprised I wasn't struck dead right there.

18

SCOTT COULD HEAR Sprite barking as soon as he got out of the car. They would finish the pasture today. The barn was up and all the fencing was done except the gates, and they should hang those pretty easily. He realized with a pang he was going to miss having a reason to come down here every weekend.

When he first started, he figured he would have to ignore a lot of preaching from Nate, but that wasn't the case. Soon, he let his guard down and relaxed. In fact, working at Nate's was about the only time in the week he felt relaxed.

Scott walked up the steps and Nate opened the door. "Hey, man," Nate said. "Good to see you. Come on in." He gestured toward the couch. "Have a seat. I'll be right out."

The leather creaked as Scott sat down. Absentmindedly, he picked up the book Nate had been reading and thumbed through it. For a thin book, it had some pretty deep thoughts. He put it down again.

"All right, let's go," Nate said, entering the room again.

"I'm ready."

They worked for about three hours in the hot sun, setting the gates, making sure they swung just right. There were two gates wide enough for a vehicle, one near the barn and one down the hill at the end of the "L" near the driveway. Then there were two smaller gates about four feet wide.

"Barn looks good," Scott said, when they stopped to wipe the sweat off their faces. "It's handsome."

"She wanted it done right."

"It's got water?"

"Water, electric, a loft, and a tack room big enough for a bed. Scares me. I might end up in there."

Scott smiled. "I don't think you have to worry about that."

"I don't know. These women, they get their ideas."

"Yes, they do." That triggered a thought. "How's Jess?"

Nate picked up a wrench and tightened a bolt. "Not hearin' much from that girl these days. You ought to call her."

Scott shrugged. "I'm not good company right now."

"I ain't havin' trouble with you."

"That's because we're working."

Nate gestured toward the gate they were working on. "Hold that up while I fix this." He tightened the last bolt.

A sound from the driveway caused both men to turn and look. "Just in time," Nate said. "Here she comes."

"You bought another truck?" Scott asked.

"Nope. That's her truck."

"You married a woman with a good truck? Aren't you smart."

"Yep. Mine's about dead." Nate clapped him on the back. "Trouble is, a hoss came with her truck. I don't know. Mighta been smarter for me just to buy a new truck."

Laura pulled up, got out, hugged Scott, and kissed her husband.

"Everything go okay?" Nate asked.

"So far."

Scott could hear the horse moving restlessly in the trailer. His mind went back to his uncle's ranch. He shook off his thoughts. "You need help getting her out?"

"You know about horses?"

"Some."

"I think I'll be okay," Laura said, "but stand by."

"It's a slant load?"

"Yes." Laura walked around to the left side, pulled a mounting block out of the back of her pickup, and set it down near the front of the trailer. Then she climbed up on it, reached in, and untied her horse.

Lead rope in hand, she moved around to the back, unlatched the tailgate, and swung the door wide open. "I'll get that," Scott said, and he held the door, keeping it from hitting Laura or the horse. He glanced over and saw Nate looking at him curiously.

"Whoa, Abby," Laura said as she opened the divider in the trailer and secured it. "Whoa, girl." She kept her hand on the horse as she moved forward, attached the lead rope, and then put her hand on the mare's chest to move her back.

Scott watched as the beautiful chestnut Quarter Horse felt her way out of the trailer. Something caught in his chest. He took a deep breath, trying to loosen the tightness. The smell of the horse, the sight of her coat gleaming in the sun, the sound of her hooves, transported him back twenty years. He could see his sister in a saddle, the sharp peaks of the Rockies behind her. He could hear her laughing when he challenged her to a race, feel the horse underneath him, sense the exhilaration of a mad gallop across the ranch, feel his hat being swept off his head by the wind.

Laura's voice brought him back. "You want to come say hi?"

He closed the back and latched it. Scott held his hand up to the mare's nose and let her smell him, then ran his hand over her neck, and onto her withers. He felt the smoothness of her coat, the firmness of her muscles, and he fingered her mane. His throat got tight.

"Do you ride?" Laura asked, her voice soft.

"A long time ago."

"You'll have to try her out once she gets settled."

Scott didn't respond. He tried to swallow past the lump in his throat. His eyes watered.

Nate broke the silence. "Laura, you're probably tuckered out, making that drive on those mountain roads with the trailer." Nate said. "You want to turn her out or put her in the stall?"

"The stall for now."

"Okay."

Laura made a clicking noise and led the mare into the barn. Scott's head felt like a band was wrapped around it. He followed them into the barn and watched as Laura walked the horse in and removed the lead rope.

Nate grabbed a bucket. "I'll fetch water."

Scott stood watching, silent, his mind most of a continent away, and half a lifetime ago.

"I guess it's time for dinner," Nate said when he returned.

"You staying, Scott?" Laura asked.

He shook his head. "No. Do you mind if I hang out here for a while?"

She cocked her head. "Stay as long as you like."

———

"WHAT'S GOING ON WITH SCOTT?" Laura slid her hand into Nate's as they walked back to the house.

"We'll know along and along."

"He's had some history with horses. Did you see the way he was touching her?"

"Yeah, and he knew what a slant-load trailer was."

They went inside. Laura showered while Nate cooked dinner. He made a salad, microwaved corn on the cob, and grilled some steaks. As he was putting food on the table, he said, "I thought for sure the smell of the steaks would bring Scott out of the barn."

Laura put glasses of lemonade on the table. Nate had set a

third place, but it looked like it was going to go unused. "Maybe you should check on him."

Nate thought about it. "Maybe I should."

———

Scott stood with his arms draped across Abby's withers, his forehead resting on her. The emotion he'd fought for so many years had flooded him.

He heard a noise and straightened up, quickly wiping his eyes on his sleeve.

"Hey. Got some steaks ready," Nate said.

Scott moved out of the stall. "No, thanks. I've got to go."

"Been a long time since you've been around a horse?"

Scott cocked his head at the comment. How did Nate know? He took a deep breath. "Yeah."

"You want to talk?" Nate gestured toward a straw bale.

He shook his head. "Your dinner's ready."

"I don't care about that. Sit down." Nate sat on the bale and leaned his head back against the wall.

Scott hesitated, pushing against a voice inside. But then he realized Nate wasn't going anywhere, so he sat.

"Tell me about it," Nate said, pulling his pipe out of his pocket and sticking it in his mouth.

"It's nothing."

But it wasn't nothing, it was something. A big something. And despite the tight grip Scott kept on his emotions, the story spilled out. His sister. The ranch. Horses. The overwhelming sorrow he felt when she was murdered. And then the anger that drove him into law enforcement. Even now he could feel the rage. It was a constant burning in his gut.

"What was she like, your sister?" Nate asked.

"Janey was crazy fun. She loved life. She was a risk-taker. That's what got her into trouble, you know? Taking a risk to meet that boy."

Nate nodded. "We all do stupid things." He shifted his position. "He wasn't the one who did it?"

Scott shook his head. "No. Whoever found them attacked them both. He got hurt bad. She got abducted, and...you know. Raped and murdered."

"That's a hard thing."

Abby stomped her foot in the stall. Scott got up and walked over to her and began stroking her head. "Janey and I rode horses together on my uncle's ranch, skied, played ball. We had a lot of fun. But the best part was the horses. You know how girls go through that horse-crazy stage?

"Yep."

"Janey never grew out of it."

"What do you s'pose they meant to her?"

Scott pondered that question. "Freedom. Adventure. Risk." He traced his finger down the white blaze on Abby's face. "The challenge of working with an animal." He glanced at Nate. "Kinda like you with the dogs." He cleared his throat, turned, and walked back toward Nate. "Being around all this," he gestured as he sat down next to Nate, "made me remember something I loved before Janey died. Something we loved together, before...all this happened." He tightened his fist.

"And what do you think she'd say to you if she were here?"

Scott laughed softly. "She'd tell me to get off my butt and on with my life. Let go of the past. Live again. Be happy."

"Weep deeply, grieve the losses, feel the pain, then get up, wash your face, accept the life you have, and trust God."

Scott turned toward him, raising his eyebrows.

"It's something a pastor I listen to says."

Scott frowned. "I don't get it."

Nate had his eyes fixed beyond the stall, beyond the horse, to a place near the far ceiling of the barn. "When you have a loss like that, someone you love, time don't fix it. Workin' hard don't fix it. Drinkin' don't fix it. Other folk, even ones you love, cain't fix it." He sat real still. "Only the Lord's big enough to heal that pain."

Scott sagged back against the barn wall. He took in a big breath and blew it out. "Sometimes I wish I had your faith. I really do."

"It's not somethin' you can conjure up. The Lord has to show you. And I'm prayin' that he will. I believe, Scott, that he will."

19

A WEEK LATER, my phone alerted me at one in the morning. A callout. I sat up in bed, staring at the bright screen. Elderly man with dementia last seen at 11:00 p.m. in an area near the Chickahominy River.

Oh, boy. That area was full of water—creeks, bogs, swamps, plus the river itself. It also wasn't far from my house. I mentally calculated my readiness. I was feeling good. So was Luke. My pack was ready, I had boots and waders, emergency food, and, well, I couldn't think of anything I was missing except enough sleep. I had even visited Miss Lottie's that very day. She should be set for a while.

I texted our group leader that I would respond, ETA forty-five minutes.

Luke had alerted when I sat up. He stood looking at me, his tail slowly wagging, waiting to see what I would do. "You want to go search?" I asked, sending him into a paroxysm of joy. "Okay, then!"

Forty-three minutes later, I stepped out of my Jeep, coffee in hand. I walked over to the search command center and reported in. The night was soft and warm, typical for a Virginia August.

Bugs enjoyed that kind of weather, particularly mosquitos, and I made a mental note to spray both Luke and myself down well.

Three teams from Hampton SAR were responding, and Sarra, who was acting as search commander, had already recruited three deputies from an adjoining county to be our walkers.

When all three handlers arrived, Sarra handed out topographic maps covered in plastic. She'd met with the overall incident commander, identified areas for us to cover, and marked them on the maps.

"Our subject is Alan Thompson, age seventy-nine. He's Caucasian, six feet tall, a hundred and eighty pounds, with white hair and blue eyes. He has Parkinson's and sometimes hallucinates. When last seen he was wearing dark-blue pajamas. He lives with his daughter. Her house is marked with an X on your map. She went to check on him at eleven before she went to bed and found his room empty.

"Sheriff's deputies have searched the house and grounds. Our job will be to cover the woods and other unpopulated areas around it. Be advised there are copperheads in the area and water moccasins in the swamps. Any questions?"

After she answered the two questions the other handlers had, I went back and let Luke out of the Jeep, sprayed him down with bug repellent, and let him water the bushes while I used the spray on myself.

"You're going to have to watch for snakes," I told him. "You know I'm not good with them."

He wagged his tail without looking at me, and I knew he was just responding to the sound of my voice. He had no idea what I had said.

My deputy's name was Pat Callendar. I shook Pat's hand, and within three minutes, I'd decided I liked her. Her short, salt-and-pepper hair announced her personality—no nonsense, smart, and spunky.

"Are you familiar with this area?" I asked her.

"Yes and no. I've been a deputy on the Peninsula for twenty-five years, York County mostly. But I've never been in these particular woods."

I explained to her how we worked, what her job was, and I showed her the map. "Do you know how to use a GPS?"

"In my car." She laughed, knowing that's not what I meant.

I showed her the handheld. I demonstrated how to read the lat and lon, and how to mark a spot called a "waypoint."

"Don't worry," I said. "I'll use a second one to mark our beginning point. We won't get too lost."

"Good to know."

"And this is Luke. He's the brains of the team."

"Okay to pet him?"

"Yes. Thanks for asking."

Pat showed Luke her hand and let him sniff her, then rubbed his ruff. They were going to get along just fine.

"All right. Let me get Luke's vest on and we'll be ready to go."

I was glad it wasn't raining. We started at the edge of our search area. I told Luke to "seek" and he took off. Three minutes into our search, I could tell it would be a soggy night, even without rain. The area was laced with drainages—small creeks, ponds, and bogs. I couldn't move twelve steps without my boots squishing.

I had on my best boots, gaiters, long pants and a long-sleeved shirt, my hat, and my headlamp. I carried my pack, of course, and had a good, long-range flashlight, as did Pat.

Still, it was hard to see, and after a while I just had to stop worrying about snakes. Copperheads like wet areas, and they like to crawl out at night. But trying to see a snake in the dark and keep track of Luke, too, was slowing my progress.

We searched for forty-five minutes, then took a break. I called Luke back and poured him some water. The temperature, according to the weather app on my phone, was seventy-three degrees, but the humidity made it feel hotter. With the pack on my back, my energy drained pretty quickly.

I offered Pat a protein bar. I always carried extras for my walkers, because they often didn't bring food, though they usually carried water. We talked while we rested on a convenient log. I found out she was divorced, mother of two grown boys, and that she loved her job.

"It's easier now that the boys are grown," she said.

She asked me how I got into SAR, and I told her about adopting Luke, and about joining Battlefield, and about Nate. I didn't go further than that. My anxiety attacks and nightmares from my pre-Luke trauma had gone away almost completely. I didn't need to invite them back.

However, getting run off the road—now that was still fresh. I couldn't resist asking Pat if she knew Detective Hap Carroll.

She laughed. "Hap? I've met him. Seen him at some in-service courses at the academy."

"What do you think of him?"

Even in the dark I could see her eyes scanning my face, trying to decide how much to reveal.

"He's kind of a good ol' boy. A little sloppy. A little stupid. I was surprised when he made detective. You know him?"

"I met him. At the gym." I wanted to keep my cards close to my chest. I stood up. "You ready?"

"Yep."

Ten minutes later we'd reached the interim target I'd set, but not before I'd stepped in a hole and sank up to my knee in mud. Yuck! Pat had been traveling about ten feet back. I'd explained to her that would keep branches from smacking her in the face. I hadn't thought about the bogs.

Because of that space, she didn't get trapped, but I was stuck. She had to pull me out.

It took me a few minutes to recover. Luke actually came back, not to indicate he'd found someone, but to check on me after he heard me cry out.

I was okay, just wet and muddy. It could have been worse. Visions of snakes ran through my head.

After we reached our target, we began doubling back toward the neighborhood where the search had begun. We were now almost two hours into the search, which is kind of a ballpark limit we tried to maintain, depending on the terrain.

I was just trying to figure out if we could cover the rest of the area in a reasonable time, when I heard a crashing sound, and my dog came racing back through the woods and grabbed the braided cotton tug on my belt, then raced away again.

"Wow!" Pat said.

"He's got somebody!" I stepped up the pace. "Watch out for bogs."

Luke came back two more times, tugging and trying to get me to hurry. "I can't run through these woods like you," I explained, although I knew he didn't understand and didn't care. My head-lamp cast crazy shadows as we hurried as best we could. "You doing okay?" I called back to Pat.

"Just fine."

"If he's found Mr. Thompson, you will need to deal with him while I call it in and reward Luke."

"Got it."

It took us almost ten minutes to reach Luke's find. We found him dancing excitedly near an elderly man who was up to his thighs in a bog. Mr. Thompson was trapped.

I could understand that. I'm young and strong, but I couldn't get my leg out of that sucking swamp. He was still fighting it, though, and I knew the more he moved, the deeper he'd sink.

I gestured Pat toward the old man. "I'll be there in a sec!" I saw her reaching out to Mr. Thompson while I called the search commander with one hand and rewarded Luke with the other.

Then, I traded Luke the Kong for a jerky treat and turned to help Pat with Mr. Thompson.

"I called it in," I told her. "They're coming." I took off my pack and put it next to a tree in a dry spot.

Pat was talking to the man, trying to calm him down. She glanced at me. "Hand me that, will you?" She gestured toward a four-inch-diameter limb on the ground.

I retrieved it, handed one end to her, and then saw what her plan was. Together we maneuvered the limb in front of him. The end near us was on dry ground, and I think we both hoped the other end would be as well.

"Hold on to this, Mr. Thompson. Hold the log."

It took a few more words of encouragement, but eventually, Mr. Thompson gripped the log. Once he had his hands on that, he stopped struggling.

"What's their ETA?" Pat asked.

"Rescue crew should be here in ten."

When Luke started barking, we knew they were close. Then we saw their headlamps, and a five-man water rescue crew emerged from the woods.

Pat and I stepped back, and I snapped on Luke's leash. We watched as the crew used a device made of PVC tubes and an oxygen bottle to bubble a little air under Mr. Thompson's feet, breaking the suction of the swamp. Within ten minutes, they had him out, on a stretcher, and were carrying him out of the woods.

I grinned at Pat and raised my hand for a high five. "We did it!"

"Luke did it. Your dog is amazing."

———

I HAVE to admit I felt great driving home. Mr. Thompson was safe. Luke had proven himself once again, and except for dragging a lot of mud into my truck, we were none the worse for wear.

Dawn had not yet begun to break, although it wasn't far off. I had already begun mapping out how our morning would go. I'd hose off Luke and my pants and boots outside, then feed him, shower, and hit the bed again. A few more hours of sleep were definitely in order.

As I turned onto the two-lane road leading to my driveway, I saw an odd glow up ahead. Some clouds had moved in, and they looked pinkish off in the distance. I wondered what was going on.

The closer I got, the more my stomach fluttered. The pinkish glow was now more orange. Could the woods be on fire? I hadn't thought about forest fires when I'd moved here.

As I drove around a curve, I saw cars parked on the edges of the road, then trucks, and then, there at the end of my driveway, sat a police car with its lights flashing.

I pulled over, edging into a clear space. "What's going on?" I asked the first cop I saw. "Is it a forest fire?"

"Who are you?"

"I live in a house down that lane."

A deputy nearby responded. "Not any more you don't."

I turned to him, incredulous. I heard a drumbeat in my ears —*boom, boom, boom*—as my heart slammed against my chest. "Did the fire reach the house?"

"The house is what's on fire."

"No!" Shock lifted me by the ears. "No."

"Are you the only resident?" the first cop asked.

"Me. Me and my dog."

"Is he in the house?"

"No, he's with me."

"Lucky."

The roar of a truck coming up the driveway nearly drowned me out. It was a tanker truck, apparently on a water run, and I read the name of the fire department and "Engine No. 3" on the door as it passed by.

I had to see it. I had to get down there. "Can I drive down?"

"No ma'am. Fire Department only."

"Can I walk?"

The deputy hesitated. "I'll walk her down," the second deputy said.

I started to go with him, then hesitated. "Wait, my dog."

Ignoring his protest, I ran to my car, released Luke, leashed him, and ran back. I wanted my dog with me. If my life was being destroyed, I needed a friend.

It was a long driveway. We sorted our way through the trucks, with their blazing lights and loud radios, the hoses, and the people, until the house was in view. My firefighter friends would have labeled it "fully involved."

I called it "hellish."

20

THE WHITE-HOT FLAMES lit the night, licking at the siding, bursting through the roof, popping out the windows as it consumed my home. My head grew woozy. I wondered if I was going into shock. Almost everything I owned was in that house.

A firefighter noticed my look and handed me a water bottle. I fumbled at the cap. He took it back and opened it and handed it back to me.

Luke nudged my hand, giving me an excuse to squat down as if I were petting him. I needed him right then, needed to feel his fur on my cheek, have his scent in my nose, feel the warmth of his breath as he turned to lick my face.

Though I was focused on Luke, I still noticed someone walk up to me. "You the resident?" a gruff voice asked.

I stood and faced a heavyset man with a moustache wearing a fire marshal's uniform. "This was arson," I said, my voice breaking.

His eyes narrowed. "What's your name?"

I told him. I told him my name, how long I'd lived there, what my cell phone number was, and where I'd been that night. I told him the name of the owner, the name of the realty company, and that the house had been built three years ago. Then I told him someone was trying to kill me.

"He ran me off the road, now this."

He apparently didn't believe me, because he kept going with the standard questions. "Nobody else lives with you?"

"I live alone. And no one was in the house. Or at least, no one should have been. As I told you, I left shortly after 1:00 a.m."

Thank God, I had taken Luke! The thought of him dying in a fire...oh, my gosh...my pounding heart beat double-time. I put my hand to my forehead, shocked at the thought.

"Miss!"

Apparently, the fire marshal had asked me another question. "Sorry, what?"

"I asked you about the things inside the house. Was there any propane, like for a camping stove or a grill? Gasoline for a lawn mower? A candle left lit? Were the appliances and outlets in good working order? Could you have left food on the stove?"

I set my jaw. "There was nothing inside that would have started this fire. No propane, no candles, no gasoline, and certainly no food on the stove."

"How about a computer? Laptop? Cell phone charger? Those things can overheat and explode."

"I had the cell phone charger with me. I have a laptop, but it was not plugged in. I never leave it charging when I'm gone." Behind him, the fire raged, relentless in its destructive force. "Look," I said, "I told you, this was arson." What proof did I have? The security system was melting before my eyes.

"You got a degree in fire science?"

"No, of course not."

"But you're telling me how to do my job?" He hunched up his shoulders and moved toward me.

I didn't back down. "No, sir. I'm not telling you how to do your job. I'm giving you your best lead."

He stalked off, angry.

A terrible trembling ran through my body as I watched him go. A sense of panic, a fear, a horrible dread.

I'd been there before.

I retreated to the tree line and sat down on the ground with my back against an oak. Luke lay down next to me.

Shaking, I started counting the cost. All my clothes, what furniture I had, my lamps, my dishes, my pots and pans, my computer containing all my business files, my printer, my sheets, my towels, my books, and...and the brown Bible Nate had given me that had been on my night table.

A wave of sadness ran through me, then something worse hit. My box. My box!

My box from home with my father's NYPD badge, the bulletin from his memorial service, his pipe, his black book....

I jumped to my feet, totally panicked. I had the strongest urge to run into the fire, to look in the flames. My box!

Luke pawed me. Not a nudge this time. He pawed my leg. It hurt. Then he stood in front of me, almost as if he knew what I, in my distress, wanted to do.

My mind raced. Where in the house had I kept my box? "Oh, God," I said, not as a prayer, but as a cry of terror. I mentally pictured each room, and then, then, oh, sweet mercy...I saw in my mind where it was. It was not at my house. I'd given it to Nate to keep for me. I was afraid it would get lost in the move.

I sat down quickly. I pulled out my phone. I texted Nate. Yes, it was five in the morning. I didn't care. *Do you still have my box?* I asked. And then I hugged my phone close to my chest. *Oh, please, let it be at Nate's.*

Luke had settled down next to me again, apparently deciding I was no longer at risk. I closed my eyes at the enormity of the losses.

What did I have left? Luke, thank God. My car, my gun, my cell phone, my camera, and my SAR pack.

And my box, if it was at Nate's.

I'm telling you, when you're tired like I was and under stress, your mind can play tricks on you. I stared at the fire, watching the flames dance and lick the black sky. I thought I saw faces in those flames. I couldn't decide what was real and what was not.

"Miss Chamberlain?"

That voice was real. A woman in her thirties bent down toward me.

"Yes."

"You're the resident?"

"Yes." *What now?*

"I'm with the Red Cross. We provide emergency aid for families in these situations."

"I'm not a family. I'm just...me."

"Do you have family nearby? Someone who can help you?"

"No." My mother and stepfather, anyway, were on a cruise. My little sister was in Fairfax, 150 miles away. And I was not running to Nate this time. He'd rescued me enough.

"Do you belong to a church? Is there a pastor I can call?"

Another strike against me. "No."

"Did you have renter's insurance?"

Strike Three.

"Well," she continued, "I can arrange a motel for you for two nights, and here's a debit card worth five-hundred dollars so you can at least get a change of clothes."

"Thank you." My voice sounded dull. Two nights and five-hundred bucks. Wow.

"Give me your cell phone number. I'll let you know where I've arranged a room."

She left and I retreated back into my dark world. I cannot remember my throat and my jaw feeling as tight as they were that night. I watched water from fire hoses arc fruitlessly toward the flames. I smelled the smoke as it curled toward me on the wind. I listened to distorted voices give updates on radios.

Then I wrapped my arms around my legs and rested my head on my bent knees. *Oh, God Oh, God.*

"Jess?"

I lifted my head. Trooper C.E. McCoy squatted down in front of me.

"Are you okay?"

I nodded.

"I heard the call on the radio and thought I recognized the address. What happened?"

"It was arson. It had to be. He tried to run me off the road. That didn't work. Now this."

"I thought that whole thing had cooled off. Have you had contact with either Hap Carroll or Susan Larson since your car wreck?"

Contact? Oh, like stalking both of them? Like following them in my car and on social media? Like surveilling their same gym and confronting Carroll in the parking lot? That kind of contact?

"I saw them at the gym. A week or so ago."

"Together?"

"I don't know. At the same time, anyway."

"And they saw you?"

I nodded.

He muttered something under his breath. It could have been an expletive. "Have you told anybody?"

"I told the fire marshal the fire was arson. I didn't mention names."

Trooper McCoy nodded. "Where are you going to live now?"

"I have no idea." I fought tears.

He reached out and touched my shoulder. "Look, can I call that friend of yours for you?"

Nate? I shook my head. "I'll figure something out. The Red Cross is putting me up in a hotel for a couple of nights. I don't know after that. But I'll work it out."

He reached in his breast pocket and pulled out a business card. "Call me if I can help."

"Thanks."

I couldn't bear to watch him leave, the one semi-friendly face I'd seen on that horrible night.

Feeling very much alone, I dragged myself back up the driveway, found my car, put Luke in the crate, and sat down in the driver's seat. I was exhausted. I needed a shower. I needed food. I wanted to go home.

I had no home.

I wanted to cry.

But the Red Cross lady called and told me where I could stay. I asked her to text me the address. On the way there, I stopped at Walmart. I went in with Luke, because I couldn't bear to be apart from him right then. I guess everybody assumed we were some kind of security team because nobody stopped us. I bought sweats and T-shirts and toiletries with the Red Cross debit card. I also bought canned meat for Luke—I'd have to go to a pet store for his normal food, but the meat would do for now—and food and water dishes for him, and towels, for he was certainly dirty. And on the way out, I broke all my rules and got a Big Mac for myself from the in-store McDonald's and a quarter pounder for Luke. Oh, and fries.

The desk clerk at the hotel frowned when I showed up with Luke. "Dogs have to be under thirty-five pounds."

I took a deep breath, looked him in the eye, and said, "Sir, at three o'clock this morning this dog saved the life of a seventy-nine-year-old man trapped in mud near the Chickahominy River. Two hours later, we arrived home to find our house on fire. It is completely gone. We're exhausted and have nowhere to sleep.

"Not only is this dog well-trained and perfectly housebroken, he is a hero. Now, are you going to forgive him his extra fifty pounds or are you going to spend the rest of your short career explaining to your bosses why your hotel has gone viral on Twitter?"

He handed over the room key. I thanked him.

Before we went into the room, I brushed as much dirt off Luke as I could, and I took off my boots. Thankfully, I always carried an extra pair of athletic shoes in the car, so I put those on. I sure didn't have much to bring in—just my SAR pack and my Walmart bag.

I fed Luke, took a shower, and put on the sweats. When I got out of the shower, I had a text from Nate. *Sure,* it said, and he included a picture of my box sitting on a bookshelf.

I felt huge relief wash over me. I could not stand the thought of losing the last traces of my father.

Why? Nate texted. *You okay?*

A panicky thought in the middle of the night, I texted back.

That was true. Sort of.

I leashed up Luke and walked him in a grassy area behind the motel. By then it was light, and the rest of the world was waking up and moving around. I was planning on crashing for as long as I could. I hoped Luke would too.

Soon, Luke was snoring, but I didn't fall asleep right away, despite the light-blocking curtains and remembering to put the Do Not Disturb sign on my doorknob. Instead, I lay in bed trying to figure out how to recover, my mind flitting from need to need.

I needed a place to live. I needed some other clothes. I needed a new computer. I needed someone, somewhere to believe me when I said people were out to get me.

How would my business recover? Did I have enough contact information in my phone to reconnect with my open cases? Could I reconstruct what I'd done so far for them?

I felt a pang of loneliness. More like a tearing of flesh inside me. My father was dead. My mother and stepfather, who I hardly ever called, suddenly seemed very far away, off in the Caribbean, completely out of reach. I had no idea when they'd be back. My sister was too young to be of help, and I was not going back to Nate. Not this time. He'd told me confronting Carroll was "askin' for trouble."

And Scott? Something in me told me he would help, but how could I call him after I'd been such a jerk? I had complained about him being too involved with work. I didn't even bother to see how he was doing after what had to have been a trauma.

I was alone, partly by choice. Mostly by choice.

Why was that? Why did I tend to run from my closest relationships?

Lying there in the dark, exhausted, my mind went back twenty-one years to when I was eleven. It was a confusing time for me, with my body changing and hormones beginning to rise up. I was starting a new school and had to find new friends. Plus, I sensed something going on between my parents. Some coldness had invaded our home. They were each living separate lives. I was the demilitarized zone.

But I was a demilitarized zone with an opinion. Like many pre-teen girls, I adored my police-officer father and thought my mother was uninteresting and dorky. What did she even do for the Department of Defense? It couldn't have been important.

I lived for the weekends when my dad didn't have to work and would take me on adventures—to the Long Island beaches, camping, rock climbing. In my eyes, my dad could do anything. He was a hero.

And then he actually became one. On 9/11 he ran into the World Trade Center and, I'm told, helped hundreds of people out of the collapsing building.

I watched that tower fall a hundred times on the news, despite my mother's attempts to shield me, and in the end, out of the dust and rubble, I built a wall around my heart so I would never, ever experience that kind of loss again.

As yet, no one had penetrated that wall. When someone came close to breaching it, I ran.

So here I was, homeless, in a motel that didn't want me, with only my dog as a companion.

Did I tell you dogs only live about twelve years?

And Luke was almost four.

21

FLAMES LICKED at the edges of my dreams while I slept. I got in a restless four hours, waking up about noon. I took Luke out, then worked on rebuilding my life.

My savings had been nearly depleted when I bought the Wrangler. I still had about eight thousand dollars left, so I went to Best Buy and bought a new MacBook Pro, plus two phone chargers. I took Luke in with me, daring someone to challenge me. No one did.

I went to a specialty pet store and bought Luke some food and treats and a cheap crate in case I had to leave him in the motel room. Then came the hard part. I needed a place to live. I went back to the motel to access the Internet. I booted up the computer and went through all the set up. Then I started looking on Craigslist at real estate listings and even Airbnb.

One thing kept running through my mind—they were not going to run me out. They might kill me, but they weren't making me run.

Was I unnerved? Yes. Scared? Yes. Hypervigilant? You bet.

But I was also angry—angry at whoever had run me off the

road, angry at whoever had torched my house, and angry with the boatload of officials who didn't believe me.

Now where would I live? Where would they be unable to find me?

I found a small house that would accept a pet in a neighborhood not too far from where the SAR group met. It wasn't nearly what I had before, but it would do. I filled out the rental application and provided the agency with enough information so they could do a credit check. I didn't expect any problems. I'd paid my bills and my rent on time.

Six hours later, I got a call. No dice. "Your prior landlord wouldn't give you a reference," the agent said.

What? Furious, I called the guy who owned the house that had burned down. I stood there with my phone pressed to my ear, the ground under my feet shifting, as he told me he wouldn't give me a reference until I was cleared as a suspect if the fire at my former residence proved to be arson.

A suspect? Me? "I wasn't even there when the fire broke out!"

It didn't matter. According to him, I could have used some kind of ignition device that included a timer.

Sure. Right.

When I clicked the phone off, I collapsed on my motel bed in a heap of despair. Tears of fury and frustration soon soaked my pillow. Luke edged over to me, jumped up next to me on the bed, and licked my ear. In his mind, dog slobber was the universal antidote to all injuries, physical and emotional.

I let myself cry for a while, then got up, washed my face, leashed up Luke, and left. I didn't know where I was going. I just needed to get out.

While I was driving around, I happened to pass by a shabby, rent-by-the-week motel, the kind inhabited mostly by immigrants and people in need of rehab. Curious, I drove around it. In the back, I saw lawn chairs outside some of the rooms, some kids' toys, and an undeveloped grassy area.

I thought about that all evening, and the next morning, I checked out of the Red Cross-provided motel and checked into the Pinewood Inn. At least I wouldn't be sleeping in my car.

I requested a room on the back of the building. After I checked in, I examined the mattress thoroughly for bedbugs before stowing what little gear I had in the closet area. I put Luke's food and water dishes in the open space under the sink, as well as his bag of dog food.

"This is it," I told Luke, "at least for now."

Actually, I felt pretty safe. I didn't think the people who had attacked me would ever look for me in a place like this. I had my gun. Other motel residents took one look at my dog and gave us a wide berth. I could park my Jeep right outside my window, and if somebody touched it, I'd know about it. The downside was I'd have to run with Luke to keep him exercised, but I did that anyway. There was a public park nearby and a high school with a track as well.

With that big problem solved, I booted up my new Mac and ordered clothes from L.L. Bean and Lands' End—sturdy cargo trail pants, khakis, shirts, two pairs of shorts, and a jacket. I found a blazer I liked too. That would work if I had to go into an office. I also ordered new Ariat hiking boots. Mine were wearing down, and I'd need time to break the new ones in. I had everything delivered to a mailbox service nearby where I'd rented a box.

Then I started reconstructing my open cases. I began with Miss Lottie's, because I could remember a lot about that, which I was still convinced was a dead end. The others were more hazy. They had just come in before the fire. I had sent them questionnaires, but none had been returned.

That made my stomach queasy. I mean, I could live cheap for a while, but I needed income.

Stalled, I put Luke in the Jeep and drove to the park nearby. We ran four miles. Tears blurred my vision. The enormity of the losses, the fire, all piled up.

I was putting Luke back in his crate to go home when my phone buzzed. I checked the screen. Tim. "Hey, what's up?"

"Is your dog cross-trained for HRD?"

My stomach knotted. Human Remains Detection was not my favorite part of SAR. "Yes."

"Okay, we've got a distressed person call about a sixty-year-old widower who is being treated for severe depression. Missing for two days, northwest of Williamsburg. Not too far from your house."

My former house. I didn't correct him. The fewer people who knew about what happened, the better.

"The sheriff's office has done a foot search and used their bloodhound. Now they're calling us. We're short on people. Are you available?"

I checked my watch. Except for needing food and my aversion to dead bodies, I was, in fact, available. "Yes. Text me the location, and I'll meet you there."

I jumped in the car and raced back to the Pinewood Inn. I'd forgotten that my SAR clothes and boots were still muddy. I'd rinsed them out in the shower but they were not washed. They were dry, but stiff. Still, I put them on and loaded my SAR bag into the car.

Luke jumped into his crate again and we were off.

Only two teams had responded to the callout, me and Luke and a guy and his Malinois. No matter. Tim handed me a map, showed me where to search, and introduced me to my walker, a deputy named Skip. I'd been hoping Pat would have responded but that was a big no.

We entered the woods near the man's home. My stiff pants rubbed my skin, reminding me of my homelessness and distracting me from the search. My boots felt squishy. In fact, maybe it was because I was tired, or stressed, or secretly sad, or all of the above, but I kept messing up. I forgot to mark a turn, I miscalculated the wind direction, and I fell flat on my face because I failed to see a big root sticking out of the ground.

Fortunately, it was a short search. The other team found the man. He'd shot himself.

Frankly, I was glad it was them and not us. Suicides were messy, and I'd suffered through enough trauma for a while. I navigated us back to our start, thanked my walker, checked in with Tim, and headed back to my car. Down the street from where I was parked, I saw someone familiar walking toward the crime scene.

Hap Carroll. He was apparently the detective assigned to this case.

Anger filled me. Here he was, living his best life now while I was stuck in a fleabag motel with no money and no income in sight. All because of him.

It was time to confront the man. But I wanted circumstances to be on my side when I did.

All the way home, I tried to devise a plan. In the end, I decided on the semi-direct approach.

I called the sheriff. I asked for a meeting. And for some reason, he gave it to me. He told me I could come in at four on Thursday. Awesome.

22

SPRITE SCAMPERED DOWN THE STEPS, barking. Scott stepped out of his car as her tail wagged like crazy. This was the fourth time he'd come down since they brought the horse home. Something kept tugging at him, drawing him close to Nate's place. Even Sprite treated him like family.

Nate shook his hand as he reached the porch. "Come on in." He closed the front door behind them. "Laura's almost got dinner ready."

"I didn't mean to—"

"She always makes mor'n we can eat. Come on in."

Scott had a package in his hand, a brown bag that looked suspiciously like a bottle of wine. He handed it to Nate. "This is for you."

Nate opened the bag and laughed. Lemonade.

"Perfect," Laura said. "Let's eat."

They sat down and Nate said grace. "So, what's up, Scott?"

"Do you remember Gary Taylor?"

"The guy who knew Jess's dad," Nate responded.

"Right." Scott turned to Laura. "Gary was a young NYPD cop and

Jess's dad was his sergeant. They were together on 9/11. They went into the towers, saved a bunch of people, and then Jess's dad pushed him out as the tower came down. Jess's dad died. He survived.

"After he recovered, he got a degree in psychology, came to work for the FBI, and got his doctorate. He works for the Behavioral Analysis Unit and helped us on the case, the one where..." he hesitated.

"The one that brought us together," Nate said, reaching for Laura's hand.

Scott smiled. "Right. That one." Taking another bite of food, he finished chewing and said, "Gary had a massive heart attack about four weeks ago. He's back at the Bureau now, but not fully up to speed. He's doing a study of mass shootings and has asked my boss if I can be detailed to work with him. Help pick up the slack."

"And provide the boots on the ground experience," Nate added for him.

Scott nodded.

"How do you feel about that?"

"I think I'm going to love working with him."

"You'll add a lot to his project," Nate said.

"I think so."

"Is it gonna dredge up some post-traumatic stress?"

Scott shrugged. "We'll see. Honestly, I think it could help process it."

"Scott, that's wonderful," Laura said.

"I'm pretty excited about it."

Nate grinned. "That there? That's an answer to prayer."

Scott laughed. "If you say so."

They talked more, then about Nate's job, and Laura's, and the horse. Scott's phone rang. He excused himself to take it and returned a few minutes later, a puzzled look on his face.

"Everything okay?" Nate said.

He rubbed the back of his neck. "Remember McCoy, the trooper with the K9 that helped when Jess got run off the road?"

"Sure," Nate said.

"He called to tell me Jess's house burned down."

"What?" Nate pushed his chair back partway. "When?"

"Three days ago. He recognized the address and went to the fire. Saw her there."

"Is she okay?" Laura asked.

Scott nodded. "Apparently."

"And Luke?"

"They were out on a search when it happened. McCoy says he talked to her, volunteered to call me, but she said no. It's been bothering him ever since."

"Wait, what day was that?" said Nate, pulling out his phone. Scott told him. He scrolled through his text messages, then looked up. "She texted me real early in the morning, like five o'clock. Asked me if I still had her box."

"Her box?"

"A treasure box. Things of her father's. I told her I did. Even sent her a picture. At the time I thought it was really odd. But that's why! Everything else got burned up."

Laura touched his arm. "What are you going to do?"

Nate frowned. "I'm not sure I'm the one to do anything."

23

THANKFULLY, my new clothes arrived just in time for my meeting. I dressed in khakis, a blue shirt, my new boots, and topped it all off with my new black blazer. I felt nervous. I needed to look my best. Well, not my power female, sexy best. Just practical, strong female best.

I jotted down notes in the Moleskine notebook I carried. I stuck my driver's license in the pocket of my pants. I knew I'd have to show ID and go through a metal detector at the sheriff's office. I wasn't about to carry a purse.

I'd done my homework. I knew Sheriff Jimmy Montgomery had been in office for nine years. I also knew he was running for reelection and catching some heat because a lot of deputies were leaving for higher pay in nearby counties. Of course, the county supervisors set the pay rate, but still, he was the face of the department. I knew, too, that he prided himself on being a family man.

After apologizing to Luke for leaving him at the motel, I drove to the sheriff's office, went through security, and took a seat. A few minutes later, Montgomery opened the door and invited me in.

Montgomery looked younger than I thought he would. He

had to be fifty, but his hair was still dark, and he was trim and fit. His brown eyes, edged in wrinkles, seemed friendly enough.

"What can I do for you?" He gestured for me to take a seat in a leather chair.

I began my story, identifying myself as a private investigator hired to look into the death of Bob Larson. "There are doubts that his death was a suicide," I explained, being careful not to mention the identity of my client. I told the sheriff what I'd learned about Susan Larson and her former husbands. "Late one night," I said, giving him the exact date, "I was watching her house and saw one of your deputies emerge and leave in a black Ford F-150 pickup. At that point, I left as well. A few minutes later, I was run off the road."

"Oh, yeah, yeah," he said. "I remember who you are. A state trooper called me about this." Then, to my shock, he reached over, touched the button on his office intercom, and said, "Margaret, send in Carroll."

Surely, he doesn't mean Hap Carroll! My heart skipped a few beats.

But a minute later his door opened and Hap Carroll stuck his head in. "Yeah, boss. What's up?" Then he glanced over and saw me. His eyes narrowed.

"Come on in and have a seat," the sheriff said.

My heart beat wildly.

"What's this all about?" Carroll said, the chair leather creaking as he sat down.

The sheriff looked at me. "Go on," he said.

My throat closed up. My mouth went completely dry. Then I straightened my back. "I was looking into the death of Bob Larson. I was outside the house of Susan Larson. I saw you come out of the house and get into a truck parked in her driveway." I took a breath. "Minutes later I left. It was raining hard. I was on State Route 644. A big pickup came up behind me, following me way too closely. He crossed the double-yellow line, and I thought he was going to pass me. Instead, he ran me off the road."

"Okay," Carroll said.

"I read the report on that after McCoy called me," the sheriff said.

"I was run off the road," I insisted. "Whoever did it used a PIT maneuver. I think it was someone in law enforcement, someone with something to hide."

"What are you saying?" Carroll's face turned red.

"I'm saying I was working on a case you investigated. I was collecting evidence that seemed to indicate the death was not, in fact, a suicide. I saw you coming out of the victim's widow's house at ten o'clock at night. Then I was run off the road by someone who knows how to PIT a car." I glared at him. "What do you think I'm saying?"

"I didn't run anybody off the road!" Carroll said. I could see the arteries in his neck pulsating. "It's true, I was at Susan Larson's house, but I didn't see you and I sure was not the one who ran you off the road." Then he turned to his boss. "Tell her."

"I asked Hap to go over there that night," Montgomery said. "She had called, asking for a copy of some evidence we'd collected, and well, I couldn't see any reason not to give it to her."

"At 10 o'clock at night?"

The sheriff shrugged. "We had a county meeting that ran late. We were both there. Hap said he'd run it by on his way home."

I stared at Hap. "Susan Larson was in her nightgown."

"So."

"Your wife thinks you're having an affair!"

He looked at the sheriff. "You know how women get. Too many late cases and suddenly, you're having an affair."

The sheriff nodded.

I was in a cage match with the good ol' boys. My pulse pounded in my ears.

I looked back at the sheriff. "Someone burned down my house."

He picked up a file on his desk. "I got the papers on that too. Preliminary finding is arson. Fire marshal has found traces of accelerant in the back of the house." He looked at me. "Who would want to burn you out?"

"Someone who wants to either kill me or run me out of the area. Someone who thinks I'm getting too close to the truth."

"You got an old boyfriend? Former lover? Someone's wife angry at you?"

I couldn't believe what he was implying!

"Your landlord's wondering if you did it."

"Why in the world would I burn down my own home?" I was ready to explode. I turned to Carroll. "Where were you that night?"

"At home. In bed. Asleep."

"Your family was there, right Hap?" Sheriff Montgomery added.

Nice job leading the witness.

"Of course."

I set my jaw. "I don't know who did those things." I turned to Carroll. "All I know is you did a sloppy job of investigating Bob Larson's death. And I'm sure that's embarrassing to you. You had motive, means, and opportunity to get rid of me." I wrote my cell phone number on a page in my Moleskine, tore it out, and tossed it on the sheriff's desk. "Here's my number. I'd like to know who tried to kill me—twice."

I stood up to leave.

"Miss Chamberlain?" the sheriff said, as I opened the door. I turned. He stood up and hitched up his pants. "Be real careful who you're accusing of things without proof."

I shot him a look.

———

I HELD it together until I got to my car, then I yelled and pounded the steering wheel. I don't know what I had expected, but I sure didn't think things would turn around on me like that. Had I accomplished anything? Or just put my life in more danger?

When I got back to the Pinewood Inn, I took Luke for a run. Actually, it was more like a run...cry...run...cry for me. He kept glancing at me, checking on me. Twice I stumbled.

But I didn't fall. We got back to the motel, and after he cooled down, I fed him. While he ate, I decided to retrieve my SAR backpack from my car. It had gotten dirty on the last two searches, and I wanted to scrub it down. So I went out to my car and grabbed the pack. As I did, my fingers brushed against something under the front passenger seat. I grabbed it and pulled it out.

Miss Lottie's photo album. She'd given it to me the last time I saw her and I'd forgotten all about it.

I carried it inside along with the pack, guilt settling on me like dust. I put the album on the desk while I started in on the pack.

I pulled out my compass, my first-aid kit, extra clothes, emergency weather cover, small flashlight, extra food for me and Luke, and my other gear. Then I saw a small zipper opening within a larger pocket, and I unzipped it. Inside was a small pocket Bible.

Of course. Nate had helped me pack my kit initially, and I had asked him to make it just like his. After all, I was a rank beginner and he was the expert. And so, in addition to all the other gear, he'd put the little Bible in that inner pouch. Just like his.

I sat down on the motel bed and fingered the soft blue cover, engraved with a Celtic cross. I remembered those early days of SAR. Nate had been hard on me, and I had resisted him stubbornly until circumstances made us a team and tragedy opened my eyes to a world I never knew existed. Later, Nate had said losing his leg was worth seeing that.

Tears filled my eyes. Yes, I'd come to believe what was in that book was true. But had my life changed? It felt like it was getting worse.

I put the book down and went into the bathroom. I showered, scrubbing my skin as if I could wash away my anger, my loneliness, and my self-pity. My car had been wrecked, my house burned, and my only friend was an eighty-year-old woman with terminal cancer. I'd lost everything in the fire, almost. I was living in a fifteen-by-twenty room in a shabby motel that was just asking for an immigration raid. Or an exterminator visit. And I'd confronted someone I was convinced was guilty of attacking me and had only managed to put myself on the sheriff's radar.

That's the way self-pity works, isn't it? It's like a cancer. If you don't catch it right away, it spreads until all you can think about is your own sad life. Nate had a Latin phrase for it. *Incurvatus* something—man turned in on himself.

Or woman.

I didn't feel like eating, and television was just annoying. Then my eyes fell on the photo album.

Nate told me once that it's never too late to do the right thing. So I retrieved the album, propped myself up against the headboard of the bed, and began leafing through it. Luke jumped up next to me. Soon he was snoring. I guess he'd gotten used to my moods.

The book documented the life of the Thomas's adopted daughter. Instead of a sonogram picture, there was Miss Lottie and her husband, Frank, showing their plane tickets to Romania. Then there were shots of that country, some beautiful countryside scenes and some sad cities.

Apparently, they weren't allowed to take pictures at the orphanage, because the next photos were outside the courthouse with three-year-old Tamara standing next to them, a dark-haired, dark-eyed beauty, sadness writ large on her face.

What does it do to a kid to spend three years in an orphanage? I didn't know, but pages and pages of that photo album went by before I began to see pictures of Tamara smiling. Smiling at birthday parties, smiling as she waited for the school bus dwarfed by her backpack, and smiling at church dressed as an angel in a Christmas play. It wasn't until I got to Tamara's teen years that I saw something that brought me up short.

Tamara was sitting on a beach in a swimsuit. My guess was she was about thirteen. She was sideways to the camera, looking shyly at the photographer, her chin pressed against her shoulder. And on her shoulder was a heart-shaped mark.

I moved the book toward the light so I could see it better. Was it a tattoo? Not likely, I thought. It was too imperfect. And anyway, a tattoo in that era and in a Christian family in the conservative south? No. No way. A birthmark would be my guess. It was high enough to be covered by a short sleeve, so I hadn't seen it before. How curious!

I really wanted to know more. I checked my watch. Nine o'clock. Too late to call Miss Lottie?

I decided it wasn't. I swung my legs over the side of the bed, picked up my cell phone, and pressed her number in my contacts.

"Why, yes," Miss Lottie said. I could tell I'd woken her up. "It is a birthmark. We thought it was precious. It's one reason we picked her out of the agency's book."

"When she went missing, did you tell the authorities about that?"

"Oh my, yes we did. I'm sorry I didn't tell you!"

"Please don't worry about that. I'll follow up and let you know if I find anything." I clicked off my phone. Despite my miserable day, I had something—not quite a lead, but something—on my impossible case. Go figure.

When was NamUs created? I got up, opened my computer, and Googled it. The National Missing and Unidentified Missing Persons System went fully live in 2009 I found out. Long after Tamara disappeared. I had used NamUs when I was a detective. You input information (DNA, dental records, etc.) from missing persons, and the system matches it with the same kind of evidence from unidentified remains. It's a nationwide database, and it is powerful. But was it too late for Tamara? Surely, they would have entered data from earlier databases, right?

Maybe. The trouble was, I was neither a family member nor law enforcement, so I couldn't really use it. Not like when I was a detective. I closed my computer, got back in bed, and lay there thinking. What could I do?

I certainly couldn't ask the locals for help. Nobody in the sheriff's office would give me the time of day now. McCoy, maybe?

And then there was Scott. I checked my watch. Not too late. I could call him right now.

Pride and shame paralyzed me.

Troubled, I tried to close my eyes and sleep, but my mind kept flitting from problem to sin to fear to grief to anxiety and back to sin. Yes, I used that word. Thanks to Nate, I no longer could see my mess-ups as simple "mistakes," or "errors in judgment," or even "a bad mood."

I knew my lack of consideration, my failures to love, my self-focus, and even my overwrought anger emerged from something dark festering deep inside me. I guarded it like a treasure, and I dressed it up with euphemisms.

Ugh.

I remember Nate telling me once that sometimes when he got convicted of his sin, the way forward, what he called "dyin' to self," looked like death, felt like death. "But when I'd take that step forward," he'd said, "it'd be like pushing through a curtain and finding beauty on the other side."

I had no idea what he was talking about when he started waxing poetic like that.

I desperately needed some external focus to stop my racing thoughts. There was the TV. I hate TV. And then there was one book—that little Bible from my SAR pack.

Doggone Nate! I picked it up and began reading the now familiar words in the Gospel of John. Soon I became lost in stories of healings and contention and grace and rebuke and wonder. I fell asleep with the book in my hand.

Luke nudged me awake the next morning. I took him for an early run, since the temps were supposed to soar into the 90s. I treated myself to breakfast—a real breakfast—at an outdoor café on the outskirts of Williamsburg. And then I called Scott.

24

OF COURSE SCOTT was happy to give me a hand. He would call the agent serving as liaison with the National Center for Missing and Exploited Children and see if they could help.

I felt the need to apologize. "Scott, I'm really sorry about not calling you after the shooting."

"It's okay."

"How are you?"

He paused. "It's not a good time to talk about that. How about I come down sometime this weekend and we have lunch? I'd like to catch up with you."

"Scott, I don't know." Then a refrain began in my head. *Don't run. Don't run. Don't run.*

"There's that park down there, near the Yorktown historic area, with some cool running trails. You could bring your dog, we could run, and I'll bring lunch. How about that?"

Don't run. Don't run. Don't run. "I...uh...." *Don't run.* "Okay!" I blurted out. "Okay. When?"

"How about tomorrow? I'll leave early, so I can be down there by, say, nine-thirty? I'll meet you at the visitors' center. You send me everything you've got on this girl you're looking for, and I'll send you the address of the visitors' center I'm talking about. That work for you?"

———

AFTER WE HUNG UP, I carefully removed some photos of Tamara from the book Miss Lottie had given me. I scanned them using an app on my phone and emailed them to Scott, along with all of the other information I had on her.

Then I went out and bought some decent running shorts and shoes and a couple of T-shirts. I bought my usual sizes, although I could tell I'd lost weight.

When Scott's text dinged on my phone with where we should meet, I recognized it as the same place we'd done the search for the eight-year-old student—where I'd met Jason.

I told Luke all about our plans, and he seemed happy about it, although because what I said didn't include the words "search" or "seek" he wasn't what I would call elated.

The next morning I found myself oddly nervous. I fed Luke early but I couldn't stomach breakfast myself. *Don't run.* I arrived at the visitors' center early, let Luke out, and remembered to put poop bags in my fanny pack, along with my wallet and my gun. I knew FBI agents are supposed to be prepared 24/7. Had the shooting affected Scott's willingness to carry?

Scott pulled up moments later in his black Nissan Rogue. He stepped out of his car and the first thing I noticed was the bulge of his gun on his hip. The second thing was that he greeted Luke before he said anything to me.

That was a good thing. Trust me. Because before, he'd barely paid any attention to my dog. His "hey, buddy!" greeting and the way he ruffled Luke's coat made him seem relaxed, almost happy. Maybe this wasn't going to be the therapy session I'd been dreading.

When he finally looked at me, I noticed his eyes, blue like

Nate's but not as intense, and softer than I remembered. His navy-blue T-shirt stretched across his chest. It looked like he'd bulked up more in the last few months. No fat. Just more muscle.

I felt something stir, but I tamped it down. "Hey, Scott."

He gave me a brotherly hug. "How are you? I've missed you!" He looked around. "Are you ready to run? Four miles okay with you?"

Nothing like getting right to it. Still, I was relieved we weren't diving into a conversation right away. I needed to get used to being with this man. My stomach fluttered. Weird, because this was Scott, right? Serious, intense, driven, obsessive, no-time-for-fun Scott.

We set off running on a gravel-and-dirt path that led us to a paved walk that ran next to the York River. We dropped our pace a little and Scott started talking about Yorktown and the British surrender at the end of the Revolutionary War, and Washington and Rochambeau, and about this storm that came up at just the right time. He knew more—and apparently cared more—about history than I expected. There was a lot I didn't know about Scott.

About two miles into our run, we got to a place where no one was around, and I let Luke off leash so he could swim and cool off. Scott threw sticks for him, and Luke paddled out to retrieve them. They were having such a good time, I stood off to the side and watched my beautiful dog interact with him.

After five or six throws, Luke trotted out of the water and then did his crazy rolling in the sand bit. Scott and I started laughing, watching this big strong dog writhing in the sand like a puppy. When he finally hopped up, covered with sand, I pointed at my running partner.

"Go to Scott, go to Scott!" Luke raced toward him and then he shook. Scott and I both laughed so hard I couldn't catch my breath.

You know what? It felt good.

We jogged the remaining two miles back to Scott's car, parked near mine. I got Luke's water dish out of the back of my Jeep and filled it. Scott grabbed a towel from his Rogue, dumped a bottle of water over his head, and then began wiping off.

"Your car's really cool," Scott said, after he'd pulled on a clean T-shirt. I remembered he'd been in a bad way when I'd driven up to Nate's, and so he hadn't seen it. "You could throw a sleeping bag in there and camp."

"I was lucky. I bought it from a guy who used to be involved in SAR, so it's all equipped. He even threw in the crate."

Scott nodded approvingly. "Very nice."

Then I noticed someone approaching us. Jason. He apparently was working that day. I hadn't seen him since the day I got my car.

"Hey, Jess!" he called out.

Scott turned around to see who was coming. I thought he turned kind of fast, and I noticed he kept his back to the car. Was he hypervigilant?

"I thought I recognized your Jeep," Jason said.

I could tell he was scoping out Scott, trying to gauge our relationship.

"Scott, this is Jason. Jason, my friend Scott." I gestured. "Jason's about to go to Glynco."

"Club Fed!" Scott said, and then he started asking him what he was hoping to do, career wise.

While the two of them talked law enforcement, I grabbed a brush out of the back of my Jeep and began working the sand out of Luke's coat. Then Jason got my attention.

"Jess, I was going to call you."

I turned toward him.

"A guy I work with, he's got a friend, a very successful real estate broker, whose wife disappeared. Emptied their bank accounts and took off."

"Wow, I bet he's ticked."

Jason shook his head. "Apparently not. The guy I work with says he's worried about her, says she's emotionally unstable. The police haven't done much. I told him about you. You do that kind of thing, right? Search for lost people?"

"Yes."

"Could I give him your name and number?"

"Sure. Let me get you a business card." I dug one out of the glove box and handed it to him.

Jason took it, looked at it, and tapped it against his left hand. "The guy's pretty connected, from what I understand, down in Norfolk. You'd go that far for a job?"

At this point, I'd go to Alaska. "Yeah, sure. Tell him to call me. I'd be glad to help if I can."

"Will do."

After Jason left, Scott looked at me. "So, your business is doing well?"

"It's fine."

That was a lie, but thankfully he didn't pursue it. Instead, he grabbed a cooler out of his car. "Let's eat over here," he said, nodding toward a picnic table in the shade.

A good idea. It was hot.

The first thing Scott pulled out was a big chewie for Luke. "Can he have this?"

I nodded yes. "Thank you."

Luke took it from him and moved under the picnic table to begin working on it, his tail sweeping the ground, brushing acorns and leaves to the sides.

Scott had brought a tablecloth, red-checked. Most guys wouldn't have thought of that, but picnic tables are inevitably dirty and I appreciated it. He'd stopped somewhere and gotten a variety of sub sandwiches and had them cut up so we could share. In his cooler was a bag of chips, some chocolate chip cookies, and to top it all off, he pulled out a bottle of lemonade.

"Lemonade?" I laughed.

"I know. Nate's got me drinking it." Scott grinned. "He's like an invasive species."

He spread the food out on the table, then sat down next to me, rather than across the table. That surprised me, but it meant we could both look out over the river and we didn't have to shout. With the sorts of things we had to talk about, that was a good thing.

"Scott, I'm sorry I was so MIA after your shooting incident. How are you doing?"

Don't think I was being kind. I asked about his life because I wanted to add to my black box, plus keep the spotlight off of me. How could I tell this neat, organized, successful FBI agent that my house had burned, I was living in Hotel Fleabag, had virtually nothing to my name, and I could imagine myself running out of money in the not-too-distant future? The thought of it made my stomach churn.

Thankfully, he began talking. He told me how the shooting went down, using details that painted the picture vividly in my mind. He talked about his shock, right afterward, and his daughter's reaction and how that had hurt. Then he opened up about his devastation that it had been his bullet that killed the little girl.

"I fell into a deep pit," he confessed. "I almost quit."

Scott almost quit? Wow. I couldn't believe...

But wait—I *had* quit. I'd left the Fairfax PD after my traumatic incident. The sense that I'd failed passed over me again. Life is a competition, right? He didn't quit. Scott had scored and I hadn't.

I forced myself to redirect my thoughts. "What brought you out of it?"

"I'm not out of it, not all the way. But it's better." Scott's jaw shifted. "Two things have helped. Nate was one."

Of course.

"I went down there every weekend. I helped him build a

fence. The physical work, being out in the country, and hanging out with him felt peaceful."

"Did he preach at you?" I laughed softly. I meant it as a joke. And also a jab, to be honest.

Scott ignored me. "He just let me talk. Or not." He took another bite of his sandwich, gazing off toward the river.

Something he'd said had stuck in my ears. "Wait. A fence? Why a fence?"

"For the horse."

"The horse?" I put my sandwich down.

"Laura has a horse. Nate said having the horse there was part of a prenup. When she sold her own house, she had the money to have a barn built. You should see it."

"Wow." Why had I thought things would stay the same after I left? Now he's got a barn, a horse.... I felt more distance grow between me and Nate.

"Building the fence was therapeutic," Scott said. "My sister loved horses." He paused.

"Tell me about your sister." Did this count for the black box?

So he did, describing a young woman I thought I might have been friends with—smart, athletic, and too much of a risk-taker for her own good. He told me about the fun they had as kids in the Colorado mountains, hiking, backpacking, and skiing with their father and sometimes his mother, and hanging out on his uncle's ranch.

"My sister was full of life." Scott's jaw shifted again. "Dealing with Laura's horse brought back those memories, and suddenly it hit me. I never have fun like that anymore." He took a paper napkin and began fingering it. "I've been so focused on fixing her murder. Fighting crime. But some things can't be fixed. And I think Janey would be the first to tell me I need to do my job, but find a way to enjoy life too."

As he opened up to me, I felt our connection growing, and

fear swept through me, cold as a winter wind. *Don't run, don't run,* said a voice in my head.

"I've been talking to Nate and hanging out with the horse, and well, I feel different."

I nodded. "I understand the need to let go. I had to do that too. What was the second thing that helped, Scott? Besides Nate?"

"I've switched jobs. I'm working with Gary Taylor."

Gary Taylor. My dad's old friend. The man who survived 9/11 when my dad saved his life. Gary Taylor! My heart did a double beat.

"We're studying mass shootings, trying to get a handle on them so we can propose a broader, multi-agency study. Gary's got the expertise to guide the project and do the statistical work, and I'm doing the interviews."

"That's awesome, Scott."

"The first week, we did nothing but talk, about the shooting, about my perceptions, my reactions, the people around me, and about finding out it was my bullet that killed that girl." He swallowed hard. "You remember, he's a psychologist?"

I nodded.

"But you know, he's been on the street too. Been through the worst of it."

The 9/11 attacks. The World Trade Center. Shock and horror.

"He gets it, and talking to him really has helped." He looked at me. "He had a massive heart attack about six weeks ago."

"Gary did?" I said, shocked.

Scott nodded. "He's back, working about twenty hours a week. That's one reason he asked for help. But he's doing well, and honestly, Jess, between him and Nate, I'm starting to feel okay."

"That's wonderful," I said, but my voice cracked at the end. I ducked my head. Why was it that when I heard about someone getting better it just made me feel sorry for my life? Did I feel like more of a failure because he was overcoming his trauma?

"So how are you?" Scott asked. "We've talked enough about me."

I knew I had to say something. I couldn't completely avoid my life. "I have cases. The one I was working on, the suicide/homicide, that got taken away. The lawyer wants to pursue it. So I ended up not getting paid much. I've had a couple of straying husband cases and the old lady's case." I tried to sound upbeat, normal.

"What you're calling 'the old lady's case'—is that Tamara?"

"Right. Did you send that to your friend?"

Scott nodded. "Yes. My friend reminded me skin is one of the first areas to degrade. Tattoos and birthmarks are rare in unidentified remains cases. But she will explore all her options."

"I've doubted from the beginning I'd find this girl." I kept a cynical tone.

A long silence followed. I got the feeling Scott was waiting for me to say more, but I had drawn a mental line in the sand and didn't want to venture past it. He kept waiting. I offered up a few SAR stories, including the one about Luke finding the elderly man trapped in the mud.

That was a mistake. Just thinking of that night created an ache in my chest that began to grow and grow until I felt I could hardly breathe.

"You two saved that man's life."

All I could do was nod. I'd have thought saving that guy would be a lot of credit in the black box. Instead, I'd had my life knocked out from under me hours later with the fire. Tears filled my eyes.

"Jess?"

His voice was so gentle.

"What's bothering you?"

Run! I jumped to my feet, tried to swing one foot over the picnic table bench, and I tripped. He caught me. "Hey, hey," he said. "Hey, it's okay, Jess, it's okay."

His hands on my waist had kept me from falling. I sat back down awkwardly. I couldn't look at him.

"Hey, girl. We're friends. You can tell me."

I shook my head.

"Let's put this stuff away and walk," Scott said, gesturing toward our picnic lunch.

Fine by me.

25

WE WALKED down a path through the woods, Luke padding beside me on leash. It was probably five degrees cooler in the shade, but sweat still slickened my skin. The trees here were different than I was used to in the Piedmont, shorter, and there were more pines in the mix. And more bugs in the air.

"McCoy called me."

Scott's words jolted me. I felt fear, like lightning, pierce through me like an arrow. "What?" I stopped walking and faced him, my fists clenched. I felt naked, exposed.

"He told me about your house."

"He had no right!" My throat felt like someone had stuffed a box of Kleenex down it, I turned and began running. Running back to my car. Running back to safety. Running.

"Jess! Jess, wait."

I heard him. I just didn't stop.

Scott chased me down. He got in front of me and blocked my path. "Jess, wait, wait—"

Salty, angry tears ran down my cheeks. "Move!" I said, and pushed past him.

He jogged beside me. "He was worried about you."

"I told him not to call! I don't need—"

"Nate said you'd run."

"What?" I stopped. My heart pounded so loudly, I thought the trees could hear it.

"He said you're like a skittish colt."

Flustered, I didn't have a comeback. Luke had picked up on my stress. He pressed his body against my knees. Ironically, he blocked my way forward. I couldn't have moved if I'd wanted to.

Scott looked down, saw him, and grinned. He tried to wipe the smile off his face with his hand.

Red, hot anger surged through me. Then I glanced down. I caught the absurdity of it. Here I was, trying to run from a friend, a man who only wanted to help me, letting shame and failure cut me out of the herd. I could almost see the wolf lurking in the woods. And even my dog knew I was acting stupid.

I squeezed my eyes shut. "I'm sorry," I said. Then I dropped down and hugged Luke, as if a good whiff of his scent and the feel of his coat on my cheek would restore my sanity.

It did. My heart slowed. I pulled myself together, and we began walking again, Luke on one side of me, Scott on the other. In a tight voice, I told him about the fire and the loss of almost all my earthly possessions. I explained how I was convinced it was arson and the arsonist was either Carroll or Susan Larson, and I shared my frustration after my meeting with the sheriff.

Scott listened. He didn't try to fix it. He didn't say how foolish it was for me to confront Carroll directly at the gym. He didn't roll his eyes when I told him about the fire marshal. He just heard me out.

When I'd gotten through the whole story, Scott asked me what I was doing to recoup my losses.

I started listing all the things I'd done—found a place to live, bought a new computer, got some new clothes, and so on.

"Yes," he said, "that's all good. What are you doing to recover emotionally?"

We were walking again and I was glad because tears flowed down my cheeks unchecked. I'd grabbed a bunch of tissues before we left, and I needed them now to sop up my sorrow.

"Look, I don't want to wallow," I said. "And I don't need other people feeling sorry for me."

Out of the corner of my eye, I saw Scott nod. "I understand, but there's a difference between self-pity and legitimate grieving."

My eyes widened. Was this the same Scott?

"It's okay—healthy in fact— to feel the sorrow. You can't skip that step. I did, and it's hung me up for years."

He continued talking. "As for the rest of it, you and I are both loners. I know that's been self-protective for me. I'm starting to see, though, that it's not a good long-term plan. There's a time to let people in, to begin to trust again."

I stared at him and sniffed. "You've been hanging out with Nate too long."

Thankfully, he laughed. "No, most of this is from Gary. But it does sound like Nate." He reached down and petted Luke. "Did you find another house to rent? I imagine that's hard, having a dog."

I told him about being refused a rental reference, and anger and shame surged through me again. I gasped for air, my words faltering.

"Hey, it's okay. You're doing what you can," Scott said.

I just shook my head.

"Look," he said. "This might help. I told Jim about the fire, and he told me to remind you he'd set you up with a cloud backup."

I stopped. "What?"

"He said he'd told you, but maybe you don't remember. You can recover what was on your computer."

"Seriously?" I felt hope rising.

"You can download the backup. Jim told me how. What if we

go back to your place and I do it? Then all your stuff will be on your new computer."

But I recoiled from that. I mean, seriously, take Scott to the Pinewood Inn? Let him see how I was living?

"Don't you need to be getting back?" I said. It was almost three o'clock.

He checked his watch. "Well, let's see, I have forty hours and seventeen minutes before I have to leave for work. I may have a second or two to help you."

"Why don't you just email me the instructions? I should be able to do it."

"Jess…"

I was tired of fighting. I faced him. "I live in a dump."

"I don't care."

"It's got semi-homeless people, probably some illegals, potential drug abusers, and no doubt rats."

"So what?"

"Pizza places won't even deliver there."

"We just ate."

"It's a by-the-week motel on the wrong side of town."

He touched my upper arm. "Let me help you."

Ten minutes later he sat in his car, following me to the Pinewood Inn. I kept glancing back, wondering at our conversation. Something was swirling around inside me, something I didn't want to name.

We pulled into the parking lot. There were two spaces outside my door. I got out and handed him the key card. "I'm taking Luke over to the grass."

Scott nodded. He didn't seem to notice the three men hanging two doors down dressed in white T-shirts, smoking what smelled like weed to me. Nor did he flinch at the feral cats, which had scattered as we pulled up.

I got Luke out and let him water the grass, then followed Scott inside. The air-conditioning, a sharp contrast to the muggy humidity outside, raised goosebumps on my arms. Scott already had my computer up and running and was checking his iPhone, apparently for Jim's instructions. "Go take a shower," he said. "I'll get this started."

I grabbed the clothes I'd need to change into and showered, using my favorite body wash and shampoo. I smelled positively tropical. When I emerged from the bathroom dressed in sweatpants and a T-shirt, Scott was sitting back in the desk chair and my computer was working.

"The WiFi is slow and erratic," he said. "This might take a while."

"Like how long?"

"A couple of hours. But it's working. It got hung up on one of the steps, and I had to call Jim. He talked me around it."

I nodded. I hadn't taken the time to blow dry my hair. I probably looked like a drowned rat. But at least I was clean. "You want to shower? Do you have a change of clothes?"

"Do you mind?"

"Of course not."

He'd brought a backpack in from his car. He dug some clothes out and headed for the bathroom.

"You might lose the hot water once in a while."

He laughed. "Thanks for the warning."

While Scott showered, I straightened up the room a little, then blow-dried my hair. I wore it long and straight, parted just off-center. It was easy to maintain, and thankfully, it was in-style for most women my age, because I probably would have worn it that way anyway.

I put the dryer back in its holder and brushed my hair into place. All the while, I kept thinking, *There's a man in my room!* When you're single, you forget what that's like.

Scott emerged, drying his short-cropped hair with a white towel. "How's it going?" he asked.

"It's slow."

He came over, leaned down, and looked at the screen. He smelled good. Tropical. Like me.

My body responded to his nearness. A shiver ran through me. My heart beat faster.

He straightened up and moved away.

"You want this towel on the floor in the bathroom?" he asked.

"Yes. I'll have the maid come in tomorrow."

He returned and sat down in the extra chair. "I can stay until it finishes."

"That'll put you home awfully late." I really wanted him to stay.

"I'm only going as far as Nate's."

I looked at him curiously.

He shrugged. "He's got something he wants me to do. I told him I'd sleep in the barn if I got there too late."

Jealousy reared its ugly head. Nate was *my* special friend. Yes, I know I was the one who walked away. Still...

I nodded toward the computer. "I got this. You don't need to stay. Unless you want to." My voice betrayed me.

He stood up abruptly. "I'd better go. Goodbye, buddy," he said to Luke, who'd been lying on the floor at his feet. "Take care of Jess, okay?" My dog thumped his reply with his tail.

I stood up, too, and Scott looked at me, clearing his throat. His Adam's apple bobbled as he swallowed hard. "Your friends care about you, Jess. Me, Nate, Laura. You should come see us."

I expected him to hug me. Kiss me even. He didn't. He just picked up his backpack and walked out.

Suddenly, the room seemed very, very empty.

26

I LAY in bed that night, watching my computer finish populating itself with my files, feeling lonely and tired and scared. I tried thinking back over the day, cataloguing my interactions with Scott—the run, the silliness with Luke, lunch, him sharing his heart, then finding out McCoy had told him about my house.

I came across angry about that, but mostly what I felt was shame, shame at my stubborn independence, my refusal to be vulnerable, my inability to share my life with my best friends.

To his credit, Scott hadn't commented on my living conditions. He seemed to take the Pinewood Inn in stride. He seemed to take *me* in stride.

Round and round and round my thoughts whirled in my head. Finally, I stopped turning from side to side, flipped on the light, and picked up the only book I had—that little Bible. I read until I fell asleep.

I WOKE up the next morning determined to restart my life.

After throwing on a pair of shorts and a T-shirt, I took Luke for a long run. At eight o'clock in the morning, it was already hot, but it would climb into the 90s again later. The heat in Tidewater seemed particularly oppressive. Was it because of all the water? The proximity to the ocean?

I didn't know, but I'd learned to schedule our exercise either early in the morning or late in the evening, and even then I was careful not to let Luke get overheated. I'd once seen a dog suffer from heat exhaustion at an agility trial. His eyes glazed over, and he acted dazed. His gums turned gray, and he panted like crazy. Thankfully, someone knew what to do—cool him off with wet towels. We all donated water bottles to the cause, and the dog recovered.

But the dog's suffering scared me as a young teenager, and I was very careful with Luke.

When we returned from our run, I took a tepid shower and then called Nate. I forgot it was Sunday. My call went to voicemail. Of course. He was at church. I left a generic apology for being out of touch.

Nate called me back in the early afternoon. We talked for over an hour.

"I don't *feel* God!" I said.

"Feelings don't matter. You take a step toward him. I'm tellin' you, he'll be there."

I kept seeing Nate's anchor tattoo in my mind's eye. "I need proof."

"No, you don't."

"How can you say that?"

I heard him take a deep breath.

"Jess, you already believe some things to be true from reading the book of John. Remember? You told me that. You told me you loved how Jesus interacted with people. Now, you need to walk further in. So pick up that Bible and read. And keep reading. Ask God to show you who he is. He will, and by-and-by, you'll know just how much he loves you whether you feel it or not."

Nate steadied me. He always did. I swallowed, trying to regain control of my emotions.

"Trust me," Nate said.

"I do." I sniffled "You're my anchor."

He didn't respond at first. The only sound between us was me blowing my nose.

Then he spoke. "You know I love you, Jess. You're like a sister to me. You're the best search-and-rescue partner I ever had. I always say, you got grit."

I soaked in his praise.

"But I'm not your anchor, Jess. Jesus is your anchor. And now, you need to learn to relate to him."

"I can't even relate to you!"

He laughed. "Now that's sure enough true. Look at you, running off like that. Not calling. Not tellin' me about the fire." I could hear amusement in his voice, not anger. That was grace.

"Remember my tattoo?" he said.

"I can't remember what it's for," I confessed.

"It's Hebrews 6:19: 'We have this as a sure and steadfast anchor of the soul, a hope that enters into the inner place behind the curtain.' That's Jesus, Jess. The same Jesus you read about in John. Now go read some more."

Nate could convey more authority in his quiet voice than anyone else I ever met. I clicked off the phone. I didn't see how Jesus could help my anxiety, my loneliness, or even my anger. But obediently, I did what Nate said. I picked up that little Bible, let it fall open, and this is what I read from a book called 1 John: *There is no fear in love, for perfect love casts out fear. For fear has to do with punishment, and whoever fears has not been perfected in love. We love because he first loved us.*

I read that over and over. Why should God love me? I didn't deserve the slightest bit of attention from him. I knew that. I was as stubborn with him as I was with my friends.

And how does love cast out fear? I had no idea.

Still, I read those verses until they became a prayer.

———

Two days later, I received a call from a man named Colton Danville. It took me a minute to realize this was the guy Jason had told me about.

"I understand you're a private investigator," Danville said. His voice dripped social confidence.

"Yes, that's right," I replied.

"I wondered if you might help me—help my wife, actually. She's disappeared and...and I'm worried about her."

Great. A new case. Income!

I asked him the basic questions: when, why, where might she have gone, what had the police done—and as he answered them, I became intrigued. This woman had been missing for about a month. She was emotionally unstable, according to Danville, and he was afraid she might even have fallen in with some bad company. Maybe even traffickers. That seemed a little extreme to me.

"I lie awake at night worrying about her," he said. I heard him take a deep breath. "Look, this isn't about getting her back with me. If she's finished with our marriage, well, I guess I'll have to deal with that. I just want to know that she's all right." He paused. "I don't know what you charge, but I'll make it worth your while. And I'll pay you an advance. The money, well, it doesn't mean much to me now that she's gone."

I liked the sound of an advance.

On the spur of the moment, I decided not to go through my usual questionnaire process. Instead, I arranged to meet Colton Danville at the place he suggested, in his office in Norfolk, in two days. In the meantime, I got online and did my homework.

Colton Danville was not just a successful businessman in Norfolk, he was apparently a pillar of the community. He served on the board of several charitable foundations and the vestry of a local church. A graduate of Old Dominion University with an MBA, his bona fides were impeccable. The real estate firm he'd inherited twenty years ago was now a multimillion-dollar business. He was married, according to his bio on his website, to Elise, but they had no children.

I also found newspaper articles about him—mostly about his participation in charity events and several business deals he'd closed. I saw he was a runner and had participated in a local marathon. He played tennis and golf. And he'd made a major contribution to a YMCA.

All in all, Colton Danville seemed like an all-around upstanding citizen. So what was with his wife? I ran an online search for her and found practically nothing. Amazing. He's such a public person and she's what? A recluse?

———

I HAD A BUSY WEEK. We had an SAR meetup on Tuesday night, and I went to see Miss Lottie on Wednesday. She looked paler to me, and weaker. I bought groceries and put them away for her, then made another one of my easy meals—a nourishing soup made from rotisserie chicken and fresh vegetables.

While I was there, a well-dressed woman named Rachelle Bennett came by. She wore a burgundy business suit and had pulled up her auburn hair in a severe bun. I noticed her fancy nail-polish job—something I'd never think to spend money on.

We talked for a little while as the soup cooked. Rachelle went to Miss Lottie's church. Her mother, who had died six months before, had been one of Miss Lottie's very closest friends, so Rachelle checked in on her now and then.

"Oh, so you knew Tamara," I suggested.

Rachelle shook her head. "No, I didn't grow up here. I came here for a job as an adult and moved my mom here to be near me.

Lottie and Mom didn't meet until," she looked at the older woman, "maybe five years ago."

"But it was like we'd known each other forever," Miss Lottie said. She patted Rachelle's hand. "Your mother was very dear to me. And she was so proud of you!"

Rachelle smiled and then turned to me and asked about my life, my work, and search and rescue. I shared the highlights, but not the horrible mess I made of nearly all my relationships.

After that I excused myself and retreated to the kitchen. I ladled some hot soup in a bowl to take out to Miss Lottie, put some in the fridge, and froze the rest in meal-sized portions. Rachelle had declined my offer of soup, so after I gave the bowl to Miss Lottie, I said goodbye.

In the evening, I took Luke on a good run. I'd have to leave him in the crate in the motel while I went to Norfolk the next morning. It would be a long day for him penned up.

I'd picked a trail in York River State Park. The views were spectacular. We ran for over an hour. At one point, the trail dropped close to the water, and I let Luke cool off. I never got tired of watching him swim. Or run. Or do just about anything.

27

THE NEXT MORNING, I showered and put on my best clothes. I'd actually gone out and bought dress pants. They were gray, and along with a white silk shirt and my black blazer, I thought I looked pretty good. Of course, I had to buy dressy shoes to go along with my outfit. I swear, I hated wearing heels, but for this, I would. I was slightly desperate to make an impression.

I put Luke in the crate. He flopped down, sighing with resignation. I'd bought a water bottle—the kind they use for hamsters, only bigger. It hung on the outside of his crate, and he could lick the tube for water. I'd shoved the thermostat down to 65 degrees. I doubted the room temperature would actually go that low, but I did it anyway. Then I said goodbye to my best friend. Remembering to put the Do Not Disturb sign on the door, I left, swallowing the guilt I felt. I tried hard not to imagine what would happen if the hotel had a fire while I was gone. Just the thought was enough to make me nauseous.

To get to Norfolk, I had to travel down Interstate 64 and then either take the Hampton Roads Bridge Tunnel or the Monitor Merrimac Bridge Tunnel or the James River Bridge. I was familiar enough with the area to know any of those routes was a roll of the dice. My navigation program could tell me which one was fastest right now, but let some idiot run out of gas in one of the tunnels or drive into a bridge abutment and all bets were off.

The trip should normally take about an hour and a half, no matter which route I chose. I allowed two hours and fifteen minutes. I would much rather kill time in a coffee shop or sit in my car than be late.

After rolling the dice in my head, I chose the HRBT. I breathed a prayer of thanks when I got through it with just one slowdown, right at the beginning.

Hampton Roads is what they call the area surrounding Norfolk, where the Chesapeake Bay, Atlantic Ocean, and the James, Elizabeth, and Nansemond rivers join. "Roads" is an old British nautical term for a sheltered anchorage. I knew that because I'd looked it up, not because I'm Jeopardy-smart.

As I emerged from the tunnel and drove on the flat bridge crossing the James, I was once again impressed by the size of the port. Huge Navy ships and commercial cargo vessels dwarfed what I called "normal-size" boats. Ice-free and sheltered, I could see why the deep-water port was a tremendous asset to the entire country.

I wound my way into downtown Norfolk and pulled into a parking place thirty minutes early. Nervous, I decided to walk a little. I picked up the new black business tote bag I'd bought, stepped out, locked the Jeep, and walked around the block.

Glancing at my reflection in a storefront window, I barely recognized myself. I was a lot more comfortable in cargo pants and boots than the way I saw myself now.

I arrived at Colton's office ten minutes early. I announced myself to the receptionist and, minutes later, a secretary ushered me into Danville's inner sanctum.

It looked just like what you would expect—all leather and

wood and brass with a stunning view of downtown Norfolk through a huge window. A "me wall" behind the desk displayed pictures of him with people I probably should have recognized and lots of plaques trumpeting his sales accomplishments.

Colton Danville stood up as I entered. He was fifty, as I knew from his bio, fit and trim and movie-star handsome in his dark suit. A shock of brown hair hung over his forehead, giving him an impish look. His brown eyes smiled at me. I was glad I wasn't wearing khakis and boots.

"Mr. Danville?" I said, extending my hand. "Jessica Chamberlain."

"Let's have a seat." He gestured toward a leather armchair, one of two in a conversational grouping. I made a note to myself to recreate that idea if I ever opened my own office. I found it cozy, almost relaxing.

"Tell me about yourself," he said.

I gave him the short bio. He kept his eyes on me like I was the most interesting creature in the world. He asked me some questions, and I found myself telling him more about my time as a Fairfax County detective, about Luke and SAR, and about some successful cases I'd had as a PI.

"Fascinating!" he said.

But I knew this shouldn't be about me. "So how can I help you, Mr. Danville," I said, moderating my tone. "Tell me about your wife."

He shook his head. "She is a fragile one, my Elise. I think of her like a doe. She frightens easily. This time, she ran."

"How long have you been married?"

"Twenty-one years," he said. "No kids. That's the way she wanted it." He sat back and stared upward. "Maybe I got too involved at work. Or in these boards and all." He gestured helplessly. "I just...I just wanted to give back to the community, you know? But maybe it was too much for her."

"When did you see her last?"

"A month ago on a Thursday. It was hot and muggy. I had a golf date at one o'clock. When I left, she had gone upstairs to rest. She wasn't feeling well. When I returned home, she wasn't there."

"Where did you think she'd gone?"

He shook his head. "I had no idea. She never did work. I thought maybe she'd gone to one of her appointments. A doctor's appointment or something. I had a board meeting, but expected I'd see her that evening. When I got home—"

"About what time?"

He frowned, trying to remember. "Late. Eleven." He pursed his lips and shook his head, as if trying to get back on track. "Anyway, when I got home that night, she was still MIA."

"Her clothes?"

"Some missing, some still in the drawers and closets."

"And what else was gone?"

"Personal things. Her jewelry. Some cash we had in the house. Her purse, wallet—that sort of thing." He laughed softly. "Then I discovered she'd cleaned out our savings account." He looked surprised at what he'd said and held up his hands in surrender. "But I'm not angry about that. Like I said, the money doesn't mean anything to me if she's not here."

"How much money is missing?" I asked.

"Tens of thousands."

"Enough to live on for a while."

"Yes." He ran his hand over his head.

I felt sorry for the guy. I really did. "What did you do then, Mr. Danville?"

"Call me Colton."

I really did not feel comfortable with that but I went along. "What did you do when you realized she was missing? Did you try her cell phone?"

He nodded. "It went straight to voicemail. Then I called the police. Filed a missing persons report. Started checking hospitals and clinics and even rehab places."

"Rehab? Was she an addict?"

"No, not that I knew of, unless you count keeping the house spotless an addiction." He laughed softly.

"So why did you call rehab places?"

He shrugged. "Just in case. She was secretive, you know. She had a hard time opening up to people."

"Even her friends?"

"She hardly had any friends."

I pondered that information. "You called the police and filed a missing persons report. Then what happened?"

"They asked me to talk to a detective so I did." He gestured. "They all know me down there at the police station—know my name anyway. I told them all that I knew, gave them a couple of names, and then I think they had uniformed officers checking traffic cams and our security cameras and the neighbors'." He rubbed his knee. "I don't know what all they did. All I know is two weeks later they said they hadn't found her, and I just needed to wait for her to come home or call me. They said they believed she had left voluntarily."

"What brought them to that conclusion?"

Danville's shoulders heaved as he took a deep breath. "She sold her car."

"What?"

"She had a nice little roadster, a BMW. Her choice. White. Tan leather interior. Only had about ten thousand miles on it because she rarely went anywhere. She sold it, or traded it in at a dealership in Virginia Beach. The cops interviewed the salesman and the manager. There was no evidence of foul play. No indication she was forced into selling it."

"So you're left hanging."

"Yes, they won't go any further. Not without some indication she's a victim." Danville looked at me. He definitely had tears in his eyes. "I miss her, Miss Chamberlain. And I will not be able to live with myself if...if I stand by and do nothing and something terrible has happened to her. She's naïve! And fragile."

I know I winced. "Do you see this as your fault?"

"Oh, absolutely."

I cocked my head.

"I didn't pay enough attention to her. I failed to love her well. No question, it's my fault."

I found myself wanting to reach over and pat his hand. I refrained. "Don't blame yourself."

"Thank you," he said, his voice low.

I asked a few more questions, got information on what she did all day, where she liked to go, where she shopped, that sort of thing. And the name of one friend. That's all he knew.

And I thought *I* was isolated.

Danville's intercom buzzed. I checked my watch. We'd been talking for an hour.

"Yes?" he called out.

"Sir, your next appointment is here."

"Thank you, Cara." He looked at me apologetically. "I'm sorry. I need to move on. Does that give you enough to start with?"

"Yes, sir." I slid my notebook into my bag and stood. "Oh, a picture would help."

"Of course." He turned to the console behind his desk and slid a five-by-seven picture of his wife out of the frame. "Take this."

"Is it fairly recent?"

"Two months ago. I had a bunch taken for our anniversary."

I looked down at the picture in my hand and saw a woman with long blonde hair and beautiful dark eyes. She was smiling, but the smile seemed stiff, forced, and I wondered what pain lay behind it.

I heard a noise and looked up. Danville removed an envelope from his center desk drawer and handed it to me. "This is for you."

I slid the photo into my tote bag, opened the envelope, and found a check for five thousand dollars. I caught my breath.

"That should get you started," Danville said.

"Yes. Thank you." I shouldered my bag and pretended I was used to people handing me large checks. "I'll be in touch soon."

28

My HAND SHOOK a little as I sat in my car fingering that check. I knew a lot of it would go toward expenses, but still it doubled my net worth.

I'd seen a branch of my bank nearby. I went through the drive-thru and deposited the check and automatically started home the same way I'd come. That was a mistake. The HRBT had been brought to a stop by a broken-down car.

I glanced at the dashboard clock. I'd left Luke almost four hours ago. I needed to get back. But I was at the mercy of the Hampton Roads Bridge Tunnel and, as far as I knew, the HRBT showed no mercy to anyone.

I pulled a small notebook out of my bag and began writing a to-do list:

Interview Elise's one friend. Walk through her house. Talk to the minister at their church. Talk to the police investigators and to the used car dealership where she'd sold the car.

As I inched my way forward while writing notes, my phone rang. Brooke. My little sister. "Hey, what's up?"

"Mom and Dad are home. I thought you should know."

"Oh, good," I said, as if it made a difference. Brooke was a lot closer to them than I was, geographically and in every other way. I considered my mother and stepfather her responsibility. "What are you up to?"

"I've decided what I want to do. For a career."

"What's that?"

"You know I've been working as an EMT while I finish school. Well, I'm applying to get more training. I want to become a paramedic. I may even go on to medical school."

This, from my sister who, last I heard, was majoring in communications. "Sounds good, Brooke. So what's your plan?"

"I'll graduate in December, keep working as an EMT, and get my paramedic's license, then cardiac-care tech. I think I can do this, Jess. I'm excited about it."

"The adrenaline rush does wear off after a while."

"I know, but after...after that night with you and the fire and Nate, I couldn't get my mind off being a first responder. But I knew mom would have a heart attack if I tried to become a cop, especially after what happened to you."

Not to mention my father.

"So I'm going the EMT route. So far, I like it!"

"Well, then, go for it!" I hoped that sounded encouraging. "Brooke, I'm about to go into a tunnel. I'll lose my signal. Gotta run."

"Okay, I want to come see you. Call me!"

Five hours and forty-five minutes after I had left Luke, I drove into the motel. Poor guy.

As I stepped out of my car, I noticed the Three Amigos standing at the end of the row of motel rooms, smoking. They stopped talking and stared at me. I opened the room door and shut it quickly, throwing the bolt.

Poor Luke was overjoyed to see me. That was the longest I think I'd ever left him in the crate. I released the door, and he jumped all over me, squeaking like a girl, his tail wagging madly.

"Hey, buddy. Hey, hey," I said, thumping his side. I kicked my heels off, slipped on my athletic shoes, grabbed the room key and his leash, and took him out to water the grass.

As soon as I stepped outside, I realized I should have brought my gun. I did not like the way those guys were looking at me. I'd seen them talking to the maids, too, joking around with them. If they were able to get their hands on a master key, I could be in trouble.

Luke did what he needed to do, then we went back inside. I changed into running clothes, and we left again. He needed a run. I drove to a nearby park, and while we ran, I mapped out a game plan in my head. If I could get in to see the police investigators on Friday, I would. If not, then Monday. And if I could interview the car salesmen, I'd do that on the same day. That would mean leaving Luke again, but what else could I do?

On Saturday the SAR group had a practice scheduled all day at York River State Park, which Luke and I planned to attend. I'd need to see Miss Lottie on Sunday or maybe Monday.

The thought occurred to me that Miss Lottie might like going to church. I imagine that habit dies hard with people like her. I decided to call her when we finished our run.

After about forty-five minutes, I was ready to quit. Luke was panting like crazy. This park had a splash pad for kids, a concrete area with all kinds of waterspouts and showers that kids could run and play in and get wet without concerns about drowning. I decided it would work well for my dog, too, especially since there were no kids using it.

I walked Luke down to it, and he thought it was great, biting at the spurts that emerged randomly from the ground, raising himself up on his hind legs to try to catch the water as it flowed down from the showers. I tricked him, positioning him under the bucket that, once filled, tipped and soaked him. He shook the water off, soaking me, and I thought it was hilarious and fun until a man walking by reamed me out.

"That's for kids," he yelled. "What do you think you're doing?"

I said a few things back that I probably shouldn't have, and the man continued his rant. Some people seem to be experts at taking the joy out of life.

When Luke and I returned to the motel, I gave Luke the chewy that Scott had brought for him. Then I called the Norfolk police detective who had worked on Elise Danville's disappearance. He actually sounded friendly and said he'd be glad to see me the next morning at nine. I put off volunteering to take Miss Lottie to church. I'm not sure why. Instead, I called and arranged to see her on Monday.

My life was coming back together, getting organized into neat little manageable boxes. I had work. I had good deeds. I had exercise. I had SAR.

Now if only I had dinner.

I reviewed my options. Put Luke back in his hotel room crate while I went out to get something. Take Luke with me. Starve.

I rejected all of those.

I looked in my phone at nearby restaurants. I chose an Italian place. I called and ordered a huge chicken Caesar salad. Then I told Luke to wait, and I'd be back soon. I grabbed my keys and my gun bag and left.

Twenty minutes later, I arrived back at the motel. All of the spaces in front of my room were taken. I thought that was odd. I parked in the next closest space, grabbed my food, and, hotel room key card in hand, I got out of the car.

I was about to slide the key card in the lock when a voice said, "Yo, pretty mama, whatcha doin'?"

When I turned, I saw one of the Three Amigos on my right. The hair on the back of my neck stood up. Where were the others? Behind me?

I got aggressive. "Get away from me!" I yelled. My hand went to my gun. Inside the room, Luke started barking ferociously.

The guy held up his hands in surrender. "Okay, okay." Grinning, he backed away.

I turned my back to the door to make sure no one was behind me. Then I slipped the key card the rest of the way in, stepped inside, and closed and bolted the door.

"Good boy, good boy!" I said, crouching down and petting Luke. "Good boy!"

Still, the confrontation had shaken me. I slept that night with my gun on the night table and the light in the bathroom on. My dreams were full of darkness and fear. I woke up the next morning knowing one thing—I had to move.

———

I'D GOTTEN up at five so I could run Luke, shower, dress in my power clothes, and leave by seven. I had to be at the Norfolk police station by nine. All of that made me wonder if my next place of residence (I couldn't say "home") should be on the Norfolk side of the HRBT. Farther away from Nate and Laura. Farther from Scott.

Detective David O'Connor looked as Irish as his name. Barrel-chested and broad-faced, he had big brown eyes and a friendly smile. Most detectives come across as reserved, observational, even skeptical. It comes with the territory. Constantly dealing with criminals and violent crimes makes a person guarded. This man was different.

He met me at the sergeant's desk and walked me back to an interview room. He had on a gray suit with a light blue shirt and a striped tie. We sat down at the table in the room, across from each other. That's when I noticed his brown hair was flecked with gray.

"You were with Fairfax," he said, delivering the first pitch.

I raised my eyebrows. Clearly, he'd done a little research. "Yes."

"And now you're out making the big bucks as a PI."

I laughed out loud. The look on his face told me he was joking, and my guess was he knew why I'd left Fairfax.

"I was with the Metropolitan Police," he said. "Had a shooting incident I couldn't get past. So I took a break and ended up down here at the training academy, doing firearms training, until I realized I really missed hanging out with dead people. His self-deprecating humor instantly put me at ease.

"Well, if you ever run short, I have a dog who has a knack for finding them. Just let me know, I'll bring him around."

"Really?"

"We do volunteer search-and-rescue."

"Tell me about it."

I told him about Luke, about a couple of cases we'd been on, about water training and climbing mountains and some of the other things we did. "We get between fifty and seventy-five call-outs a year," I told him. "Many more than ever get reported in the press."

"And you do it all for free." By this time, Detective O'Connor was rocking on the two back legs of his chair, looking like a fourth-grade boy about to be called out by his teacher. "That is very cool," he said. Then he moved forward, resting his forearms on the table. "Tell me about this case you're working on."

I pulled out my notes. "Colton Danville has hired me to find his wife. You all saw no signs of foul play, but he's broken up about the fact that she's missing. Worried because she's mentally fragile. I'd like to know as much as you can tell me about the case. I understand you were the lead detective?"

"Yeah, that's right. I caught the ticket. Danville called us on 18 July at 22:53. On the 911 call he sounded upset. The dispatcher sent uniforms over. They did a preliminary search, then I got called out."

"You responded right away?"

"Danville's connected. Well thought of in the community. He's got money, so we had to rule out a possible kidnapping. So yes, I went over immediately, along with my partner, Sara Benson."

I wrote that name down.

"She's off today. But anyway, Sara and me, we did the usual routine—interviewed him, sent uniforms door-to-door, had dogs search the area."

"Do you have your own dogs?"

"Yep. Tactical canines."

He picked up a pencil from the table and began fiddling with it. I got the feeling he was the kind of guy that had a hard time sitting still.

"The dogs didn't find anything. But Danville, he has security cameras, as do a lot of the neighbors. It's a pricey zip code. We collected all the information we could and helped him file a missing persons report. The videos show her leaving the house on her own, nobody compelling her."

"What time was that?"

"The time stamp on the video was 14:23. Those can be off, as you know, but it jives with the other security cams."

"She left in her car?"

"In her car. A 2016 BMW 530xi, white, tan leather interior," he said.

I was impressed he could remember so many details without notes. "Did you follow that with traffic cams?"

"Yep. We tracked her through Norfolk to Virginia Beach, where she sold her car."

"She sold it?"

"Yes."

"And what did they say?"

"The car dealer? He said she had the title, the car was cleaned out, and she had decided the price she wanted. They went over the car, and *boom*...it was a done deal in less than an hour."

"So she leaves there on foot—"

"Nope. She Ubers over to another dealership, buys a cheaper car—"

"Which is?"

"A 2018 Kia Forte, silver, gray interior. She gets that car and pockets about $25K."

"Money to live on," I said.

"Exactly. By this time, me and Sara, we're thinking this lady is just walking out. The BMW was in her name. She had a perfect right to sell it. There's no crime. We don't see anyone compelling her. The last thing we saw on video was her driving over the CBBT."

The Chesapeake Bay Bridge-Tunnel is a nearly twenty-mile span over the mouth of the bay. It connects the mainland—Norfolk and Virginia Beach—with the Delmarva Peninsula. A lot of people take Route 13 up the peninsula to get to Philly or New York.

Where could she have been going?

I thought of something else. "Danville said she cleared out their savings account."

O'Connor laughed. "She took exactly half of what was in there. I saw the withdrawal."

I tapped my pen against my lips. "What did the car salesman or the bank people say about her mental state?"

He shrugged. "Said she was real quiet but knew exactly what she wanted. I don't know...it seems to me she just walked. Seems strange, given who Danville is, but people do weird things." His phone rang. He checked the number. "Excuse me."

"Sure." I studied my notes while he talked.

He clicked off the phone and stood up. "Sorry, that was my wife. We've got two little kids and one of them just threw up at preschool. I've got dad duty. She's on a case."

"Is she a detective?" I asked, gathering my things.

"No. FBI." He grinned. "I get the bodies, she gets the big bucks. It all works out."

29

I DROVE BACK to the motel after leaving David O'Connor. I could have gone to the car dealership, but he'd given me enough information for now and I knew I had work to do today.

I pulled into my parking space, thankful the Three Amigos were nowhere in sight. I took Luke over to the grassy area, then headed inside to pack up our stuff. All of it. The last thing I did before I checked out of the Pinewood Inn was use their WiFi to check out other places we might live.

I'd decided to stay on the Williamsburg side of the HRBT. I can't explain why. I drove around to the three best prospects and checked into the third one, the Red Coat Inn. It was at least one step up from the Pinewood Inn. As I got us settled, Luke thoroughly inspected the room, his nose working hard. He always knew more about the places we checked into than I did.

As I worked, I thought of three reasons why I'd probably made the decision to stay in the area. I'd be closer to Miss Lottie, closer to the SAR group meetings, and closer to the sheriff and fire marshal. I could keep bugging them about the house fire and my wrecked car.

Down deep inside, I also knew I didn't want to move farther from Nate. And Scott.

The SAR practice for the next morning started at eight. Luke and I pulled up to the parking area at 7:45. As soon as I got him out of the crate, I saw his head go up like he smelled something. I thought maybe there was a cat around. As I reached into the back for my SAR pack, all of a sudden he took off.

Alarmed, I yelled for him, but he ignored me, so I chased him. Then I saw what he was after—Sprite! Nate was here. I had no idea he was working this training. I ran to him and hugged him so hard I nearly knocked him off his feet.

"Hey, easy on the crippled guy!" he said, laughing.

"I didn't know you were going to be here. You didn't tell me!"

"Yeah? And how does that feel?" He grinned.

My face grew hot.

"I'm just kiddin'. Tim had somebody cancel on him at the last minute. He called me last night, and I told him I'd come. I barely had time to get my stuff together."

He pronounced "barely" like "barley." I missed his crazy accent.

Nate gestured toward our two dogs. "Look at that." They were wrestling and mouthing each other, happy to be together.

Tim called out, "Nate!"

He looked at me. "Gotta run. What say we get together when we're done?"

"I'd love that."

The fifteen of us who were there divided into three groups. Nate took experienced handlers who were having a problem with their dogs to a different area of the park to help them. A woman named Joyce took new handlers and/or new dogs off to do the basics. The rest of us were doing water training with Tim.

Soon I found myself in a jon boat with Luke. This time the boat had a platform built into the bow. Luke had laid down on it, keeping his center of gravity low. "Find the body, Luke. Body!"

He found the first diver quickly and got his hot dog reward. Then Tim wanted to take the next step—bring in multiple boats and people on shore to try and distract him.

That did not go well. One of the other shepherds was on another boat and barked nonstop. Luke seemed confused about whether he was supposed to be barking too. He cocked his head, looking at the other dog, like he was wondering if Caesar had found something and was about to get his reward, probably the last hot dog on earth.

Then we heard thunder. Tim called off the water work, and we made our way back to shore.

My mood plummeted. I wasn't used to failure with Luke. We usually pulled off whatever test was thrown at us. We got out of the boat and he shook off, even though he wasn't wet. He looked at me with those big brown eyes, like he was searching my face, reading the disappointment there.

I bent down and rubbed behind his ears. "It's okay, buddy. We'll try again." At that moment, we both heard a noise and looked up. Nate's group was returning to the parking area.

Nate! *Sprite!* If I had a tail, we both would have been wagging.

Off to the side, Tim checked his iPhone. "That's it for today," he called out. "Weather calls for storms the rest of the afternoon."

That was fine with me.

———

NATE FOLLOWED me to an Italian place I knew of that had a covered patio. It would provide protection from the predicted storms and yet let us keep the dogs with us. He insisted on treating me to lunch, but it was just pizza so I didn't feel too bad.

"Have you done water rescue?" I asked him as we waited for our large "everything" pie.

"Nope."

There was something behind that, I knew. "Why not?"

"Don't like boats."

"Why don't you like boats?"

His eyes narrowed. He sat back. "Just don't."

The devil got into me. "That really surprises me," I said, "because I thought you did every part of SAR." I knew I was goading him. I also knew I was trying to avoid his commentary on my life. "Why don't you do water searches? You seem to know a lot about them."

"Knowin's one thing. Doin's another."

"So..."

He sighed. Then he leaned forward. "Up in the hills we didn't have swimmin' pools and lessons and all. We had creeks." He pronounced it "cricks." "One summer my family visited an uncle. Lived on a lake in Tennessee. Had a couple of canoes. His boys piled into one, and me and my brother took t'other. But we didn't know what we were doing. We didn't have it balanced right. Wind came up and dumped us and I 'bout drowned. I can still hear those boys laughin'."

"Who saved you?"

"I had to swim for it, but I knew the current was pullin' me toward the dam. Scared the daylights out of me."

"Were you wearing a life jacket?"

He shook his head.

"What happened to your brother?"

"He stayed with the canoe. Hung onto it 'til our cousins could tow him and it back to shore."

"And you?"

"Somehow, I made it to a little island in the middle of the lake. The others thought it would be real funny to leave me there."

"And you were how old?"

"Eight. It was near dark before the adults figured out what was going on and my uncle came to get me." He turned his head, stretching out the tension in his neck. "So yeah, I pretty much hate boats."

I looked across the table at my friend. I felt bad that I'd pushed him. "Your brother should have been looking out for you."

"We weren't close. Still aren't."

I wondered if that's what Brooke would say about me.

The pizza came, hot and steaming, distracting us. Nate said grace, and we moved on to happier subjects while we ate. He told me about Laura and her horse and said he was thinking about getting another dog. And he told me about his fear that he wouldn't be able to train a dog being one-legged.

"It's one thing standin' still and telling other folks how to do it. It's another making all those quick moves, teachin' 'em to heel and all."

"You'll figure it out. I know you will."

He just looked at me, and I knew my knee-jerk encouragement wasn't touching the core of his concern. I took a deep breath and conjured up something that might. "God has given you this gift...this way with dogs that you have. From the time you were a kid, through the military, and now in SAR. Your handicap can't stop that gift. Not when it's from God."

A slow smile spread across Nate's face, as if he'd just won a kind of victory. "Well," he said, "I thank you for that. Now, tell me what's going on with you."

I told him about Miss Lottie, my moves, and my latest case—the realtor's missing wife. I told him about Scott coming down and, in an effort to be transparent like him, I told Nate about wanting to run when Scott got close, and even about Luke blocking my path.

He laughed at that. Then he got serious. "When are you comin' back home?"

"I'll be up to see you sometime. I want to meet the horse."

"I don't mean to visit. When are you moving back home?"

I started to say something, but my throat closed up. An awkward silence followed, then Nate broke it with a laugh. "Someday you'll quit runnin'."

I raised my chin and grinned at him. "I'll let you know when that happens. You can come visit me wherever I end up."

———

LATER THAT NIGHT back at the Red Coat Inn, I thought about how I answered him. I couldn't think of a statement more flip and dismissive. Why did he put up with me?

But as usual, Nate's comments convicted me. So to prove I wasn't isolating, I called my parents.

My mother answered the phone. "Welcome home!" I said in my cheeriest voice. "How was your trip?"

She seemed flustered at first to hear my voice, but my question soon launched a review of their cruise—the weather, the entertainment, the food, their fellow passengers, and the waiter who served them daily. I heard about St. Thomas and St. Kitts and places in between, as well as the shopping and a waterspout they'd seen from a distance. I asked a few questions and, twelve minutes later, concluded the call without revealing a single one of my current traumas. For all my mother knew, her older daughter was happy, healthy, and safe.

I had a feeling Nate would just call that a different way of running.

———

I LAID out my plans for the week. See Miss Lottie, look at the Danvilles' house, gather what information I could about his wife, talk to their pastor, and visit Elise's one friend.

I checked the time and put in a quick call to Danville. He said I could come by on Tuesday at noon to see the house. He gave me email addresses for the others, and within an hour, I had appointments set up for that same day.

I went to see Miss Lottie on Monday. After putting away groceries and getting her some soup, I asked her if I could see Tamara's room again. I'd looked at it once before, but I needed something to indicate I was trying to make progress.

I found it odd that Miss Lottie never pressured me. She actually told me she was trusting God to guide me. Realistically, I think she was just lonely and enjoyed my company. Logically, she couldn't have had any expectation I would succeed in finding Tamara.

Like many grieving parents, Miss Lottie had kept Tamara's room much the same as when the girl lived there.

Posters of NSYNC and the Backstreet Boys hung on the walls. I found school pictures of her friends on her desk and a couple of issues of TEEN magazine, as well as unfinished homework. From her papers, I doubted that Tamara ended up as a history major. Or a mathematician.

When I joined Miss Lottie in the living room, I asked, "How'd she do in school?

She shook her head. "Very much a B/C student. She just seemed not to care."

"Did she have a favorite subject?"

"Art, maybe? Music? None of the academic subjects." She shook her head. "We denied her so many things. We were saving for her college. Looking back, that was foolish."

I reached over and patted her hand. "You couldn't have known."

Tiger jumped up in her lap, and I wondered if he sensed her sadness. I liked to think of Luke as brilliant and particularly sensitive, but I had to admit, even a mutt like Tiger could pick up on an owner's emotions. It was the nature of dogs. "God's great gift to mankind," Nate would say. I thought it probably had more to do with their domestication over thousands of years as they followed our hunter-gatherer ancestors and a mutually beneficial relationship developed.

———

ON TUESDAY MORNING, I had a ten o'clock meeting with Mr. Danville's pastor, a man named Carter Bolinbroke. You couldn't get much more old Virginia than that name.

I stepped into his church office, all deep red carpet and cherry wood, and he invited me to sit on a couch. The Reverend Doctor Bolinbroke had snow-white hair, a deep tan, and the good looks of a TV preacher. I noticed he closed the door completely when we entered his office.

"What can I do for you?" he asked as he sat down.

"Colton Danville hired me to find his wife," I began.

"Oh, yes, a terrible shock, her disappearing like that."

"Dr. Bolinbroke, how well did you know her?"

He frowned a little, trying to think. "I saw her at church events, occasionally, and on Sunday morning. She wasn't one of our more involved parishioners. Very quiet. Almost shy. Nothing at all like Colton." He smiled. "Colton told me why you were coming in. I asked my wife if she knew Elise. She said Elise kept to herself, that she didn't participate in any of the women's events. She didn't really know her. Kind of sad."

Bolinbroke continued. "Now Colton, he's a great guy. Always willing to jump in. Ran our charity golf tournament. Serves on the vestry. We play tennis together every Saturday morning and often golf on Thursdays. Usually he beats me."

I ventured out onto thin ice. "So you would know if they were having problems."

He raised his eyebrows. "Problems?"

"You said they were such opposites."

"Well opposites attract, don't they? I never got the impression there were problems." He picked up a pen and tapped it on his hand. "Elise disappearing was a complete shock. I never saw that coming. Colton is well-liked, well-respected. He's a good provider. I mean, have you seen their house?"

"That's next."

"Any woman would be thrilled to live there."

"Then why'd she leave?"

"I think she must have snapped. Had a nervous breakdown." Bolinbroke sat back. "I've urged Colton to be patient with her. See if she'll come back. I guess he hired you because he couldn't wait."

"He's concerned about her."

"Quite right. That's the kind of person he is."

30

COLTON DANVILLE'S house was in an upscale part of Norfolk. A big, boxy colonial, it stood on a grassy lawn surrounded by mature trees. Two chimneys sprouted from the rooftop, and a driveway led to a garage behind the house and to the right.

I rang the bell and a middle-aged maid dressed in a white uniform let me in. "Mr. Danville call. He be here soon. He say please wait. I give you tea?"

"Tea would be nice," I said. I followed her past a beautiful curved staircase and down the hall to an immaculate, updated kitchen. I sat down at a classic farmhouse trestle table (nicer than anything I'd ever owned) and watched her boil water and place tea leaves in an infuser. "What's your name?" I asked her.

"Rosa."

"How long have you worked for the Danvilles?"

"Three years."

"So you know Mrs. Danville well."

She frowned. "She stay quiet. In her room most of the time."

That was weird. Elise didn't connect at church and didn't talk to the maid. Who did she talk to?

I sipped my tea while staring at the glossy, natural-hardwood floors, the classic cabinets, the beautiful granite countertops. The place looked like something from a real estate design magazine. Mr. Danville had said Elise kept an immaculate house, but this was beyond immaculate. No kids, no dog. Plus she had a maid. What did Elise do all day?

Rosa had left the kitchen. I was alone. I set down my tea, walked over, and opened a drawer. Kitchen utensils perfectly in place. Another one held neatly folded, perfectly unstained, tea towels. Behind cabinet doors I found china, crystal drink ware, and spices in alphabetical order.

Growing obsessive, I checked the dishwasher, which was empty. And I was staring into a half-empty, perfectly ordered refrigerator when Mr. Danville walked in the rear door.

I know I must have turned six shades of red. "Just looking for some milk," I said. I grabbed a quart and poured some into my nearly empty teacup.

"Rosa should have offered you some. I'll have a word with her."

"Oh, don't bother. It's fine," I said, replacing the milk and smiling.

He had on a gray shirt and black tie with dark gray pants.

"It's a beautiful house," I said.

He visibly relaxed and glanced toward the ceiling. "Yes. She has a gift for design, my wife does. Seems empty now without her." He looked at his watch. "Look, I don't have a lot of time. What did you want to see?"

"Whatever you can show me. I'm trying to get a feel for who she is."

Danville walked me through the first floor, with its classic dining room, living room with a fireplace, and a library in what might have once been a breakfast nook. Oriental carpets covered the floors, and art adorned the walls.

Upstairs he showed me three bedrooms. One was a study, the other a guest room. The master bedroom had a large, king-sized sleigh bed in dark wood and an en-suite bathroom with a walk-in shower. On the vanity, I saw makeup, cleansers, and hair ties.

"May I?" He nodded. I opened a drawer and found neatly folded scarves.

"Oddly, she didn't take any of this," Danville said, opening a jewelry box. My guess was what I was looking at wasn't fake. He closed it again. "Go ahead and look around," he said, gesturing. "I'll be downstairs."

I took advantage of the invitation. I looked through her drawers, the closet, even under the bed. I found nothing that would clue me in on what she was thinking when she left that day, or even who she was.

Ten minutes later I found him downstairs in the kitchen, sipping something that smelled to me like whiskey. "I'm sorry," he said, gesturing with the glass. "I find this whole thing depressing."

"I get that," I said.

"I have clients again, beginning at two…"

"Of course. I'm finished here. Thank you."

———

ELISE'S ONE FRIEND, Allison Brewster, looked about forty. She wore her dark hair chin length, and her lipstick was perfectly applied. I met her at a coffee shop in downtown Norfolk. We sat outside, catching the breeze as it came in off the harbor. I was thankful for the breeze. It had to be at least ninety degrees.

"So, how long have you and Elise been friends, Miss Brewster?"

She took a long drink of her iced tea, handling the glass with perfectly manicured and stylized nails. "Two years, maybe longer."

"Where did you meet?"

"At the Chrysler Museum. She was sitting perfectly still,

staring at a painting of a slave cabin. She was hauntingly beautiful, and I sat down next to her. At first she seemed startled, but I
just stayed quiet and she settled down. After a while I asked her
what she saw, and her words opened my eyes to things I'd never
noticed before, although I'd seen that painting many, many times.
I think she is brilliant, an undiscovered talent."

"You know art?"

"I teach at ODU."

Old Dominion University was just a few miles away. "So, you
became friends."

"Yes. We'd meet on Fridays, either at the Chrysler or somewhere else. Sometimes we'd have lunch."

"Did she tell you about her family?"

"Oh, she didn't have one. Only her husband. When he found
out we were meeting, well you'd have thought she was having an
affair." Allison giggled. "He actually followed her to the museum
one day. But as soon as he realized what was going on, he relaxed.
Bought us lunch. Turns out he was just worried about her. She
doesn't have many friends and rarely goes out. He was
concerned."

"Was she angry that he'd followed her?"

"She didn't seem to be." She sipped her drink, and the way
she did it made me wonder if she'd ever gone to finishing school.
She continued, "What a charming man. I adore him."

"Did Elise give you any indication she was going to
leave him?"

"Oh my, no. And I can't imagine why she would. He gave her
everything. Cared for her. Worshipped her, even." Allison took a
deep breath. "Elise is fragile, like an artist, and, well, I guess she
simply snapped."

———

I PONDERED that as I drove back to the Red Coat Inn. I couldn't get past the "what did she do all day question." Yes, there were books in the house, but she had a maid and aside from a small garden, I couldn't imagine what occupied her time. She had to be mentally ill.

I pulled into my parking space at the inn and stepped out of my car. I could hear Luke barking. As I slid my key card into the slot, my phone rang. Miss Lottie.

"Hello? Miss Lottie?" I said, pressing the phone to my ear. "Miss Lottie?" I couldn't hear a thing, but then, Luke was going ballistic. I leashed him up and, cradling the phone on my shoulder, took him to the closest grass, all the while trying to hear my friend.

I could hear Tiger barking through the phone. I could hear what sounded like scratching. But I could not hear Miss Lottie.

I looked at Luke. "We need to go."

31

As I RACED to Miss Lottie's, I called 911. "I need someone to check on an elderly cancer patient who lives alone." I answered the dispatcher's questions until she asked for the address. I didn't have it memorized. I tried putting her on hold while I accessed my contacts but I accidentally hung up on her. All this while screaming down the road at twenty over the speed limit.

Thankfully, a garbage truck forced me to slow down. I got the address, called 911 again, and finished giving the information. Then I rounded two corners and pulled up in front of Lottie's house.

What to do with Luke. It was ninety flippin' degrees outside. The only thing I could do was leave him in the car with the engine running and the AC on.

"I'll be back!" I promised as I jumped out of the car.

Of course, the front door was locked, but I'd noticed Miss Lottie often left the back door unlatched, so I jumped the chain-link fence and ran around to the back. Success. I pushed it open. "Lottie? It's Jess. Are you all right? Lottie?"

Tiger came barking and dissolved into wags when he saw me. "Where is she?" I said, addressing Tiger's inner Lassie. I walked through the kitchen, glanced in the dining room, then saw her in the living room, lying on the floor, her phone still clutched in her hand.

"Lottie!" My heart raced. I crouched over her and felt for a pulse. Thankfully, I found one. I grabbed my phone and called 911 again, this time for the rescue squad. I jumped up and opened the front door for them. Then I knelt again next to Lottie. I called her name. I stroked her gray hair. I fought back tears. And I prayed, out loud, like Nate would have.

Tiger wiggled around me. I reassured him with a confidence I did not have. Then I heard sirens.

When they arrived, I told the EMTs everything I knew. One of them found a "File of Life" on Miss Lottie's fridge, which included her medical history and doctor's information. Very smart of her.

Oddly, as I watched the EMTs work, I thought of my sister Brooke, doing this same job.

As the ambulance took Miss Lottie away, the welfare check deputy arrived. I might have been a little short with him.

Then I was alone with the dogs.

Luke and Tiger had never met, but I was sure they'd smelled each other's scent on me enough that they weren't total strangers. Still, I'm always cautious when introducing dogs. Little dogs can be feisty and territorial, and we were meeting on Tiger's turf. Luke would obey me, so I put him in the backyard, then I brought Tiger out on leash.

Sure enough, Tiger was stiff legged at first. "Easy, Luke. Easy," I said, as my dog towered over the little guy. They sniffed, then Luke did his "let's play!" bow, and Tiger's tail started wagging. I let Tiger off leash. As they began to play, my emotions finally let down. Tears flowed from my eyes. The dogs became racing blurs.

Tiger was old, and I didn't want Luke to wear him out. After a while, I called them and we headed inside.

Luke sniffed in every room. I spied Miss Lottie's phone on the table by her chair. I must have put it there, but I didn't remember. It was unlocked. I scrolled through it. Most of her calls were to or from me. In her contacts, I found the number for her church. I called and left a message for the pastor. Then I found the information for the niece in California, called, and left another message. Likewise, Rachelle Bennett.

At that point, I faced a quandary. I wanted to go to the hospital, but what would I do with the dogs?

In the end, I took both back to the motel. I put Luke in the crate and Tiger on the floor next to him, almost snoozing on towels I'd brought from Miss Lottie's house. I told them both to wait, and then I left.

On the twenty-minute drive to the hospital, I called Nate and asked him to pray. He said he would and asked me to call him back when I knew more.

After I hung up, I realized that Miss Lottie had changed from being a black box project to someone I truly cared about. And I thought about Nate and how he'd helped his friend, Beth, through her cancer right up to the very end. At the time I'd rolled my eyes and called him a glutton for punishment. Now here I was, doing the same thing.

But I was still not a candidate for First Class Saint like Nate. No. My knees shook as I pulled into a parking space at the hospital. I was afraid to walk in that place, fearful of what I'd find. I did what I was sure Nate would tell me to do. I prayed.

Miss Lottie was still in the ER. I explained to the front desk who I was. I showed them the important personal items I'd brought for her—namely, her phone and her insurance cards. Eventually, they let me go back to see her.

Miss Lottie was hooked up to an IV. She appeared to be sleeping, but I could tell from the monitors she was breathing on her own and her heartbeat was regular. That was awesome.

I wanted more information, but no one would tell me anything because of HIPAA privacy laws.

So frustrating. Finally, a nurse dredged up some sympathy. "People on chemo, especially older people, get dehydrated sometimes and can pass out. We give them an IV to restore fluids. They may be admitted for a few days so we can make sure they are okay." The way she looked at me, I knew she was talking about Lottie.

After she left, Miss Lottie's eyes fluttered open. I moved closer to her. "Hey, Miss Lottie, how are you feeling?"

Her mouth curved into a tiny smile. "You sweet girl." Her voice was barely above a whisper. "I knew you'd come."

I patted her hand. "I'm not going to stay long. You need to rest."

She nodded. "Tiger..."

"I've got him. I'll take care of him 'til they let you go home."

She smiled again. "Thank you."

I told her I'd be back in the morning. Then I left, leaving my number with the staff.

I had no sooner arrived back at the motel and begun leashing up the dogs when there was an insistent, loud knock on the door. I scooped up Tiger, checked the peephole, saw who it was, and opened it to see what the manager wanted.

His eyes widened. "Two dogs? Two?"

I started to explain about Miss Lottie and that this was just temporary, but he shook his bald head emphatically. "No, no, no. I've been getting complaints about howling all day. I want you out, now!"

My heart pounded. Tiger squirmed in my arms, and Luke kept trying to push past me. "I can leave tomorrow..."

The manager's nostrils flared. "Out. Now. Or I'm calling the police! You have one hour." Then he stalked away.

Honestly, I felt like letting Luke take a dump right there in the room. How dare that guy!

But then I started thinking, who'd been howling? He said "all day"—did that mean Luke? Luke had been howling all day?

My dog had never settled in that room, incessantly sniffing, restless at night. Was he smelling something that disturbed him? Drugs? Death?

Plus, we were still in Sheriff Jimmy Montgomery's territory. Did I really want to pop up on his radar again?

We were better off leaving. I walked the dogs, packed our stuff, and threw the key on the manager's desk forty-seven minutes later.

Anger had driven me to move fast, but deflation soon followed. Where would we go? I was homeless again. It was nearly seven. I needed to feed the dogs, and the only place I could think of was Miss Lottie's house, where Tiger's food was handy and where he could sleep in a familiar environment. I'd locked it, but I'd kept the spare key I'd found on a hook in the kitchen.

With no better plan, I drove over there. The dogs ate in separate corners, under my watchful eye, then played in the backyard until about eight, when a violent thunderstorm drove us inside. Poor Tiger shook like crazy. I sat down on the couch, and he snuggled close to me. Luke eyed us like he was wondering if he could get up there, too, but I short-circuited his plan. "Go lie down."

With nothing else to do, I called Nate back. No answer. That was odd. He hadn't said he was going anywhere. I waited fifteen minutes and tried again. Still no answer. So I called Laura.

"He's on a search. They had a callout."

My anxiety soared. "What? Is this the first..."

"First since his amputation. Yes." She took a deep breath. "They said they needed him for something specific, and he agreed to respond."

Something specific. What could it be but rappelling? With one leg! And he was worried about training a new dog? "Where'd they go?"

"Hawksbill Mountain. Near Syria."

Definitely a rappelling job. "Are you getting storms?"

"One round came through about an hour ago. We may get more. I hope not."

Great. Nate was rappelling off a mountain in a thunderstorm with one leg. I choked down my fear, tempering my voice for Laura's sake. "Would you tell him to text me when he gets in? Even if it's late? He asked me to update him on my elderly friend."

Laura's voice brightened. "Oh! What's her name? Lottie? He told me about her. How is she?"

I relayed the story and decided to end our call on an upbeat note. Laura was probably as worried about Nate as I was. "They'll hold her for a few days and release her, they said. In the meantime, Luke and I get to babysit her little dog, Tiger."

The critter next to me thumped his tail appropriately.

"Lucky you," Laura said. "I'm going to bed soon, but I'll leave a note for Nate."

As I clicked off my phone, I noticed my stomach had twisted into a knot. I called a couple of friends from Battlefield SAR and learned a little more. The subject was a despondent fourteen-year-old boy threatening suicide. He'd been spotted on a ledge, but searchers couldn't get to him.

Of course, Nate would respond. He'd learned rappelling in the Marines. He was the only one of the group who could do it. And to save someone's life, he'd gladly risk his own.

I should be with him, helping him. But I wasn't, and for the third time that day, I clutched at my one option—prayer.

At ten o'clock, I roused the dogs and let them out one more time. The storm had diminished to a light rain, but I had a feeling more was on the way. The air felt thick and muggy. Tiger didn't want to leave the porch, but I made him.

I'd decided to spend the night at Miss Lottie's. It felt weird, since I really didn't have permission, but I didn't know where else to go and I was too stressed to figure it out. I didn't feel right sleeping in the beds, so I curled up on the couch with Tiger. Luke sprawled on the floor. Soon the two of them were snoring, and I drifted off.

Sometime around two in the morning, another thunderstorm rolled through. All of my current traumas coalesced into a toxic brew in my dreams. I heard sirens and saw flashing lights. I saw Miss Lottie's body on a gurney being rushed down a hallway. I saw Nate falling from a cliff, arms outstretched, lightning high-lighting the fear in his face. My limbs seemed made of cement—I couldn't get to him! I saw my house on fire, and a silhouette of my dog in the doorway. Deputy Hap Carroll (or was it the motel manager?) began yelling at me, and then my car began spin-ning...spinning. When Nate landed on the hood, I woke up screaming.

The dogs both jumped up, barking. I sat up quickly, trying to figure out where I was, who I was, and where the threat was coming from. My heart raced. My teeth chattered like a squirrel. I shook all over as I rose to my feet.

Luke was the first to realize the threat was not anything exter-nal, that it was coming from within me. He moved to my side, pressing himself against my legs. He whined and nudged me with his nose. I dropped to a crouch, burying my face in his fur, holding onto him for dear life. He licked my ear.

Then I felt other little paws on my back and realized Tiger was trying to comfort me as well. I sat down with my back to the couch, a dog on either side of me, cataloging the horrible images in my dream. When I got to Nate, I remembered the SAR callout.

"Nate!" I scrambled to find my phone. It had fallen between the couch cushions. I jerked it out, turned it on, and cried out with relief when I saw his text: *Home safe. Got the kid. Call you tomorrow.*

The time stamp was 1:56 a.m.

32

THE NEXT MORNING after I took care of the dogs I went to the hospital. Miss Lottie was better. The docs planned to release her the next day.

I told her I'd stayed at her house, and she was fine with that. We agreed I'd stay there another night and then help her get home the next day. She was well enough that she'd even thought to add me to her very short HIPAA list.

On the way back to the house, I stopped and picked up some food and cleaning supplies. I planned to give Miss Lottie's house a thorough cleaning, plus have meals and fluids (with electrolytes) waiting for her. For the first time in my life, I looked at Pinterest. I found some recipes that would work well for her.

While I cleaned, my mind shifted to Danville's case. I still did not understand what his wife did all day. Either she was quite mentally ill, or she watched TV, or she was the most introverted person in history.

Near noon, Nate called me. Relief brought tears to my eyes as he told me all about the callout. He said other searchers had located the boy, who was on a ledge about thirty feet down a cliff.

With thunderstorms predicted, they needed someone to get to him as fast as possible, and so they'd called Nate.

I fought to keep my emotions out of my voice as I asked questions. "Was the boy suicidal?"

"I would call him depressed. His dad died last year. They used to hike up there. I think the kid was taking risks, challenging God, seeing what would happen. He slipped and ended up on that ledge."

"How'd you do it, with the artificial leg?"

"It weren't a problem. I used my right leg to keep me off the cliff. And I was careful to balance before I took the harness off once I landed."

"It was dangerous for you to join him on that ledge."

"Yeah, a little. I could tell right away he weren't gonna jump. So I just sat down and talked to him for a bit."

"Did you show him your scars?"

He laughed. "Some. Mostly we talked. When he was ready, I buckled him in the harness, and the others pulled him up. Waitin' by myself down there 'til it was my turn, I realized how lonely it was. I was glad I'd been called out. Glad I could help."

Sometimes after I've prayed for something, I forget to thank God. It's like, the pressure is off and I take the results for granted.

Not this time. After I clicked off the phone, I *did* thank God—for Nate's safety, Miss Lottie's improvement, and even for giving me a safe place to stay for a couple of nights.

But I hoped I wouldn't be keeping God so busy in the next few days. It seemed selfish.

Scott called me over his lunch break. It was the third time he'd called since he'd been down. We talked for half an hour, some about him and his new job, and some about my adventures.

He sounded happier every time I talked to him. His work was fascinating—to him and to me. As a prelude to pitching the Bureau on a much more extensive study of non-ideologically driven lone shooters, Gary and Scott were looking at fourteen cases in which people committed a mass shooting in a public place. They were interviewing subjects, victims, relatives, friends, and law enforcement investigators.

Many people reported that "he just snapped," but Scott said there were always precursors. Some kind of loss like death or divorce, a traumatic event, a money problem, bullying, or some other stressor.

"The cause may be hidden," Scott said, "but nobody just snaps. Our goal is to find out why the perpetrator thought shooting others was the best solution to his problems."

Which prompted me to tell him about Elise Danville. "I can't figure it out," I said. "She apparently lived this way for years, then suddenly, she leaves."

Scott listened carefully. "What we've found is there's a process our subjects go through—a triggering event, then fantasizing about harming others, then planning, building an arsenal, then carrying it out. Maybe you could find a similar pattern in the woman you're looking for."

That gave me a lot to think about as I finished cleaning Miss Lottie's house and making her food.

———

EARLY THE NEXT MORNING, I received two phone calls that totally upended my life.

The first was from the hospital. Miss Lottie had taken a turn for the worse. A really bad turn for the worse. When her doctor called me back, he told me it appeared the chemo had stopped working. Her cancer was growing. Her heart rate had dropped, and her respiration had as well. No way could she leave the hospital anytime soon.

While trying to regroup from that phone call, I received another one, from Detective David O'Connor in Norfolk. "Hey, I wanted you to know we've had an Elise sighting."

"Elise Danville? When? Where?"

"Got a call from someone on the Eastern Shore who saw one of our old missing-person posters at a Royal Farms over there. She said she saw someone who looked a lot like Elise at Cape Charles. She was drawing."

"Drawing?"

"Yeah, you know, like doing art. On the beach."

My mind raced. Could that fit? She apparently knew a lot about art, but I didn't have any evidence she was an artist herself. "When was this?"

"Got the call a few minutes ago. The woman saw her last week."

Last week! She could be anywhere now. "Are you following up?"

"No. We think she left on her own. There's no crime to investigate. I'm just passing this on to you."

"Did you tell Danville?"

"He's my next call."

"Can you hold off, for like an hour? I've got to figure some things out."

"No problem," David said, and he gave me the contact information for the woman with the tip.

I hung up and began to pace. Luke looked up at me with his head cocked. I knew he was assessing my mood. "I'm okay," I said. He put his head back down.

But my adrenaline was pumping. Okay—I had to go to the Eastern Shore. Miss Lottie was staying in the hospital. I could take Luke with me, but I couldn't see taking Tiger. What should I do?

I knocked on the doors of neighbors. I called Miss Lottie's church. I could not find anyone to dog-sit Tiger.

The thought of putting him in a kennel was too sad. So, desperate, I called Nate.

Of course, he would take him. And because he'd taken the day off, he could meet me halfway, near Richmond.

I raced around the house packing up everything I thought Tiger would need—food, bowls, blanket, toys, leash, and yes, a little striped sweater Lottie had knitted for him. The two dogs followed me, perplexed at my speed. Then I went into the kitchen and froze the food I'd made for Miss Lottie's return. I checked the stove to make sure the burners were off and let the dogs out back.

"Go poop!" I told them.

Then I took everything out to the car. When I was finished, I hurried back inside, locked the front door, hid a key out back, and loaded up the dogs. Twenty minutes after hanging up with Nate, we were on the way to meet him.

"This is a big ask," I said to my friend when we each stepped out of our cars at a Chick-fil-A.

He hugged me and peeked into my car. "Don't look too big to me." He grinned. "I know you're in a hurry, but what do I need to know about this dog?"

I gave him the rundown on Tiger, but I noticed his questions went further. He wanted to know Miss Lottie's full name, what hospital she was in, the name of the realtor whose wife I was chasing, the name of the cop I'd been talking to, and how long I'd be gone.

You'd have thought he was my parent. This was the guy who once surreptitiously turned on the location sharing app on my phone because he didn't trust me to tell him where I was going (with good reason). I watched as he wrote down my answers in his little notebook, and then I handed off Tiger and his gear and hugged Nate goodbye.

Soon Luke and I were headed south again, down Interstate 64 toward Norfolk. On the way, my phone rang. Trooper McCoy. I answered and listened as he asked me to bring my laptop in.

"Cooper told me about the backup he installed for you. There's a chance," he said, "that it could include security camera footage if it happened to back up before the cameras burned. If you'll let me have it, it could help with the arson investigation."

"Sure!" I told him I was on my way out of town, but I was on 64 eastbound near Busch Gardens. He said he'd meet me at the Jefferson Avenue exit.

Ten minutes later, I pulled off the highway at the designated spot, dug my computer out of the back of the Jeep, wrote down the passwords he'd need, and handed it to him.

"I'm not sure what we'll find, but we will take a look," he said.

I took off again, kicking myself for not thinking of that myself. But then, I wasn't exactly a techie. I had no idea how to access those files.

———

As I approached the HRBT, Danville called. I explained I was on my way to the Eastern Shore, but he asked if I could make a quick stop at his house. He had something he wanted me to give Elise if I found her.

We stood in his driveway a short time later. He was wearing his golf clothes. Danville handed me a thick envelope. "There's a letter in there, apologizing for anything I've done to drive her away," he said, "and also some cash. I just want her to be safe, Miss Chamberlain, that's all."

I nodded. Luke had been whining in the car this whole time, and the thought occurred to me that he might need to stretch his legs.

"I'll make sure she gets it," I said. Luke barked twice. I gestured toward the car. "Do you mind if I let my dog out for a minute?"

"Is he friendly?"

"Yes."

I opened the tailgate and the crate and Luke jumped out. He

sniffed Danville briefly, then I directed him to the backyard. While he sniffed around, I asked Danville some more questions.

"Does Elise know anyone on the Eastern Shore?"

He shook his head. "No."

"Has she taken art lessons?"

"No, no. Never did. She doodled some, that's all."

"Was she on medication? For depression or anything?"

He stroked his chin. "She did try a serotonin uptake inhibitor for a while. That's an antidepressant."

"And?"

"She stopped taking it. I'm not sure why."

Colton Danville began reminiscing about his wife, telling me why he worried about her and how he tried to encourage her. The next time I looked over at Luke, he was lying in the middle of the yard, looking at me, his tail sweeping the ground.

Danville finished his story, and I said I really needed to get going. I wanted to get over the bridge and find a place to stay before it got too late. I whistled for Luke, then turned to open the back of the Jeep. When I looked up, my dog was still lying there. Irritated, I called him. I finally had to go get him.

Irritated, I told my dog to "kennel up" and closed up the back. I said goodbye, shook Danville's hand, climbed in my car, and headed for the Eastern Shore.

33

THE DRIVE over the Chesapeake Bay Bridge-Tunnel took my breath away it was so beautiful, water stretching out on both sides, sky meeting sea in a blue-gray canvas.

Although I'd lived in Virginia for two decades, I'd never taken the CBBT. When we wanted to go to the beach from Northern Virginia, we'd gone over the Bay Bridge in Maryland, near Annapolis.

Beneath me the waters of the Chesapeake Bay merged with the Atlantic Ocean, the two great bodies of water converging with the tides. I could see huge commercial vessels bound for Baltimore churning their way north through the bay and gigantic Navy vessels chugging away from the port of Norfolk into the Atlantic. Around the pilings of the bridge, all sorts of small boats bobbed in the waves, people fishing as much for the beauty and peace of it as the food. At least, that's why my dad said he fished.

The sun glinted off the waters stretching to my left and right. On nearly every light post, seagulls sat facing into the wind. My dad had taught me the names of the different species, and I reached back in my memory for them—fishing gull, herring gull, laughing gull, terns.

Nostalgia swept over me in a warm wave. I hadn't thought of those gull words in years.

The Delmarva Peninsula is a neck of land extending down from Delaware, through Maryland and Virginia. As I drove up Route 13, the Chesapeake Bay would be on my left, the Atlantic Ocean on the right. Like my Long Island childhood home, the peninsula was on the Atlantic Flyway. Migrating birds traveled up in the summer and down in the winter, providing an ever-changing parade of interesting transients.

I remembered going out with my dad early in the morning, each of us with our own binoculars, to watch for newcomers. I must have been about eight. He carried an Audubon Society bird guide and a notebook to record what we saw. That's what got me started on carrying a Moleskine.

It might seem strange that an NYPD officer was into birds. I think he found it a relief from his job.

I wondered momentarily what had happened to dad's notebook. My mother probably threw it away. It wouldn't have meant anything to her. I vowed to get a bird guide and a new notebook as soon as I could.

As I neared the end of the CBBT, I saw a broad, flat, sandy, shrub-covered island, waves breaking on the edge. One small boat lay just offshore. I passed a sign that read "Fisherman Island," and I rolled down my window and inhaled the salt air.

In that one brief action, I was home.

But I quickly checked myself. I was not on the Eastern Shore to revisit my childhood. I had a job to do.

The woman who had called in the tip had agreed to meet me at 10:00 a.m. the next day in a coffee shop in Cape Charles. I needed to find a motel that would accept Luke, preferably in that town. I pulled over to the welcome center just off the CBBT, got the information I needed, and drove on to Cape Charles.

Route 13 is a shortcut between places like the Outer Banks and northern cities. I knew from my work with the Fairfax police that it was also a major drug-trafficking corridor. I saw a lot of cars pulled over by police and reminded myself to watch my speed.

Taking a left off of 13, toward the Chesapeake Bay side, I found a hotel, a little place in Cape Charles called the Bluebird Inn. I let Luke check out the room and when he seemed okay with it, I brought in all our stuff. By then it was getting dark. I was tired, but I recognized Luke had spent the whole day in the car. I needed to take him for a run.

Beach towns are generally flat, and Cape Charles was no exception. Luke and I ran down the darkening streets toward the Chesapeake. He fell into an easy pace next to me. I inhaled the salt air and began to relax. We ran a backwards "L" pattern, west to the bay, then along the dunes to a big marina. After that, we turned back. The air had cooled off. I guessed it was about seventy degrees, but humid. I found a foot-wash station and cupped my hands under the running water so Luke could drink. Then we walked along the deserted beach under a rising moon. I sat down on a dune with Luke next to me and listened to the small waves lapping on the shore.

What would my father say about me now?

That question jumped into my head out of nowhere. I tried to shove it aside. I couldn't. So I thought about it.

My dad would have been proud I'd pursued a career in law enforcement, but he'd be disappointed I left Fairfax. On the other hand, he'd be furious at the bullies who'd harassed me. He'd be interested in my SAR work and disappointed I was doing it for free. He wouldn't like the fact that I was working as a PI for income. He'd want me on a more stable career track. And although he'd be proud of me for making it so far on my own, he'd secretly wish I would find someone and get married.

My dad would have made the most awesome grandfather.

I picked up a small shell, ran my thumb over its ridges, and tossed it. Luke pricked up his ears but didn't move. I took a deep breath. "Well, buddy, let's go."

Luke and I walked back through the darkened and mostly empty streets. Outside the hotel, I brushed as much sand off of him as I could. We entered our room, I fed him, and, after one more outing at ten o'clock, we both fell into a sound sleep.

————

PEACH STREET BOOKS, where I was meeting Suzanne Bergstrom, was a combination coffee shop/bookstore within walking distance of our hotel. I got there early, bought my bird guide and a new Moleskine, and was savoring my cinnamon latte when a fifty-something woman dressed in Under Armour workout gear walked in. Our eyes connected and I rose. "Ms. Bergstrom?"

"Yes. You must be Jessica." She extended her hand and I shook it.

"What would you like to drink? It's on me," I said.

A few minutes later she sat across from me, the scent of her Earl Grey tea drifting across the table. "So, Detective O'Connor tells me you think you saw a missing woman."

"I think so. That's why I called."

I explained who I was and why I was looking for Elise. I assured her Elise's husband just wanted to be sure she was okay. "Tell me where you were when you think you saw her."

"I was down at Kiptopeke State Park. I often go down there to walk."

"How often?"

She looked surprised. "Several times a week."

I nodded. "You saw her there?"

"I was walking down the beach, and I saw this woman. She was sitting by herself in a camp chair—"

"What kind?"

She cocked her head.

"Color?" I said. "Was it foldable? Did it have a carry bag?"

Suzanne focused on her tea. "Green," she said finally, "with a green carry bag. She had that secured on the back of the chair."

"Okay."

"Anyway, she had a sketch pad on her lap."

"A sketch pad?"

"Yes, about this big." She gestured. "I made it a point to walk behind her. She was sketching the curve of the beach."

"Pencil? Charcoal?"

"Pencil. But that wasn't the unusual thing. The beach she was looking at was actually empty, but she was drawing in children, ten or fifteen of them, all playing on the sand and in the water."

It was my turn to be surprised. "Children?"

"Yes. It struck me as, I don't know...sad."

Trying to regroup, I pulled three pictures of Elise Danville out of the file I'd brought with me. "Is this the woman you saw?"

Suzanne studied them. "Yes." She pushed the pictures back to me. "She's very stylish. And thin."

After talking more and assuring Ms. Bergstrom that Elise had not done anything illegal, I asked her to call me immediately if she saw her again. As I walked back to my hotel, I thought about what she'd said. Why children? Was she obsessed with them? Had Elise wanted children so badly it had pushed her into a deep depression?

But Danville had said Elise didn't want kids. Then why would she fill her sketch with them? It didn't make sense.

I changed into shorts and a T-shirt and took Luke for a short run. It was too hot to go far. As we ran, we dodged tourists strolling in and out of the little shops lining the main street. Young teenagers in groups walked toward the beach, joined by retirees driving golf carts. It all seemed so normal.

After our run, I made sure Luke cooled off properly. Then I put him in the crate and left. I walked around the block to a little shop, where I bought a neat, Army-green rucksack I'd seen in the window when we were walking by. Back at the Jeep, I loaded it with my camera, my bird guide, a pen, my notebook, and a snack.

While I drove south to the park, I called Nate to find out how Tiger was doing. He didn't answer, so I called Laura.

"Nate's with that boy he took off the mountain this week," she said. "Tiger's fine. I think Sprite likes him."

"What's Nate doing with the boy?"

"He lives not far from here. You know his dad died. I think Nate wants to see if he can help him."

Of course he would. "How's the horse?"

"She's settling in well. I rode her through the woods this week. She did fine."

Laura asked me a few questions about my case. I updated her and told her where I was staying and said I was going out to the state park later. I was about to say goodbye when Laura stopped me. "Are you paying attention to the weather?"

Her comment surprised me. "Not really. Why?"

"There's a hurricane down in the Caribbean. Right now they're forecasting it to run up the East Coast."

I frowned. "When is it expected to hit here?"

"About six days."

I took a deep breath. "They make such a big deal out of these storms," I said, blowing off the entire cadre of professional meteorologists.

"I know. But check the forecast once in a while. Just to be safe."

I promised her I would, then hung up and called the hospital to check on Miss Lottie. Her condition, the nurses told me, was much the same. At least she was stable.

A few minutes later, I pulled into Kiptopeke State Park. While I paid the entrance fee, I showed the gate attendant Elise's picture and asked if he'd seen her.

"No," he responded, "but I don't usually work the gate."

"Who does?"

He gave me three names. I went to park headquarters to look for them. Browsing at the brochures while I waited for the desk person to finish helping someone else, I discovered there was a dog beach at the park, and that dogs were allowed in the cabins and camping areas. I filed that information in my brain.

Finally, it was my turn. Adopting what I hoped was an open, friendly expression, I showed the middle-aged woman a picture of Elise and asked if she'd seen her. She hadn't, but maybe Shawna, who was outside, had.

I chased down Shawna, who also hadn't seen her. But maybe Tina, who was off that day, had.

And that's how my unproductive day went. How frustrating.

34

I LEFT my phone number for Tina, figuring I'd never hear from her and would have to chase her down tomorrow when she was on duty again.

Oh me of little faith. She called me! I couldn't believe it. I almost didn't answer because I didn't recognize the number.

"Is this Jessica Chamberlain?" she asked.

"Yes."

"Hey, this is Tina Patrick...from the state park."

"Thank you for calling me," I said, and three minutes later I had an appointment to meet her at the coffee shop in Cape Charles at five o'clock.

"Is she in trouble?" Tina asked me over iced caramel macchiato.

Tina, I suspected, was in her fifties, but she had one of those perpetually young, apple-cheeked faces, a little on the chubby side, framed by stylishly cut, nutmeg brown, highlighted hair. Her light-yellow tunic top fell gracefully over black capris.

"Her husband is worried about her," I responded. "She left totally unexpectedly, and she's emotionally fragile."

"I saw her first at the gate, but we rotate, you know? So next I was at the desk. She came in asking a lot of questions about the park and the birdlife. She was kind of quiet, but I remember she was excited, too, like a little kid. At lunch an hour or so later, she was sitting on the bench outside, drawing. I went over and sat down, and we struck up a conversation. I asked her what she was drawing, because the beach she was looking at was empty. She showed me and on that empty beach she'd drawn..."

I expected her to say "children."

"...birds! Hundreds of birds—seagulls, herons, sandpipers. More birds than could fit on that beach."

The surprise must have shown on my face, because Tina said, "I know, right? It was like that empty stretch of sand bugged her so she filled it."

Or her empty life. "How long did she stay?"

"At the park? 'Til five. I saw her again as I was leaving."

"Did she say what she was doing, or where she was going next?"

"No. But she was definitely on a trip. She asked me about other interesting places."

"What did you tell her?"

"Oh, let's see...The Barrier Island Center up the road, Onancock, the ferry to Tangier, and Chincoteague."

Chincoteague. As in *Misty of Chincoteague*. I'd read it when I was ten. What girl hadn't?

We chatted a little more. I asked her about the park and how often she worked. I was actually trying to get an idea of when Elise might have moved on. When I'd captured all the info I thought I could, I thanked Tina and we stood to leave.

"Oh, one more thing," she said as I gathered our trash.

I raised my eyebrows.

"She asked me who did my hair."

"Really?"

"I told her Peggy. Right here in town. Peggy's Cute Cuts. I've been going there for years."

That was curious. I thanked her again and she left. I put our trash in the can. Still puzzling, I turned to the barista. "Where is Peggy's Cute Cuts?"

"Two blocks north, one block east," she said. "In a private house, around the back."

"Thanks." I started to leave, then caught a glimpse of a book on display near the register. *Mere Christianity* by C.S. Lewis. "I'll take this," I said, pulling out my debit card. Nate would be proud.

As soon as I walked outside, I took out my cell phone and called Peggy. Yes, she could take me if I got there quickly.

Five minutes later, I was reclining in a chair letting Peggy massage Apricot Wonder shampoo through my hair. I felt myself relax. There's something about having someone else wash your hair.

Like many hairdressers, Peggy was chatty. She told me about her late husband, her grown children, her aunt, and half the town, or so it seemed. By the time she got around to asking about me, I decided to tell her the truth.

"I'm a private investigator."

Her eyes got big. "Well, now, that is just fascinating."

While she combed out my wet hair, I told her about a few of my interesting cases, ones with happy endings. Then, while she trimmed my hair, I told her about Elise.

"Her husband is worried about her," I explained. "If she's okay, well, so be it."

As I got up to pay her, I pulled Elise's picture out along with my wallet. "This is the lady I'm looking for." I handed Peggy the picture along with two twenties, double her rate for a shampoo and cut.

She looked at the picture and then at me. "She was here a week ago. We did a complete makeover. It came out great."

I smiled. "What did you do?"

"She wanted to lose the blonde, so we did. Went back to her natural color, a really dark brown. Almost black. Oh my, it brought out her skin tones and her eyes. It made her come alive! She wanted it shorter, so I did a choppy bob, with bangs, and she loved it. It absolutely fit her personality—a little bashful, but cute." Peggy grabbed her cell phone. "It came out so good, I took a picture of it. I wished I'd taken a 'before' shot."

"Well here, we can fix that," I said, just as her next client walked through the door. I grabbed Peggy's phone, took a shot of my picture of Elise, and then, while Peggy was focused on her other client, I emailed the 'after' shot to myself.

I walked away from Peggy's Cute Cuts grateful, because without that stop, I never would have known I was looking for a brunette. Now I had a current picture.

I picked up Luke at the hotel and dropped off my rucksack. We went for a run, then sat on the west-facing beach and watched an orange sun drop into the Chesapeake Bay.

"Well, buddy," I said to my dog, "it looks like we're checking out tomorrow and heading north."

He thumped his tail in agreement.

35

EARLY THE NEXT morning while driving up Route 13, I received a call from Miss Lottie's doctor. I soon found myself listening to medical options for a woman I barely knew. I told the doctor Lottie's niece in California should be making those decisions, but he had already tried talking to her. Since she hadn't seen Lottie in five years, she didn't want to get involved.

I answered his questions as best I could, giving him my best guess of what Lottie's decisions would be. I told him I was on a business trip about two hours away but that I'd be back in town as soon as possible.

Just as I hung up with the doctor, Danville called. I updated him on my search. When I told him Elise had changed her hairstyle, he grew strangely quiet. I attempted to reassure him.

"It may be a good thing," I said. "The hairdresser said she seemed very happy with it."

"It doesn't make sense. None of this makes any sense! She knows I like blonde hair. Why would she do that?"

His emotional outburst shocked me. I tried to calm the waters. "It sounds to me like a midlife crisis, Mr. Danville. Hopefully, she'll get it out of her system and come back better than ever." His silence was the only response. "I don't think I'm far behind her. Let me see if I can find her in a day or two and then we'll know more."

After I hung up, I thought about his reaction. It was the first display of temper I'd seen from him. Maybe that was good. Maybe he was feeling what he'd lost.

I turned into a long lane leading to a large white house in the middle of farm fields. A former almshouse, this was now the home of the Barrier Island Center, a museum documenting the lives of the families who once had lived on a string of islands just off the peninsula on the ocean side. Walking in, I felt a knot in my chest—pressure to find Elise so I could report to Danville. Miss Lottie needed my help more right now.

I told the woman in the gift shop why I was there, and she pointed me to the director, who invited me into her office to talk.

Ellen Wilson was stiff at first, suspicious. It took some schmoozing to get her to open up. I did it by expressing interest in the museum, sharing my love of the beach and its wildlife, and telling her about growing up on Long Island. When I saw she was still reticent, I played my trump card. I told her about bird-watching with my father, an NYPD officer. And then I mentioned he'd died on 9/11.

Did I feel guilty? You bet. And also a bit desperate. I was anxious to solve this case.

"This is the lady I'm looking for," I said, showing her the cell phone picture of Elise. "Her husband is a much-admired businessman in Norfolk. Naturally, he's worried about her."

"Why didn't he call the police?" she asked.

"He did. But they found no evidence she'd been abducted and no indication of foul play."

"If she left on her own, why should I help you find her?"

I settled back in my chair, masking my anxiety. "Well, that's a good question. My instructions are to find her, give her a letter from her husband expressing his love and remorse for anything he might have done, and then let her decide what she wants to do."

Ms. Wilson took a deep breath. "Does he know you're looking for her at The Barrier Center?"

"No. He wants the big picture, not the details. He knows I'm on the Eastern Shore, that's all."

She still didn't respond.

"Look," I said, finally. "The woman in the gift shop told me Elise was here—"

"Who was here?" she demanded.

"Elise. Elise Danville."

"She told me her name was Ann."

Surprised, I quickly regrouped. "She may be using her middle name. Anyway, the lady in the gift shop told me that you'd talked to her. All I'm trying to do is deliver the letter and assure the husband that his wife is safe. Could you please help me?"

The clock on the wall ticked off the seconds.

Finally, Ms. Wilson spoke. "Ann was here. She was fascinated by our exhibits, asking so many questions that our volunteers finally sent her to me. She wanted to know everything about family life on the islands, the watermen, how the women lived. She watched our movie about Hog Island, and it moved her, I could tell." Ms. Wilson picked up a pen on her desk and stared at it, as if gathering her thoughts. "I don't know why she was so interested. She was shy, guarded, but thirsty, too, for knowledge. She stayed all day until I had to leave at four to take my daughter to Hope Ranch."

"Hope Ranch?"

"Yes. It's an equine therapy place up the road. My daughter has struggled since her father left, and interacting with the horses has really helped. I guess you would know about trauma."

I nodded.

"I...I got that same sense with Ann, that there's something

going on in her life. So I told her about Hope Ranch. I invited her to come see it."

"Did she?"

"Not that day, but I've seen her there several times since then." Ms. Wilson's eyes seemed to implore me. "I don't know why I decided to tell you about Ann. I'm trusting you to help her, not hurt her. She seemed fragile, like a piece of fine china teetering on the edge of a shelf. I felt like I needed to help her move back."

"I promise," I said, "I won't hurt her."

I walked back out to the parking lot, an uneasy feeling dogging me as I tried piecing together what I'd learned. I'd left Luke in the Jeep with the AC running. I let him out, turned off the car, and played ball with him for a little while. Then I put him back in the car and we left.

———

HOPE RANCH WAS another hour or so up the road, near New Church. I decided to get a motel room before arriving at the ranch, because I wasn't sure they'd be happy about me bringing Luke. I checked into one just over the state line in Maryland, set up Luke's crate, got him settled, and then left.

I called Nate because I'd promised to keep him updated. I thought I'd have to leave a voicemail because it was midday and he was usually cutting grass at that time. But he answered and listened while I told him where I was and what I was doing.

"Did you ever hear of equine therapy?" I asked.

"Cain't say I have, but I'll tell you one thing. You should see what Abby's doing for Scott."

"What do you mean?"

"Seems that being around her is connecting with something deep inside him, healin' it. Like what dogs do with you and me."

I had ridden a long time ago as a kid, but I'd never had what I would call a relationship with a horse. I couldn't understand what that would look like.

We talked a little longer, and I gave him the name of the motel where I was staying. Then when I reached the ranch, I said goodbye.

36

THE FIRST THING I noticed as I approached was a carved wooden sign at the end of the driveway that read HOPE RANCH. It had a Christian fish at the bottom. Interesting. I wasn't sure what that was about.

Straight ahead of me stood a large white house with a big, wide front porch laced with hanging ferns. I saw a traditional red barn off to the right, and white stables with hunter-green trim to the left. I parked out front in a lot that I figured would hold at least thirty cars. Hope Ranch was bigger than I expected. I looked around for Elise's car in the lot, but didn't see it.

I had called ahead to see if it would be possible to get a tour. I wasn't completely honest about why I wanted to see the ranch. I didn't tell the director about Elise. I simply said I was interested in equine therapy.

As I walked up to the house, the front door opened and a woman about fifty walked out. She wore jeans and a blue-and-white checked, short-sleeved shirt and low boots. Her short blonde hair and bangs and the way she carried herself instantly told me this was a practical woman.

"Jessica?" she said, extending her hand as she reached the bottom step. "I'm Kate McClellan."

"Mrs. McClellan—"

"Kate, please."

"Kate. Thank you for letting me visit." I shook her hand and looked around. "It's so peaceful."

Kate smiled. "That's what we work on here, creating an atmosphere of safety and security that helps horses and people overcome trauma."

"How long have you been here?"

"The ranch has been in existence for twelve years. We've been at this location for five." She tilted her head. "Would you like to look around?"

"Sure!" I hesitated. "Is it okay to take pictures?"

"Of the horses and grounds, yes, but not of clients."

As we walked toward the stables, she told me her story. "My husband died quite unexpectedly fourteen years ago. His light plane crashed into the ocean. People saw it go down, but it sank and there was nothing to recover.

"I was devastated. We'd been married for thirteen years and had never been able to have children. In fact, we were in the process of adopting. Suddenly, I was alone. My future was gone."

"Wow. That must have been hard."

"I was more fortunate than many widows," Kate said. "My husband had been a successful businessman. He left me relatively well off, and I was working, too, at a bank. But money couldn't lift me out of my sorrow. I prayed, asking God to show me what to do, how to heal."

A copper-colored horse stood in a corral outside the stable, along with a white-and-tan pinto pony. Kate stopped at the fence, and the horse walked over.

"One day, someone from my church approached me. She knew of a horse that needed a home—a mare that had been neglected. At the time I lived on five acres. The people before us had a pony, so two acres was fenced with a run-in shed. Ellen convinced me that it was just temporary." Kate rubbed the horse's head. "Here she is thirteen years later." She turned to me and smiled. "This is Penny."

I laughed. "That's a different definition of *temporary*."

"I know!" The horse nudged her. "When she came to me, she was so underweight I could count every rib. She had bad teeth and overgrown hooves. She was a mess."

"She's beautiful now. Can I pet her?"

"Yes," Kate responded. "Let her smell you first."

I held the back of my hand under the horse's nose. Then I touched Penny's neck, stroking her smooth coat.

"Penny forced me to get outside myself, to focus on something other than my own grief and loss. She needed me. She saved me from being endlessly absorbed by my own problems," Kate continued.

The phrase Nate used popped into my head. "*Homo incurvatus in se,*" I said. "Man turned in on himself." I saw Kate's eyes widen. Hearing those words come out of my mouth surprised even me.

Her head cocked. "Are you a believer?"

I laughed. "Not a very good one."

That was the truth. My Bible reading was erratic, my prayer life consisted of dramatic cries for help mixed with the occasional plea for someone I cared about, and the thought of walking in cold to a local church sent shivers down my spine. Even worse, a lot of times I purposely didn't pray because I didn't want God interfering with what I wanted to do.

All I had on the credit side was Nate, the Gospel of John, and a deep thirst for the kind of purity and love and acceptance I'd found in both of them.

Kate continued her story as I fingered her horse's mane. "As Penny drew me out of myself, I began thinking of how horses might help other people. I drove down to Raleigh to visit Hope Reins, an equine therapy place I'd heard about, and I decided right then to see if I could start something like that here. This guy," she said, gesturing toward the pinto, "is a Chincoteague pony. He is the sweetest, gentlest pony ever. The kids adore him."

"Okay," I said. "I understand how dogs help modify stress. I've experienced some of that firsthand. But how do horses help? I don't understand. They can't exactly crawl into bed with you."

Kate smiled. "Let me show you the stable, and I'll tell you all about it."

I glanced toward the parking lot to check again for Elise's car, then followed Kate into the large white building. Inside, as my eyes adjusted, I saw there were five good-sized stalls on either side of a center aisle, each with a Dutch door to the outside. Two young women were working at the far end of the aisle, mucking stalls. Several horses stuck their heads out as we walked in.

"Most of these horses are rescues," Kate explained, leading me to the right. "This girl's owner became ill," she said, petting a white mare, "and couldn't care for her. She hadn't been around people for a long time, and it's taken quite a lot to get her used to being handled. This one," she said, gesturing toward a brown pony in the next stall, "is blind." She kept walking. "Timber here," she said, putting her hand on the neck of a beautiful brown horse, "is a former show horse who survived a barn fire."

I moved closer and saw scars on Timber's back and legs. I thought of Nate and wondered if horses dream, if they had night terrors.

"It took us months to get him to even walk into a barn, much less stay in one. We leave his outside door open so he knows he can always get out. But he is a very sweet soul."

I asked Kate who came to the ranch, and was it just for children or did they help adults as well?

"It's geared toward children, but a lot of adults find healing here too. You know, about half of all American children experience trauma before age twelve. It could be an accident, a divorce, the death of a parent or close friend, a serious illness...a lot of things."

Like losing your dad in a terror attack.

"They come here with all kinds of challenges—anxiety, depression, trust issues. Some may be unable to speak. All of them have difficulty in relationships.

"When they first get here, a volunteer takes the child's caregiver off to talk, and we introduce the child to the horses. We tell each horse's story, and then the magic happens. The child identifies with one of them. We can see it. They move toward a horse, they may ask questions, they won't want to leave that horse, or they keep going back to him.

"So then we start teaching them. There are two kinds of animals in the world—predator and prey. We humans are the ultimate predators. The horse is a prey animal, and they know it. They are constantly on the lookout for who will eat them. See how their eyes are on the sides of their heads?"

I nodded.

"That's so they can see what's coming for them. They have two main defenses—the speed at which they can run away and their physical strength.

"The horse is naturally anxious and hypervigilant, just like traumatized kids. They pick up on the tiniest signals, body language, sounds, and so on. But they also have a strong herd instinct. They will bond with people they trust. If you're scared and anxious, they'll pick up on it—maybe you shouldn't be trusted. If you're gentle and calm, they'll read that too.

"Traumatized children learn to modify their emotions as they bond with the horse. They develop confidence as they care for this huge animal. They learn to trust and ultimately to love. And once they've experienced love with the horse, they'll begin to bond with people, and then God. That's our end game—to connect traumatized kids to the love of Jesus."

While she talked, we walked through the barn and outside.

Behind the barn, I saw a medium-sized round corral with height extenders on the fencing. A gorgeous black horse with a white star stood inside.

"What's going on here?" I gestured toward the tall fence.

"This," Kate said, "is Nightcap. We call him Cap." We peered through the rails, looking at the horse. He stood just out of reach, his head high, nostrils flaring.

"He doesn't look very calm," I said.

"No. He just came to us. He's a former show horse, a hunter/jumper. Coming back from a show, they were involved in a terrible accident. His rider was injured and so was her mother, the driver. He was too. You can see his scars there on his hindquarters and his neck. But the worst result was his post-traumatic stress."

I looked at her, surprised.

"Yes, horses can have it too. He became difficult to handle, dangerous even. He refused to enter a trailer. He'd jump their pasture fences and escape. Of course, running away just put him in more danger. Can you imagine him on the road at night? The owners tried all sorts of things, including calling in outside trainers, even meds, but when he threw his young rider for the umpteenth time and she broke her arm, that was the last straw. Her dad said Nightcap had to go."

"Why did you take him?"

Kate gave a little smile. "I wanted to see if our way of handling problems would give him another chance. We practice natural horsemanship, a way of relating to the horse that doesn't involve force."

Suddenly, someone called out from the barn. "Hey, Kate! Can you come here for a second?"

"Excuse me," she said. "I'll be right back."

I watched her leave, then turned back to the beautiful horse. How sad, I thought, that his fear made him run. He was stuck here all alone, away from the other horses.

I looked around, spotted some grass, picked a handful, and stuck it through the fence. "Hey, Cap, hey, buddy. Come get this," I said softly. I could see his nose working. He stomped a front foot. "Hey, guy, c'mon." I wiggled the grass. "C'mon, boy." He raised his head, half-reared, and turned away. My heart sagged. It was like he wanted the grass, but not enough to come close.

Kate appeared next to me. "You tried. He's just not ready."

We walked on uphill, toward a pasture where five horses grazed. I kept glancing around, looking for Elise and wondering if I was on a wild goose chase. I felt anxiety tugging at my gut.

Kate gestured toward the horses in the field, but I was only half paying attention. One of the horses was a Clydesdale. I caught that much. He was big and his white feathering set off his dark coat. "A gentle giant," Kate said, as I tried to focus. "He lived on a farm near Baltimore."

I asked her more about Cap—about how long ago his trauma occurred, and if she thought he'd ever get out of that pen.

Then she turned to me. "Jess, why are you really here?"

Her question shocked me. Had searching for Elise been that obvious? I heard a noise, glanced back, and saw Cap half-rearing in his pen, trying to get out. I swallowed hard.

"Let's go into my office," Kate said.

37

I FOLLOWED her back to the house, composing answers in my head to the questions I expected her to ask. Who was I really? Why was I looking for Elise? Who had hired me? What were his intentions?

My gut fluttered as we walked in the back door and into the kitchen. I liked Kate, and I had misled her. Guilt dogged me.

We walked into her office in the former dining room. She closed the door leading to the kitchen and the French doors connecting to the living room. I expected her to take a seat behind her large wooden desk. Instead, she gestured toward two armchairs. I sat down, an apology on my lips.

"So Jessica," she said, before I could speak, "who or what are you running from?"

That was not the question I expected. I felt my face grow hot.

"You related to Cap's story."

I didn't want to go there, but I didn't want to explain about Elise either. I pressed my lips together.

Kate leaned forward. "When you called, you said you were interested in equine therapy. I think there's more to it than that. What's going on? Why are you running?"

Right there, I could have told her the truth. Confessed my deception.

But did I? No. Instead, I played all my cards except the actual truth card. I played the 9/11 orphan card. The critical incident/PTSD card. And the totaled car/arson victim card. Then, to my own surprise, I laid down one more—the sadly still-single card.

In card games, that's a complete book. I sat back and waited for her response, half-wishing I could muster up some tears right then to enhance my believability.

Kate remained quiet, as if she were mulling over what I said. She pushed a wisp of hair behind her ear. Then she looked at me. Her blue eyes were remarkably like Nate's. "You said something that bothers me."

"What's that?"

"I asked if you were a believer and you said, 'not a very good one.' You do realize, don't you, that you could never be good enough. You are loved by God based on faith, not your behavior."

Sure. Sure I knew that. I just mostly didn't believe it. I started to respond but felt my throat close up.

"Tell me how you came to know Christ."

I took a deep breath, then laid out the whole story—Nate, my resistance to his faith, struggling with PTSD, then getting my father's Gospel of John, a book he'd been given by an NYPD chaplain not long before he was killed on 9/11. "I read it, and somewhere along the way, I knew it was true."

"And so you ran."

I raised my eyebrows. *What?*

"Knowing God is both wonderful and terrifying. You see the purity of his love and realize how dreadful your own sin is and how dangerous. So you run. We all run." Kate got up, retrieved two bottles of water from a mini-fridge, and handed one to me. I certainly needed it by then. My throat was a desert.

She sat back down. "What happened when I left you at Cap's corral?"

Good, she's changing the subject, I thought. I relaxed a little. "I felt bad for him. I didn't want him to be scared. I looked around, saw some grass, and offered it to him."

"How did he react?"

"I think he wanted it, but he wasn't willing to risk coming close."

"And what would you do if you were in charge of helping him overcome his fear?"

"Be very patient." I took a drink of water. "I wouldn't give up on him. He's a gorgeous horse."

"It's a dance," Kate said.

I cocked my head.

"You initiated with him because you're the one without fear. You reached out because you cared. Someday, if you kept it up, he would respond, because horses are herd animals and want to be in a group. Then you would initiate again, and he would respond again. One day, he would initiate with you, and you would respond. And so it goes, one small step at a time." She looked at me, smiling. "It's all like that, Jess, all of life. It's a dance. We're built for relationship, with each other and with God. We are created to dance."

Her words landed on me like a bomb, disrupting me, disturbing my interior landscape. Dance? I didn't want to dance. That sounded scary.

"We are all made to dance and we're all afraid of it on some level, until we get a taste of love and learn to trust."

Just then someone arrived for a session, a blonde-headed girl of about eleven, and Kate had to go. I asked her if I could come back. She said yes.

I never did tell her about Elise.

———

Back at the motel, still mulling Kate's words, I rescued Luke from his crate. He was so happy to see me. "Want to dance?" I said, joking around. I patted my chest to invite him to jump up. He did, and we danced, and his tail wagged like crazy. I collapsed on the bed, laughing. "See, I can do this!"

I leashed up Luke and popped him in the Jeep. We drove to a nearby town that had a pretty brick walk along a river, and we jogged for a while. Puffy white clouds dotted the bright blue sky. Crape myrtles, heavy with deep-pink blossoms, lined the walk. A few people strolled through the small stores or sat snacking at outdoor café tables. And as I jogged, the memory of running with Scott along the York River flashed through my head. I stumbled. Luke looked up at me.

"I'm okay," I said.

But I wasn't. I couldn't get Kate's words out of my mind. I'd jumped all the fences and now I was far from Scott, from my family, from Nate and Laura. I was out in a field dancing all by myself, longing for connection, yet afraid of it at the same time.

I had to try something different.

That evening, back in the motel room, I laid a big beach towel on the bed and invited Luke up next to me. With his weight pressing against my legs, I did something new. I reached out to Scott.

He sounded glad to hear from me. He was happy about his work. He and Gary had established some preliminary findings and avenues for research. They were hard at work on their proposal for a broader study.

Nate would say God was redeeming Scott's trauma.

Scott asked me about my case, and I told him where I was and all about Hope Ranch. "I'd like to see that someday," he said.

"It's only three hours away," I joked. "You could come tomorrow."

Part of me wished he'd take me up on it. But no—he had something scheduled. Of course.

"Where are you staying?" he asked me.

I told him, and there was a long silence.

"What?"

"Where's your gun?"

That's when it hit me. Maryland's gun laws were among the strictest in the nation. How could I have forgotten that? I had no permit to carry in that state.

"Unload the gun. Put the ammo in one place and the gun in another. And go back to staying in Virginia when you can," Scott said.

I started to make a smart mouth comment. Something stopped me. "I will. Thanks."

I cannot deny that I was wide awake after talking with Scott. So I picked up *Mere Christianity*. Nate had recommended it to me long ago. "Maybe you won't argue with a book as much as you argue with me," he'd said.

Flipping through it, I came to a section near the end where Lewis was differentiating between trying to be a good person and true Christianity.

I saw in a flash why Nate talked about "dyin' to self." And why he scoffed at the whole black box idea. Faith wasn't a matter of doing good things. Trying to behave. It was about letting go of your will and letting God change you. Of joining the dance—and letting him lead.

I had a lot to learn. I went back to the beginning of the book and started reading. And lying there in that hotel bed, with Luke snoring beside me, I asked God to show me how to die to myself and how to live—and maybe even how to dance.

———

THE NEXT DAY, life got better. Scott called and asked if he could come over. He'd changed his schedule and could leave early in the morning. I responded, "Sure!"

Then, as I drove over to Hope Ranch, Trooper McCoy called. A forensic review of my computer back-up files picked up one pre-fire image of the front quarter panel of a large, white pickup truck. He checked vehicle records and found Susan Larson owned a similar truck. McCoy was getting a search warrant for her house.

Meanwhile, he'd noticed some anomalies in the original investigation, enough to refer the case to state police investigators. "The autopsy showed the trajectory of the bullet that entered Bob Larson's brain was horizontal. In most suicides, it's upward," he told me.

Of course, I knew that and had pointed it out to Sam Larson's lawyer, along with the fact Susan Larson's hands were never swabbed for gunshot residue.

"I'll let you know as more develops," McCoy said, and as I clicked off my phone, I felt a rush of adrenaline.

Could it get any better? Yes.

On my second visit to Hope Ranch, I spotted Elise. She was sitting in a green camp chair up by the pasture. She had a sketchbook in her hand. My heart jumped. Finally!

I hung out by Cap's corral for a while, then casually strolled up to the pasture. Just three of the five horses were visible. I leaned on the fence, watching them. Overhead, puffy tropical clouds dotted the sky thanks to Dora, the hurricane tracking offshore four hundred miles to the south. Forecasters were predicting it would move north until it hit the Outer Banks of North Carolina, then swing east out into the Atlantic. We'd get rain and wind but that was about it.

As I turned to walk back, Elise glanced up at me, her large brown eyes peeking out shyly from beneath her bangs. She was wearing a short-sleeved, black T-shirt and tan capris. Around her neck hung a pendant. It looked like it had words on it, but I couldn't read it.

"Hi!" I said, adopting my most non-threatening tone of voice. "I'm Jessica. Mind if I look?" I gestured toward her sketchbook.

She turned the pad toward me. "I'm not very good." Her voice surprised me. It sounded high, childish.

On the pad she'd sketched the pasture before us, but she'd filled it with horses, reminding me of the sketches she'd done of the beach that people had described to me. "Wow, good job!" I said. "Do you always work in pencil?"

"Yes. So far."

"Can I see what else you've done?"

She handed me the pad. I flipped over to the other pages. They were similar—multitudes of horses in corrals, the stables, the barn. One even had horse-shaped clouds in the sky. I thought that was creative.

But then I saw something that stopped me short—a drawing of Nightcap in his corral, but the corral was smaller than in real life, barely big enough for him to move in, and the fence loomed above him. His eyes were wide with terror, his nostrils flaring. A chill ran down my spine when I saw it. He was imprisoned, not corralled.

I handed the sketchbook back to her. "I feel sorry for that horse," I said, smiling to mask my emotions.

"He's terrified."

"Nightcap is in that corral because he jumps fences. He could get killed on the road."

"He still wants to be free."

Something in her voice sounded more than fragile, it sounded a little crazy. "You must love horses," I said to keep her talking. "Do you ride?"

"No."

"How long have you been coming here?"

"A couple of weeks."

"Do you live nearby?"

"No."

I could sense she was starting to get uncomfortable. "I'm writing a book about horses for kids. I heard about this place and wanted to see it." I smiled for the third time, covering my lie. "I'll leave you to your work. Keep drawing. You're very good." I started to leave, then turned back. "What's your name?"

"Ann," she said. "Plain Ann."

"Okay, Ann, I'll see you later." I turned and started walking away, but she stopped me.

"You should go see the ponies on Assateague."

I looked at her and smiled.

"They're really free."

"Good idea. I'll do that." I walked back down toward the stable. I stopped by Cap's corral. I grabbed some grass and tried feeding him again. "You are stubborn," I said to him when he refused to come close.

I was still studying Elise from a distance when a young woman appeared at my side, one of the ones I'd seen mucking stalls. "Are you making progress?"

Surprised, I turned to her, eyebrows raised.

"With him." She gestured toward the horse.

"Not yet," I said, relieved my cover with Elise wasn't blown. "Are you a volunteer?"

"A volunteer and a client."

She had blonde hair and perky blue eyes. I would have pegged her for a cheerleader. "What do you mean?"

"I started coming after my dad left us. I was angry and scared too. Actually," she said, lowering her voice, "I was cutting."

I nodded.

"My mom heard about this place and brought me here. At first I was like, what do I care about smelly horses? But then, I met Baron."

"Baron?"

"He's the Clydesdale." She nodded toward the pasture. "He is the biggest, gentlest goofball ever. He came from a broken home too. The dad left and the mom couldn't afford to keep him. Kate got him, and well, I found out how cool horses are."

"That's great."

"I taught him to play soccer."

"You what?" I laughed.

"I got this big oversized beach ball and kicked it toward him. Eventually, he learned to kick it back."

"That's hilarious."

She shifted a bucket to her left hand. "I'm Rachel, by the way." She extended her hand, and I shook it.

"Jessica."

"I saw you talking to Ann."

"Yes." I calculated my response.

"Her husband abused her."

"She said that?"

Rachel nodded.

I sure didn't catch any hint of that in my dealings with Danville. "Oh, wow," I said. "Like what did he do?"

"She didn't say, and Kate says we shouldn't pry. People tell their stories when they're ready. But that's why she's always drawing."

I nodded. "That makes sense. How often do you get to come?"

"Whenever I can get a ride. My mom, she works at the Barrier Island Center. She's the director."

Ellen Wilson! Rachel was her daughter. Instantly, an arrow of fear raced through me. I'd told Ellen why I was looking for Elise. Had I blown my cover?

"Is Ann a client?" I asked.

"No. The ranch is mostly for kids. But it's clear she needs some help, so Kate lets her hang around. Kate's like that." Rachel smiled.

Just at that moment, Kate walked up. "I'm like what?"

"A sucker," Rachel said, grinning.

"Oh, you." Kate pretended to be annoyed. "Don't you have a stall to muck out?"

"Actually, I do. See you!" Rachel took off.

"She's a hoot. What a change in six months," Kate said after she left.

"She told me she taught Baron to play soccer."

"You should see it. They are amazing together."

I changed the subject. "Hey, a friend of mine is coming over tomorrow. He'd like to visit the ranch. Is that okay?"

"Yes, of course."

"There's another thing. I need to check out of my motel in about an hour. I've got another place lined up, but I won't be able to get in until four. Can I stash my dog in his crate in the shade somewhere around here for a couple of hours? He's not aggressive."

Kate frowned. I thought she was going to say no. "He's the one who does search and rescue?" she asked.

"Yes. A German shepherd. He's well-trained and usually well-behaved."

"Sure," Kate said. "Don't crate him. Bring him with you. I'd like to see the horses' reactions. I've been thinking about getting a dog."

38

My stomach churned as I drove back to the Maryland motel to pack up and get Luke. I needed to call Ellen Wilson, Rachel's mother, ASAP and ask her not to blow my cover. I pulled over to look up the phone number.

I had to leave a voicemail. I explained the situation as best I could. I could only hope she'd comply.

It bothered me that I had lied to Kate about my reason for visiting Hope Ranch. I mean, when I was a detective, shading the truth to trip up a criminal during questioning was a technique. You'd exaggerate the amount of evidence you said you had, or indicate you'd flipped the criminal's buddies and they were going to testify against him. You played all kinds of tricks to pressure the bad guy into confessing.

But that was in pursuit of justice, of getting a murderer or a rapist off the streets. Now, I was lying to get information for some guy about his wife. It didn't feel right. I liked Kate and what she was doing for people and for animals. And I had deceived her.

I decided right there and then I would not approach Elise with Danville's letter at Hope Ranch. The ranch was a safe harbor, a place of peace. And I would not break that. Of course, that would complicate things. I'd have to follow her to see where she was staying, or invite her to have lunch, or use some ruse to meet her off the ranch grounds.

When I got to the motel, I packed us up, put Luke in the car, and then checked out. I took him for a run at a nearby park. I wanted him calm when we got to Hope Ranch.

There, he was the best-behaved dog ever. He was interested in the horses, but he didn't bark. He actually went nose-to-nose with Cap through the fence, which gave Kate the idea that maybe Cap was used to dogs and a dog would help him calm down.

The only bad thing Luke did was almost roll in a pile of horse poop. I'd kept him on leash, but I was talking and distracted. I felt a little tug and looked just in time to keep him from dropping on top of it. That crazy dog.

I left not long after that. I'd found a new motel south of the state line, back in Virginia. Checking in, I paid for two rooms, including one for Scott for the next night. People of my generation would think I was crazy. Why get a second room? Sex with friends was as common as having a drink together.

I'd lived that way, too, once, but not now.

The next morning at 6:00 a.m., Scott texted me that he was leaving. I figured it would take him about four hours. I was wrong. He arrived in three hours and fifteen minutes.

My second thought was *Wow, he drives fast,*

My first was *Wow. He looks good.*

He wore jeans and a short-sleeved, light-blue chambray shirt, and boots. His short, dark hair looked freshly cut. As he came close, I noticed a little silver around his temples. Had it been there before? Then I caught a whiff of his sandalwood-scented aftershave.

He greeted Luke first, then gave me a hug. "How are you?" he said. "You look great."

Me? In my jeans and T-shirt? "I'm fine. I'm anxious to finish this case so I can get back to real life. Are you hungry? Have you eaten?"

"I ate on the way. That's what took me so long."

My eyebrows shot up.

He laughed.

We put some of Scott's gear in my motel room for safekeeping, since he wouldn't officially check in until later. Then we loaded Luke in the back of the Jeep. It was hot and Scott wore his shirt out. I wondered for a moment if he wasn't armed. Then he leaned over, and I saw the bulge of the gun at the small of his back.

Fifteen minutes later, I pulled into a parking place at the ranch. Before we got out of the car, Scott said, "Show me the picture of the woman you're tracking." I found it on my phone and turned it so he could see it. "Text that to me, would you?" I wasn't sure why he wanted me to, but I did, along with a stock photo of the type of car she was driving.

As we walked up toward the house, I explained the ranch's mission, where they got their horses, and who their clients were. I saw volunteers finishing up morning chores and a few kids who I was sure were clients, but on the whole, the place was pretty quiet.

"I didn't see the car," Scott said in a low voice.

"No, she's not here. Not yet."

Kate must have seen us walking up because she emerged from the house. "Welcome."

I introduced them, and she offered to show Scott around. We did a rerun of the tour she'd given me, except that Scott asked more intelligent questions than I had. Clearly, he knew things about horses. And when we got to Cap's corral, I saw him stop short.

Kate told him about Cap's background while I tried fruitlessly to lure the horse with fresh green grass. He stood well away, stomping his foot and glowering at me.

"How long have you had him?" Scott asked.

"About three weeks," Kate said, "and so far, we've not made much progress."

"Mind if I try something?"

Both of us stared at Scott.

"We use natural horsemanship," Kate said. "Nothing harsh or punitive."

Scott grinned. "You don't just ride 'em 'til they're broke? Okay, no problem. I'd like to give it a shot." When Kate hesitated, he added, "At my own risk."

Scott had charmed Kate, I could tell. "All right," she said. "At your own risk. Just don't hurt the horse."

"No ma'am," Scott said. "Can I use that lead line?"

Kate handed him a long, white rope with a clip on the end and he slipped quietly into Cap's pen. The horse snorted and stomped his foot, then backed away. Scott kept his eyes on him, talking quietly. "Hey, boy, hey there. Whoa now, whoa." Then he started swinging the end of the rope as he moved slowly toward the horse, angled slightly toward his rear end. "Let's go, now," he said, and he made a clicking noise with his mouth. "Let's go." I felt Luke tense up next to me. He must have wondered what Scott was up to, and I put my hand down to calm him.

Scott flicked the lead toward Cap's haunches. The horse started moving in a circle around the pen. Scott stayed in the middle, swinging that rope and Cap started trotting. Then he ran round and round. I guessed what Scott was doing was giving Cap an outlet for his nervous energy, pushing him to do the natural thing—run.

Scott kept it up for a while, then all of a sudden, he stopped swinging the rope, turned his back on the horse, and walked away from him. I held my breath, but then, amazingly, the horse stopped. He stood still for a minute, then dropped his head and followed Scott. Slowly, Scott turned around and started petting him, stroking his cheek, then moving back along Cap's neck. When he reached his withers, Cap turned his head toward Scott.

In the course of about fifteen minutes, I'd seen a frightened, angry horse become calm and relaxed. Next to him, instead of an uptight, aggressive man, I saw a gentle leader. I could hardly wrap my mind around it.

I think Kate was as surprised as I was. "Where'd you learn that?" she asked as Scott slipped out of the pen.

"My uncle had horses, some of them rescued wild mustangs. At first, he broke them the traditional way, but then he learned about natural horsemanship. He introduced my sister and I to it. My sister, Janey, she was really into it. We even went to clinics around Denver."

I noticed the ease at which "my sister" slipped from Scott's mouth. No bitterness.

"I'd forgotten how much I enjoyed horses," Scott went on to say. "Lately, I've started working with one again, and, I don't know, there's just something about that I find relaxing."

"That technique you used is exactly the kind of thing we do," Kate said. "I didn't think Cap was ready for it. I guess I was wrong." She turned toward me. "And you, you've been keeping secrets from me." Guilt flashed through me. "You didn't tell me your friend knew horses." Kate smiled. "Come on, let's walk up to the field. I want to show him Baron."

I followed them, half listening to their horse talk, half processing what I'd seen. Something had changed inside Scott. He was a different man.

———

THE REST OF THE MORNING, Scott and Kate talked horses, me following behind with Luke, listening to them but also looking for Elise.

And then I saw her, over by a far paddock where an

Appaloosa and a Quarter Horse were chewing hay. She was sitting in her chair, her sketchpad in hand.

"I'll catch up with you, guys," I said to Scott and Kate, and I turned toward her.

"Hey, Ann," I called out. The two horses' heads went up and looked in my direction.

Ann turned as well. "Oh!" she said, spotting Luke. "Does he bite?"

"No, not at all. Would you like to pet him?"

She would. And she did.

"You like dogs?" I asked.

"He's beautiful." She stroked Luke's coat as he sat quietly, his tail sweeping the ground.

"He likes you." Anything to keep her talking.

Her eyes stayed focused on Luke. Then she glanced up at me from under those bangs. "I always wanted a dog."

"Why didn't you get one?"

"He said they were dirty."

"Who said that?"

Her eyes widened, as if she realized she'd let something slip. She pressed her lips together. I tried to decide whether or not to pursue it. I saw her eyes flick past me and widen. I turned to see what she was looking at. Scott.

"That's my friend, Scott," I said. "He just did the most amazing thing. He went into Cap's corral and calmed him down. It was so cool!"

That seemed to make her relax a little. "Scott," I said as he drew near, "this is Ann."

"Hi, Ann," he said, his voice gentle. "Can I see what you've drawn?"

She turned the sketchbook toward Scott.

He flipped through it, hesitating at the picture of Cap, then handed it back. "You're very good. A natural artist. I especially like the clouds." Then he turned to me. "Ready to go to lunch?"

———

Scott and I stayed silent as we walked back to my car. We put Luke in the back, and I climbed in the driver's seat.

"Well," he said as he fastened his seatbelt, "something's sure going on with her."

"I don't get it," I said, turning on the ignition.

"She was scared of me."

Scared of him? Like a man had abused her? I wasn't ready to agree with him on that. Danville seemed concerned, not abusive. "What do you feel like eating?"

"Barbeque, steak, seafood—any of that sound good?"

I drove to a barbeque place. A few minutes later, we were eating pulled pork sandwiches at an outdoor table, with Luke lying underneath hoping for spills. I'd ordered mine messy, which means with coleslaw. Scott had ordered a bunch of sides, including fries. That man could eat.

But all the while I was mulling over Elise and her weirdness. "You know, all I want to do is finish this crazy case and get back home. I'm worried about Miss Lottie. I think Elise is weird, and all I know about Colton Danville is that he pays well and I need the money." I took a big drink of lemonade, all sweet and tart and cold. Then I looked at Scott. "You and Kate sure hit it off."

He shoved his plate over my way. "Have some fries."

I took a few and transferred them to my plate. "You surprised me."

He laughed. "I enjoy horses."

We talked about what he'd been doing at Nate's and what my next move with Elise should be and what Kate was doing at the ranch while we ate.

"Hey, Kate told me I ought to go see the ponies on Assateague while I'm here," Scott said. "You want to go do that? They're pretty interesting. It's only about half an hour away."

"Sure. Why not?"

"The only problem is you can't take the dog. No pets are allowed on the refuge where the ponies are, not even in cars."

"I can give Luke a good run, and he'll be fine in my room."

———

BETWEEN RUNNING, cooling down, and showering, it was three o'clock before we left the motel. Scott drove. We went past the big NASA satellite dishes and onto the causeway leading us over marshes and waterways between the mainland and Chincoteague Island.

I read Scott some information from my phone. "Chincoteague lies about four miles off the mainland, is about seven miles long, and has about three-thousand full-time residents. Assateague is about thirty-seven miles long, and that's where the ponies live." I scrolled to a map. "Assateague looks like it's cradling Chincoteague in the crook of its arm."

"So Chincoteague is protected from the Atlantic."

"I guess so."

"How do you get to Assateague?"

"You drive across Chincoteague, and there's another small bridge that takes you over."

"Is there a bookstore—some place we could get information?"

I checked. "There's one on Main Street. Sundial Books."

As we drove over the causeway, I could see the cattle egrets were out in number, fishing in the shallows along with great egrets and herons, terns and gulls. I found myself naming them, telling Scott about my father and his interest in migratory birds. I could smell the marsh and the salt air, and memories long submerged resurfaced. It felt good sharing them. Scott didn't seem to mind.

Once on the island, we took a right on Main Street to Sundial Books to get what information we could on the ponies. The owners told us all the ponies had names and a huge following online. Who knew?

The store's stock included guidebooks, postcards, framed pictures, and pony T-shirts, alongside other books, music, and artwork. Scott bought a couple of books and a video of Pony Penning. I made him buy *Misty of Chincoteague*, even though it was a kid's book.

"It's a classic," I told him.

We got the name of a couple of good people to talk to about the ponies, and by the time we'd returned to the car, Scott had arranged to meet one of them on Assateague. I wasn't sure why Scott was doing all this, but I was happy to get away from my Elise problem for a couple of hours and just be with him.

We met Dana on the shoulder of the beach road. She lived on Chincoteague and loved the ponies enough to brave mosquitoes and the heat and hike all over Assateague, photographing them and documenting the births of foals. She knew every pony's name, which band they were usually part of, and where they hung out.

"There's two herds," she said, "the northern herd and the southern herd, about a hundred and fifty adults altogether."

"How many stallions?" Scott asked.

"Right now, fifteen. You're seeing two bands there." Dana gestured toward the marsh. "A couple of stallions and their mares. The rest are either up north, or they're just not visible."

"The mares foal every year?"

"Pretty much, and the foals are auctioned off in the summer at Pony Penning."

I knew about Pony Penning from reading *Misty of Chincoteague* so many years ago. I didn't know that the fire department, which owns the ponies, is limited in how many they can keep, nor did I realize how much they cared for them during the rest of the year, with vet checks and so on.

"They're acclimated to the climate and the marsh grass,"

Dana told us. "The salt's why their bellies are so round. Tourists want to feed them, but they shouldn't, not even apples or carrots. It messes them up. And they shouldn't pet them either. The ponies are wild. We want them to keep all the wildness they can. If people want to pet horses, there's a zillion out there they can pet." She gestured vaguely toward the mainland.

"So you never get close enough to touch them?" I asked.

"I photograph them with my long lens. Every once in a while they'll come close, and yes, I want to pet them, but I don't. For their sake."

"What do they do during storms?" I asked. The wind had definitely picked up, and the clouds, once scattered, were now a continuous layer overhead. I was starting to wonder if we were going to see more of Dora than the experts had said.

"The ponies are smart. They know how to stay safe," Dana explained. "The Fish and Wildlife Service is responsible for the refuge. When a big storm is coming in, they open up all the gates and let the ponies find their way to high ground. They know where the high places are up in the north, and down here, too, like the area around the lighthouse. They huddle together and turn their butts to the wind. They do all right."

Dana pointed out the bands in the distance. She handed Scott a pair of binoculars. "If you look on their rumps, you'll see a freeze brand, for example, '17'—that's the year of their birth."

Scott peered through the binoculars, then handed them to me.

"How are the ones that are sold, the babies?" I asked, handing Dana her binoculars. "Are they difficult to gentle?"

"People say they're smart and become wonderful pets."

Scott had a ton of questions about hoof trimming and floating teeth and parasites and even something called swamp cancer. When he had exhausted all of them, he asked Dana for her number in case he thought of something later. Then she left, and we continued on to the beach.

"Wow, you really got into these ponies," I said. "I know what to get you for Christmas."

He laughed. "I know it seems weird. But maybe it's just like your dad and the birds. Maybe it's something to take my mind off killers and guns and politics and mortgages and a daughter who barely speaks to me. Maybe it's something natural that I can relax into."

I understood that. We pulled up to a space in the beach parking lot. The Atlantic looked rough. "Let's sit for a while," Scott said.

So we sat on the beach, watching the breakers roll in one after another, watching them crash on the sand and slide back out again. Sandpipers and sanderlings skittered at the water's edge, dodging the waves and finding food. Scott started talking about his shooting incident and confessed he was worried he wouldn't react quickly the next time because the fallout was so painful. I talked to him about my case and confessed I felt guilty because I hadn't been upfront with Kate. He talked about forgiveness, and I recounted what Nate said about grace.

And when he reached over to take my hand, I didn't move it away.

39

I BARELY SLEPT THAT NIGHT. I knew Scott had to leave after breakfast. I didn't want him to go.

Over a seafood dinner on Chincoteague the night before, Scott had made a suggestion that blew me away. "Maybe it's time for you to give up this PI work."

"I don't want to leave Luke all day."

"Have you ever thought of trying out for a professional SAR team? You and Luke? Don't some disaster teams have them?"

No, I hadn't, but the more I thought about it, the more I liked the idea, if it was salaried. And full time. And I could work with Luke. I'd have to check into all that.

Wow, give up PI work? Move back near Scott?

I had a lot of questions, most of which couldn't be answered from a motel room at eleven o'clock at night. But I did all the research I could on the Internet from my phone, and then, well, I prayed about it. Nate said God cares about these details of our lives, right? So I prayed about that and my relationship with Scott. And for good measure, I texted Nate and asked him to pray, too, because he had a better track record of hearing—and actually listening to—God, and maybe he'd help me out.

The next morning, Scott came to my room after he'd packed his car and checked out. I'd walked Luke and was just waiting to say goodbye, my gut already hollowed out. I realized I always ran to keep from re-experiencing the haunting losses from my past. If I ran first, I figured I wasn't being left. In the middle of my sleepless night, I'd decided this time I'd stand my ground. Maybe even join the dance.

I heard a soft tap on my door, opened it, and Scott walked in. I could smell the scent of sandalwood. I felt his presence like a wave buffeting me.

"I'm packed," he said.

"Okay. Thank you for coming. It was good to see you."

"Yes." He bent down to say goodbye to Luke. As he straightened up, I impulsively captured him in my arms, and I kissed him, passionately, right on the lips.

I surprised him. I surprised myself! After a moment's hesitation, he kissed me back, his mouth exploring mine, his hands gripping my waist, his strength almost overwhelming me. Then he embraced me, kissed me behind my ear, and whispered, "Do you know how long I've wanted to do that?"

"No?" I said, weakly.

"A long time." He kissed me again on my mouth, on my neck, behind my ear, and I felt my world shift and change, morphing into something new and exciting and scary and fresh.

I could barely breathe. I felt the brush of his freshly shaven cheek on my face and lightning raced through me. The scent of sandalwood made my head spin.

Then he cradled my face in his hands and kissed me on both cheeks and on my mouth. His blue eyes looked deeply into mine. I could barely hold his gaze as I stood before him, shaking.

"If you want this," he said, "just know, I won't play games. No running from it, either of us. We work it out. Understand?"

I nodded, fear and passion fighting for control.

"It's too important, Jess, too real. Don't run."

I swallowed hard. "Right."

He laughed softly. "You've got that deer in the headlights look. Don't be scared. I'm not going to hurt you. I promise." And he kissed me again and my heart pounded like a kettledrum. When I kissed him back, my whole body ignited.

I think both of us knew we couldn't stay in that motel room. There's only so much temptation a body can stand.

"Come with me to breakfast," he said.

A little longer with him. "Okay."

Poor Luke had to stay behind. But I brought him my leftovers, because I could barely eat.

———

WHEN SCOTT DROPPED me back at the motel, it was nearly noon. We'd had a lot to talk about.

As I walked Luke, I immediately began working out my plan for today. Reach a resolution on this case. Get back to Miss Lottie. Decide what I wanted to do for the rest of my life.

I needed to know if Elise had really been abused. If so, I would drop the case immediately, even if I had to return Danville's money. If not, I would follow her and gently give her Danville's letter somewhere away from the ranch.

Either way, I was ready to go home.

But first, I had to do a hard thing. I had to tell Kate I'd deceived her.

I was on my way to the ranch when Scott called. "I just wanted to say you're amazing and I miss you." His tender voice made me smile even though my stress was ramping up.

I brought Luke with me to the ranch, more for comfort than for anything. When I pulled into the parking lot, I saw Elise's car. Good. This could be quick. I jogged toward the stable and found Kate in a stall.

"Could I talk to you in your office?" I asked. My head felt like a snake had wrapped itself around my skull.

"Sure. Go ahead in. I'll be there in a minute."

A knot pulled tighter in my chest. *Telling Kate,* I texted Scott. *Please pray.*

Why did I ask him to pray?

Kate came in, closed the door, greeted me and Luke, then sat down in the leather chair opposite me. "What's up?"

"I haven't been totally straight with you," I began. I felt an anxiety attack stalking me, crouching in the weeds. I clasped my hands together to keep them from shaking.

Luke sensed my stress, stood up, and put his head on my knee. I began stroking him, but my movements were jerky. I tried to do my relaxation breathing, but couldn't.

Then, as words tumbled from my lips, anxiety hit me. I started shaking.

Kate knew what I was experiencing. She reached over and touched my shoulder. "It'll pass. Just breathe in for four, hold for seven, out for eight."

My eyes widened. She knew Nate's calming technique. I did it...twice...then tried again to spit out my story.

"I'm a private investigator." Four—seven—eight. "Colton Danville of Norfolk hired me to find his wife, Elise. She disappeared five weeks ago." Luke put his paw up on my knee. "Police believe she chose to leave and are not investigating."

I took a deep breath. "I believe Ann is Elise Danville. I tracked her here, and I'm very, very sorry I wasn't upfront with you." I looked for anger on Kate's face.

"You should have been honest," she said.

"I wouldn't have found her."

"Still..."

I waved my hand. "I know. I know. I'm sorry." I stood up and paced the small office. I felt like I was going to throw up. Luke stuck right next to me.

Abruptly, I sat back down, and Luke followed, leaning on my leg. "I met Danville in Norfolk. He has great bona fides— he's a respected businessman, a leader in the community and in his church. I spoke with his staff, his minister, a friend of Elise's. I had no reason to suspect anything beyond what he told me, that his wife had serious mental health issues and that he was worried about her. He gave me this." I pulled out the letter. "He said it was money and a letter of apology for anything he might have done to make her unhappy. And he asked me to give it to her." I looked Kate straight in the eye. "I swear, I had no reason to suspect that anything else was going on."

"And your friend? Is he a PI as well?"

"Oh, no. He's FBI." Then I realized how that sounded. I shook my head. "He was here strictly for the horses. He has no interest in Elise."

Kate stayed silent for a time, as if she was mulling over what to do. "Well, I'm sorry," she said finally. "Hope Ranch is a sanctuary, a place of peace. I'll have to ask you to leave."

"I understand," I said, "but could you tell me this, please? I need to know if Danville is abusive. If he is, I'll drive home, return his money, and keep her location a secret. Can you tell me? Has Ann been abused?"

"She's not a client. How would I know?" It was a sidestep.

"You knew something was going on with me. You called me on it, the first day I was here."

"And all that you told me, about your father dying on 9/11, being run off the road, your house burning down—is any of that true?"

"All of it," I said in a whispered voice.

She looked at me. "What's causing your anxiety?"

"All of it," I repeated, "but mostly not being forthcoming with you. I'm sorry."

She studied my face, then her eyes relaxed. "Ann has not

spoken to me about it, but others have told me she says her husband was abusive."

I closed my eyes and shook my head. "I'm sorry. I never suspected him."

"We don't want to see these accomplished, charming people for who they really are. Ann is very fragile. I'm concerned about her."

I stood to leave. Luke stood up too. "I need to make this right."

Just then we heard loud knocking on Kate's door. "Yes?" she called out.

Rachel stuck her head in. "Come quick!"

Kate raced into the outer room. I followed. "What's going on?"

A gray-haired woman named Vetta, nearly out of breath, said, "We were near the barn. Ann was showing me her drawings. Suddenly, she looked up and saw a man coming up from the parking lot. She took off through the barn." Vetta gasped for breath. "I walked toward him. He said he was looking for someone. Over his shoulder, I saw Ann had run through the woods and was getting in her car. He heard the motor start and turned to chase her, but I...I tripped him."

Good for her! "Is he still here?" I ran for the door, Kate right behind me. When we got outside, both Elise and the man were gone.

"What did he look like?" I asked Vetta.

"Well-dressed, about fifty, dark hair. Brown slacks and a white golf shirt. Driving a black car. Might have been a Mercedes."

I looked at Kate. "That's him."

"How'd he find her?"

"I don't know! I'll try to catch them." I ran past Elise's spilled papers, past her green chair, down the walk, and to my car. Quickly, I crated Luke, then took off down the driveway, turned right onto the road, and hit the accelerator.

I wasn't fast enough. Within five minutes, I realized I'd lost them.

Where would she have gone?

I didn't know, so I drove back to the ranch. Maybe somebody there would have some ideas.

I left my car running and jogged back to where a cluster of ranch people stood around Elise's tipped-over chair.

"I lost them."

"How did he know she'd be here?" Kate said. Her voice had an edge.

"I have no idea. I never told him about the ranch. He only knew generally where I was."

I looked at the faces around me. "Where would she have gone? Any ideas?" They murmured among themselves, but nobody spoke up. Then I saw the papers scattered before me on the ground. Her artwork. I picked them up, rifled through them, then stopped when I came to something I recognized.

"Can anybody tell me about this?" I said, holding up a picture of ponies grazing in a marsh. My jaw had tensed.

"That's Assateague. She was obsessed with the wild ponies," Vetta said.

I turned to Kate. "Where does the road go if I turn left out of your driveway?"

"It's a shortcut down to NASA."

"And the road to Chincoteague? The causeway?"

She nodded.

I ran for my car.

"Jess," Kate called out.

I turned around.

"Be careful."

"I will." I jogged to my car and started to step in.

But a thought rolled through my mind. How did Danville know about the ranch? I dropped to my knees, then laid on the ground and used the flashlight on my phone to check the underside of my car. And then I saw it—a tracking device. He'd used me to find his wife.

I jerked the thing off and threw it toward Kate, who had walked down the hill. "Evidence," I yelled. She picked it up and waved at me.

At the end of the driveway, I turned left. In my rearview mirror, I saw a sheriff's car headed for the ranch. Kate must have called 911.

Twenty minutes later, I entered the causeway to Chincoteague. The cloudy skies opened and rain splatted on my windshield, obscuring my view of the island. The waves on the channel between the mainland and Chincoteague were tipped with white. A few seagulls fought the wind, but the other birds had found shelter somewhere out of the storm.

How close was this hurricane? Wasn't it supposed to veer offshore? I prayed. I prayed I was doing the right thing by chasing Elise. I prayed Danville wouldn't find her. I prayed that I would.

40

SCOTT STOPPED for gas just short of the Bay Bridge. This northern span would take him to Annapolis, Washington, and then ultimately to his home. But he felt uneasy as he pumped the gas. A long line of cars were waiting to fill up and the road to the bridge was jammed.

Was it the hurricane? Were people evacuating? He'd been thinking about Jess, not listening to the radio, and he suddenly felt out of the loop.

The filler hose clicked off. He finished his transaction, pulled up to the store, and walked inside. He listened to a few people talking about the weather, picked up some food and water, and found a clerk stocking shelves. "What's with all the traffic?"

The young man glanced at him and kept working. "People going crazy, that's all. Storm's shifted west. Now they say we're gonna get it. Everybody's panicking."

"Does it get that bad over here?"

"Some places. We ain't Louisiana, but it can flood."

"It looks like everybody's headed to the bridge."

"They're probably worried about them closing it."

"The bridge?"

The kid nodded. "Before they do that, they'll make all the lanes westbound, move as many people over as they can." He looked at Scott. "The ones stuck on this side, well, they'll all be in here buying stuff. Ice and all."

"If they close the bridge, how long will it stay closed?"

The kid shrugged. "As long as the wind's high. A day? Two days? Depends on the storm. They've already closed the CBBT, down Norfolk way." He put the last item on the shelf and picked up his empty box. "I'd get out now if I were you."

Scott mulled over that information as he checked out. The more he thought about it, the tighter his gut felt. Back in his car, he called Nate. "Hey, man, I'm not coming back yet."

"What's up?"

Scott told him. "If they close the bridge, or even make it one way westbound, I won't be able to get back here to the Eastern Shore. I don't know, I just don't feel right leaving Jess over here by herself. It bothers me. They've already closed the bridge-tunnel. She won't be able to go home even if she wants to."

"Follow your gut." Nate hesitated. "You want company?"

Scott considered it. Nate coming to the Eastern Shore would leave Laura alone, and really, why did he need him? He didn't. "No, man. You guys hunker down. I'll keep you posted."

He hung up, pulled out of the gas station, and turned his car south. While he drove, Scott made a mental list of hurricane preparations. *Keep the phone charged. Get some extra water. Food. Maybe a gas can? Call Gary.*

Then he flipped on the radio. "...winds are expected to reach seventy miles per hour with higher gusts. Expect tidal flooding up to seven feet..."

Scott increased his speed.

41

BY THE TIME I reached Chincoteague, the rain had stopped, temporarily anyway. I'd been through other hurricanes. The rain comes in bands at first.

At the stoplight, I drove straight across the island, toward Assateague, where the ponies lived, and where I suspected Elise was headed.

There were only a few parking lots on Assateague—the big ones at the beach itself and smaller ones at the nature center, the pony pens, and some trailheads. My plan was to quickly check each one, looking for Elise's car. If I didn't find it, I'd come back to Chincoteague and check motel and restaurant parking lots.

The problem was Luke. Dogs weren't allowed on Assateague, not even in cars. Maybe if the entrance gate was unmanned, I'd get by with it. Maybe I should throw something over the crate, a jacket or blanket. Maybe with the wind and rain, nobody would really be looking to enforce the No Dogs Allowed rule.

I decided to chance it. I mean, what was the worst that could happen? I wasn't going to take him out of the car. I wasn't putting any other creatures at risk. Still, I pulled over short of the bridge and disguised Luke's crate as best I could with a couple of beach towels.

The gate was unmanned. My lucky day. I checked the parking lots close by and then headed to the beach. I saw some ponies grazing in the marsh like nothing was wrong, and I wondered when they'd head for high ground. The wind had picked up. By the time I got to the beach parking lot, I could see the ocean was crazy rough. There were a number of cars—a bunch of people had come out to see the waves—but I didn't see Elise or her car.

Discouraged, I headed back. The rain started again and wind buffeted my Jeep as I crossed back to Chincoteague. I looked in a couple of motel parking lots, then pulled over to think.

Luke moved restlessly in his crate. Rain or no rain, the boy needed to relieve himself. I remembered the island map Scott had given me, and I fished it out of the glove box. Yes! A dog park.

Five minutes later I stood in the rain throwing a ball for my crazy dog. We were all alone, and that was a good thing. I wasn't going to be there long. I had to find Elise. Luke would have to be patient with me.

We played for fifteen minutes, then I gave him seven minutes of sniffing time. While he sniffed, I decided to text Scott and include Nate on the text in case the towers were out wherever Scott was. I told them where I was and that Danville had shown up and that I was doing my best to find Elise. I told them I'd make a decision soon whether to stay on Chincoteague or go back to the motel near Hope Ranch.

When I called Luke because it was time to leave, he looked at me like, *That's it?* I explained the situation as I was crating him. "I'll make it up to you, I promise."

I climbed into the driver's seat and glanced at my phone as I connected it to power. Already I'd gotten a TEXT FAILED message.

42

ALL THE WAY down the peninsula, Scott kept trying to call Jess. She wasn't answering, and after three times, he stopped leaving voicemails. Sometimes the calls didn't go through. He guessed some of the cell towers were down, or maybe just overloaded by calls from people panicking because of the approaching hurricane.

Near Salisbury, bands of heavy rain began rolling over the area, filling ditches and flooding streets. When he crossed into Virginia, Scott tried Jess again, but the call failed—again. Frustrated, he navigated to the motel where he'd seen Jess just a few hours ago. Where was she?

He strode into the office. The desk clerk looked up, alarmed. Scott leaned over the counter. "Jessica Chamberlain. Has she checked out?"

"Sir, I can't tell you that. We don't give information on our guests."

"I'm her friend. I stayed here last night. She may be in danger. I need to find her."

Still, the clerk hesitated. Scott resisted the urge to pick him up by his collar and shake it out of him. Instead, he violated policy and flashed his FBI creds. "I need access to her room."

"Okay, all right!" The clerk grabbed a master key and led Scott around to the room. He opened the door and Scott peered in.

Jess's stuff was still there—clothes, Luke's crate, her toiletries, and some food. But there was no sign of Jess. No car, no Luke.

He turned, gave the clerk his business card, and said, "Call me if she comes back."

"Yes, sir."

Back in his car, Scott figured out his next move. He'd seen a bit of higher ground at the ranch. Maybe Jess was there.

As he drove in that direction, he must have moved into the territory of a working cell tower, maybe one at NASA, because his cell phone rang. He answered the call, hoping to hear Jess's voice. Instead, it was Nate.

"What's going on?" he asked.

"I'm headed to the ranch. She wasn't at the motel, but her stuff is still there. Her phone just goes to voicemail." He couldn't keep the tension out of his voice. "I know she planned to go back to the ranch. Plus, she's chasing that woman and who knows where that will take her."

"I'm headed your direction," Nate said.

"Will Laura be okay?"

"Storm will be east of us. She'll be fine. I don't know why, but I just feel like I should come. I'm headed for the Bay Bridge."

"You may have trouble going eastbound."

"I'll get as far as I can."

"All right," Scott said. "I'll keep you updated."

43

THE LATEST RAIN band passed over, and I was able to turn off my wipers. Already some of the parking lots on Chincoteague were flooding. I turned on the radio for a storm update. Dora had shifted west a few degrees. It was headed straight for us, expected to hit in about six hours. I wondered how flooded the island got. I mean, the only high ground I saw were the raised graves in the cemeteries.

I checked my watch. Four o'clock. I'd look a little while longer, then decide whether I would stay here for the night or go back to the motel near Hope Ranch.

I drove down Maddox Boulevard, swinging through a couple of motel parking lots looking for Elise's car, then I turned left on Main and did the same thing. Nothing.

By this time, I wondered if I was even right about her coming here. Maybe I was totally off base.

I kept driving. The island wasn't that big, but there were a lot of roads and I could have easily missed her. I prayed hard I'd find her before Danville did. I drove all around the island and ended up back near the bridge to Assateague. That's when I made an impulsive decision. I pulled into a nearby motel and booked a room after assuring the desk clerk Luke was a well-trained SAR dog who might be needed during this storm.

Okay, that last part was an exaggeration, if not an outright lie. But it got me a first-floor room with a window looking out on the road to the refuge, along with a heaping dollop of guilt. Something just made me think Elise, in her panic, would think she could hide on remote Assateague. No buildings, no people...just ponies.

I wasn't really prepared to spend the night. I didn't have Luke's motel room crate. I had only enough of his food for a couple of meals in my SAR pack, along with two collapsible bowls, extra clothes for me, first-aid supplies, emergency food, and a flashlight.

"You need to be very good," I told him, "if I have to leave you alone here." He wagged his tail, which either meant, *I hear you* or *I'm already thinking of stuff I want to do.* I ruffled the coat on his neck. What would I do without Luke?

I decided to call Scott and tell him what was going on. I couldn't get a signal, and when I called down to the front desk, I found out the cell service was in-and-out, along with the cable.

"I 'spect the tower's been struck by lightning," the desk clerk said.

I sent another text, but that failed too. Then I called Scott from the landline in the room, but had to leave a message. I felt so isolated.

I started thinking about preparing to hunker down for the duration of the storm. The motel room had a mini fridge, a microwave, and a small coffee maker. I had my emergency food, but to supplement that, why not depend on McDonald's? I really didn't feel like getting in the car again.

Slipping into my rain jacket, I told Luke I'd be right back, and ran across the street to the fast-food place. I bought two salads and four quarter-pounders, a couple of yogurts, and four bottles of water.

I was just about to leave when something outside caught my eye. Three ponies were penned in a large corral next to McDonald's. I wondered what they were doing there. They huddled together, enduring the rain now coming down in sheets.

Then I caught sight of something else—a woman in a blue hooded windbreaker standing on the other side of the pen, watching the ponies. She had her arms crossed against the misery I'm sure she was feeling. I wondered why she didn't go into the motel or the McDonald's. Nobody would begrudge her getting out of the storm, even if she wasn't a paying customer. She turned and began pacing, then turned again, back and forth, pacing like Luke did when he was confined to a kennel.

The next time she turned, a gust of wind knocked off her hood, and I saw dark hair plastered hard to her head. Hair cut in a bob. My heart jumped.

44

Scott pulled into the parking lot at Hope Ranch. He'd tried calling, but either their phones were out or no one was there.

But would they leave the horses there alone in the storm?

He knocked on the door of the house. Kate answered. "Come in!"

"Is Jess here?"

"She was." Kate told him about Danville showing up and Ann taking off. "Jess went after her. She was headed for Chincoteague."

"Okay, good. Thanks."

But Kate continued. "Fifteen minutes after she left, Danville came back."

"Came back here?"

"Yes. Gave us the whole sob story about looking for his poor wife. He turned on the charm, but I wouldn't even admit she'd been here. He pressed me. He said he'd seen Jessica's Jeep here. I told him Jessica had been staying at a motel up Rt. 13 in Maryland." Kate straightened her shoulders. "That was true. She'd been there days ago."

"Right! Good move."

"So when he left here, I watched, and he turned right at the end of the lane, toward 13, away from Chincoteague."

"Good," Scott said. "Very smart, Kate. Take this." He handed her a business card. "Call me if she shows up here again. Call the sheriff if he does. I'm going to Chincoteague."

"But you can't!" Kate said. "They've closed the causeway."

"What?" It came out sharper than Scott intended.

"The causeway floods. They've closed it."

"And that's the only way in?"

"Yes. And you won't get a boat or a chopper out in this." Kate put her hand to her forehead. "Maybe the state police could help you?" She pulled out her phone to check something. "High tide is in three hours. Maybe it's still passable if you get permission."

"You got a landline?"

"Yes, sure. In my office."

Scott followed her, looked up a number on his phone, and dialed it on her phone. "McCoy? Scott Cooper. I need some help."

45

CLUTCHING MY FOOD, I left the McDonald's and raced over to Elise. I timed it so she had her back to me as I came near.

"Ann!" I said, when I was about six feet away.

She looked up in alarm and turned to run.

"Wait, wait! It's me, Jess, from the ranch." I slid my hood back. "Where's your car? Are you okay?" I could see she was shaking.

"We need to get out of this storm. I'm staying over there." I gestured toward the motel. "Will you come with me? Look, I have food!"

She hesitated.

"I'm by myself except for Luke, my dog. Remember him?" I saw her glance quickly away. I suspected she was looking for an escape route. "He keeps me safe. Nobody can hurt me or my friends when Luke's around." I smiled at her, like I was relaxed.

That did it. "Okay," she said. She walked with me, step by reluctant step, back to my motel. I slid the key card in the lock and we blew inside, where Luke was ready with a warm greeting.

"Whew! That's quite a storm," I said, putting the food down on the desk. "Let me take your jacket." I felt something heavy in the pocket. I assumed it was her phone. I hung both jackets in the bathroom. When I turned back, I could see she was freezing.

I dug into my SAR pack. "These are probably a little big, but why don't you go take a hot shower and then change into them? At least they're dry." I handed her my spare pants and T-shirt.

"Thank you."

When I heard the shower stop, I used the in-room coffee maker to fix a cup of tea. When she emerged a few minutes later, I invited her to sit down and handed it to her. "There's sugar if you want it."

"No, thank you." She began petting Luke, who had come over to her, his big tail wagging.

"Where's your car?"

"It got stuck."

"Oh, no. Once the rain stops, we can call a tow truck. In the meantime, you can stay here if you want."

"Thank you."

"I think the motel has a laundry room for guests so we can dry your clothes. We can check it out when the rain slows down." The street outside was collecting water. "Are you hungry?"

She looked at me as if trying to figure out the right answer.

"I am," I said. I felt like I was dealing with a teenager. I also felt that if I made a wrong move, she'd bolt like a skittish colt.

Then I remembered that was the expression Nate had used to describe me to Scott. He predicted I'd run like a skittish colt if Scott tried to get close. And I'd tried to. Luke had blocked me, and then, instead of running, I'd opened up, and Scott came back with me to the horrible motel, and he accepted me as I was, where I was, diffusing my shame, speaking words of comfort and acceptance.

Now, I wanted to speak those words to Elise, if only she would let me.

"Let's eat some of this before it gets cold." I laid quarter pounders, salads, yogurts, and water out on the desk. "Help your-self," I said. "Take what you want."

She approached the desk like a shy, suspicious child. Finally, she took some yogurt.

"Would you like some more tea?" I asked.

"Yes, please."

I took her cup, refilled it with water, and poured it into the little coffee maker. I could tell this was going to take some patience.

She had tea. I had coffee because I wanted to save the tea bags for Elise. She had yogurt and then a salad. I had a burger, and I gave one to Luke. He wolfed it down. I think he was hoping it was the new normal.

The wind and the rain buffeted the room, clicking against the windows. The TV wasn't working, I didn't have a radio, and I didn't want to use up all my cell phone battery. I wanted to hear more about Elise's life, but the only way I knew to draw her out was to prime the pump. So I started telling her about my life, about being bullied by coworkers and quitting, then adopting Luke, and about my friend Nate. I must have gone on for nearly an hour, because she wasn't jumping into the conversation. I had set out to prime the pump. Instead, I thought I must have about drowned it.

46

McCoy HAD a friend stationed on the Eastern Shore. State Trooper John Crockett agreed to meet Scott at the ranch.

Scott climbed into the passenger seat of Crockett's SUV and extended his hand. "Scott Cooper. Thanks for coming."

"John Crockett. Tell me what's going on."

So Scott explained that it wasn't an FBI case, he was just asking for a favor. "I think she could be in danger. If this client tracked her here, he may have followed her to Chincoteague. I don't know what he'll do."

"You know where she's staying over there?"

"I'm not sure."

"I checked with VDOT. We can make it over the causeway if we leave now. Tide's coming in, and in an hour, it could be underwater. What are you driving?"

Scott pointed out his Nissan Rogue. "It's all-wheel drive."

"You can follow me or I'll drive you," Crockett said. "Your call."

"You're more familiar with that area. What do you think?"

"Your car doesn't have a lot of clearance. I'd leave it here. Ride with me. VDOT will give us an escort across the causeway."

"Sounds good."

———

SCOTT AND JOHN met the VDOT emergency truck at the beginning of the causeway. John talked briefly to the driver, then they made their way across with lights flashing. The waves crashed on the bridge abutments, sending spray skyward. In lightning flashes, Scott could see whitecaps on the water and feel the wind buffeting the SUV. Ahead, the VDOT truck's orange lights lit the way. He turned to John. "You grew up here?"

"Yes, sir. On Chincoteague."

"What's it like?"

John's eyes stayed focused ahead on the road, but he smiled softly. "It's a solid place. Small town. Good people, good values. Gets busy in the summer, with the tourists coming in. The kids complain there's nothing to do, but that's kids for you. If you like the water—crabbing, oystering, fishing, and the beach—there's always stuff to do." He shifted in his seat. "When the storms come up the coast, it gets interesting."

"You surf?"

John grinned. "Yes, sir. Started before my mom knew what I was up to." He glanced at Scott. "How about you? Where are you from?"

"Colorado. A long way from the beach."

"You ski?"

"Ski, snowboard, hike, fish." Then he added, "Ride horses too. My uncle had a ranch."

"Cool."

The lights of the town emerged from the fog and rain like diamonds on a strand. "Power's still on," Scott said.

"For now."

Scott's phone buzzed. A text message. No, a series of text

messages. "We must have just hit a good cell tower. I just got five texts."

Three were from Jess. Two from Nate.

"Okay," Scott said. "She's staying on Chincoteague, so at least we're headed in the right direction."

"She didn't say where?"

"No."

"You know what she's driving?"

"Yes."

"We'll find her."

47

JUST WHEN IT SEEMED HOPELESS, Elise began opening up. She looked up from under her bangs and said, "We ran away. A long time ago." She studied her hands.

"How old were you?"

"Almost seventeen."

"And he was?"

"Twenty-nine."

I tried not to react, but really? Wow.

"We were madly in love. It was exciting."

I nodded. "I get that. What happened?"

Elise began wringing her hands, rubbing them together over and over. "He had inherited a business; I stayed home. He didn't want me to work or go to school. He said he wanted to take care of me."

She grew wistful, looking up at the ceiling, off into space. I held my breath, hoping she'd continue.

"For a while, it was okay. But then, he started getting mad at me for everything. I forgot to dust. I left a book out. I burned dinner." She raised her hands helplessly. "I tried to make him happy, but I couldn't."

"Did he hit you?"

"No. Not then. But I was never good enough for him. Never thin enough, smart enough, educated enough, or clever enough. I wasn't like the women he worked with. And he made sure I knew it."

She had moved from the chair to the other bed. Now, she seemed to grow smaller. She looked so young to me, and her voice was wispy and high. As a teenager, she must have seemed like a child.

"What about your family?" I asked. "Your parents?"

"I never saw them again."

"You never saw them ever again?" I tried to keep the alarm out of my voice, but I'm not sure I succeeded.

"He told me I couldn't and that if I tried, I'd go to jail and so would he and is that what I wanted?"

I felt sick inside. "And they didn't come looking for you?"

"No."

"Ann, when was this? What year?" A thought entered my head—a crazy thought. I needed more information.

But Ann didn't respond to my question. "He told me they were done with me. They didn't want me." Tears filled her eyes. "I'd been bad as a teenager. They'd had enough." She fingered the comforter. "I was terrified that he'd decide he was finished with me too. Then where would I be? So I tried hard to be good...to please him."

My mind grasped at straws. Surely, someone would have seen her isolation. Would have recognized her husband as abusive or at least controlling. I mean, this well-known businessman was virtually holding her prisoner, and no one came to her aid? "What about his parents?"

"Both dead. In a car accident when he was in college."

"Ann," I said, reminding myself to stick to her assumed name, "when did you marry?" Again, I was going for a date. A time reference. At the same time, I was looking beyond the thin face, the little crow's feet at the edges of her eyes, the downturn of her mouth to see if I could see any familiar features.

She shook her head. "We never did. I was too young at first, and then, he said it was just a piece of paper." She shrugged.

"Have you ever told anyone about all this?"

She shook her head. "I tried to." She took a deep breath. "My husband is a well-respected, charming, smart, handsome, successful realtor. He gives me everything. Why would anyone believe me?" She shifted her hands on the covers. "When he found out I'd gone to the minister, he was furious. Furious! He grabbed the book I was reading and threw it across the room. Then he choked me." She put her hand around her throat in a protective gesture. "He told me if I ever did anything like that again there'd be hell to pay."

I tried to stay calm, but inside, anger surged through me.

Luke sensed Ann's distress. He lifted his forequarters partway up on her bed. She stroked his head. "I had no education, no job, no friends, no family. Without Colton, I had nothing. What could I do?"

"I understand." I stood up and looked out of the window, trying to calm down, trying not to yell at God and ask him where he'd been when this was happening to her, trying to think of some way to soothe the raw wounds she had revealed to me.

The rain had blown steadily against the windows for more than an hour now. My watch said it was seven-thirty. It looked much later. No cars moved on the road, and the McDonald's was dark, like they'd closed up early. I looked toward Assateague. The lighthouse, barely visible in the rain, steadily blinked in the storm. I wondered how old it was and how many storms it had weathered. If I were out on a boat in the ocean right now, that light would be a godsend.

The light shines in the darkness and the darkness has not overcome it. The Gospel of John. I'd read it so many times, some of the phrases had stuck in my brain. *The light shines in the darkness and the darkness has not overcome it.* I tried to let those words settle me down.

"Ann, would you excuse me? I need to use the restroom." She nodded, still stroking my dog.

In the bathroom, I checked the Internet—still no WiFi, and it looked like the cell tower was still down. Still, I had to try to communicate. I texted Scott and Nate (thinking maybe Nate would get it even if Scott couldn't) and I told them where I was and what Elise was telling me. *Talking to Elise. Sunrise Beach Inn. Quitting Danville job. Will keep Elise safe!*

Then, I made a big show of being in the bathroom, flushing twice and turning on the sink water full blast to justify how long I'd been in there. I slid my phone in my pocket and walked back into the room.

"Another cup of tea?" I asked.

Ann focused on Luke, continuing to pet him. She seemed calmer. "Yes," she said. "Thank you."

"Ann, how did you live? What got you through it?"

She closed her eyes and nodded her head, as if rehearsing this part of the story. "I found art...and a friend. One friend all my own." She held up her forefinger. "We met at the art museums in Norfolk and we talked. We loved the same artists, the same style. I'd read a lot, and she taught art and seemed to think I knew things. We started meeting every Friday. It was a tiny fragment of my life that was mine

"But one day, he followed me. He couldn't bear to let me have that one little two-hour span to myself, that one friend. When I spotted him, he made some excuse about why he was there. He sat down at our table where we were having lunch. He charmed her, charmed *my* friend, and she became like all the rest. His. No longer mine." A single tear dripped down her cheek.

I popped a few tissues out of the box on the nightstand and handed them to her.

"Something broke in me that day. I finally decided to leave. Now, I'm terrified he'll find me."

"He won't." Anger stiffened my voice. "We won't let him. You're with me, and I have my dog. I have a gun. You're safe. Trust me."

I saw her eyes shift. People had said "you're safe" to me a zillion times, and I hadn't believed them. I couldn't. And I knew Ann couldn't believe me now. I had to change my approach.

I crafted some small talk, telling Ann stories about SAR and about Nate. And then, maybe it was because I was getting tired, I shared about Nate's faith. I told her about his anchor and the hope it gave him, that no matter how difficult life seemed, God was with us.

She shook her head and blew out a breath. "He killed my baby." Her words dripped out like acid.

My blood ran cold. "What? Who?" *Did she mean God?*

Elise stood up and began pacing. I sat down in the chair, trying to remain calm and as nonthreatening as possible. "What do you mean?"

"He was angry when I got pregnant." Elise jammed her fist into her thigh. "So angry. He accused me of doing it on purpose. Of deceiving him."

Her eyes flashed. "Was it so wrong to want a baby? To want something of my own to love?" She sat down, hard, on the bed. Tears streamed down her cheeks, forming tracks of sorrow and pain. "He found out when I was in my fourth month."

"What happened?" My voice was almost a whisper.

She stood and paced over toward the door, shaking her head. I could see her trembling.

"He slapped me, hard. I started to cry. I tried to explain to him that nothing would change. I would still love him. But he was enraged. He beat me." She crossed her arms over her abdomen. "He hit me hard over and over. That night, I started cramping. It hurt so bad, I screamed and cried. 'What now?' he said, and he flipped on the lights. There was blood everywhere in our bed."

I could hardly breathe.

"And then," Ann looked at me, her eyes tight with anger, "I lost the baby. Right there, in our bed, a perfectly formed four-month baby boy. Dead."

"Oh Ann! That's horrible!"

"He was this big." She held her hands about six inches apart. "Perfect tiny hands. Perfect little feet. And his face..." Her voice trailed off, then she looked toward the ceiling and wailed. "He killed my baby. He killed his own son!"

Every fiber of my being shook.

"He panicked. Yelled at me. Grabbed my arm and forced me into the bathtub. Threw towels on me. He took the sheets, every-thing, and left. When he came back, he had mud on his shoes."

I suddenly saw my dog, lying in Danville's backyard, giving me the cadaver signal. He'd smelled human remains, but I, entranced by the charming, intelligent man, had ignored his indication..

"He buried the baby, didn't he? Is that what he did?"

She looked at me, her big eyes filled with tears, and nodded.

My anger erupted.

And that's when I made my mistake.

"Elise," I said, "that's terrible!"

Her face reflected her shock at hearing her real name, turning sheet white. She looked at me like I was a monster.

"No!" she screamed. She clutched her chest.

I realized what I'd done. "Wait, no, Ann, you don't under-stand. Let me explain." But my words fell into the chasm between us that I had created.

She turned, jerked open the door, and ran out into the night.

48

LUKE STARTED TO FOLLOW ELISE. "LUKE!" I said, calling him back.

What had I done? I dashed to the bathroom, grabbed both of our jackets, and jerked my flashlight out of my SAR pack.

"Stay here," I told Luke. He barked twice in protest. "You stay!"

I slid into my jacket and ran outside, slamming the door behind me. I looked across toward the corral. I didn't see her. I wiped the rain out of my eyes and looked left. And there she was, running toward Assateague.

I took off after her. She was fast, but so was I. During flashes of lightning I saw her, running, running through sheets of rain, running as if her life depended on it.

Don't run. Don't run!

But she did run. She crossed the bridge. I sped up. The road at that spot turned just enough that I lost her. I shot desperate prayers heavenward—*please, God, help me!*

I always wondered if those kinds of shallow prayers were any more effective than wishing on a star. I still didn't have the answer, but suddenly, a flash of lightning at just the right time illuminated Elise as she dashed into the woods.

I gained on her. Now that we were racing into the woods, tracking her would be immeasurably harder. I wished I'd brought Luke.

Still, my SAR experience had taught me a few things. I used my ears, listening for her crashing through the brush ahead of me. I used my flashlight, looking for clear paths forward, broken branches, and footprints. And I prayed. I prayed with every breath in me.

I caught up to her at a boggy place. With no flashlight, she'd run full into it and was knee-deep in muck. "Ann! Stop, I'll help you."

She looked up at me, wide-eyed, and stopped struggling. Then she cried, "Stay away!"

I edged around the bog, found a tree to hang onto, and held my hand out to her. "Come on. I'll pull you out."

She wouldn't look at me.

"Ann, come on," I urged. "Please, let me help you!"

After what seemed like an eternity, she reached out. I grabbed her hand and pulled while I hung on to the tree. It worked. Released by the muck, she slid toward me and collapsed next to the tree I held.

I didn't want to let go of her. I was afraid she'd run again. But I did, sitting down next to her, trying to look as non-threatening as possible.

I handed over her jacket. "Here. I brought this for you."

She took it, slid her arms into it, and pulled up the hood.

"I'm not going to hurt you," I said. "I promise I won't hurt you. Your husband asked me to find you. I had no idea he was abusive. I'm so sorry. I won't tell him where you are, I promise. And I will get you the help you need. I'll help you, Ann."

My voice caught in my throat. A flash of lightning illuminated her face. I felt like I was looking in a mirror, seeing my own fear, my own unwillingness to trust, my own tendency to run.

"Ann," I pleaded, "don't run. Let me help you start a new life. I can do that. I *will* do that. Please come back with me. I'll keep you safe." I kept talking. I told her how I understood why she wanted to run, that I'd done that too. I recalled things Nate had said to me. I pleaded, encouraged, exhorted, begged.

She was shaking like she would fly apart. I shivered, too, because even if it was seventy-five degrees, I was wet and stressed and felt cold.

Finally, after what seemed like forever, she spoke. She talked about the ponies and being free. "He won't find me. He can't find me. Not here, with the ponies. Who would look here?"

Honestly, it was crazy talk. I wondered if she was experiencing a psychotic break.

What could I do? I persisted. I told her about how long it took for me to trust Nate. I told her about Luke helping me deal with my PTSD. I told her I'd take her back to Hope Ranch. Get her a dog. Anything to help her cope.

The wind howled. I heard a branch fall not far from us. "We need to leave, Ann. It's not safe here. Will you come with me?"

"I hear them. I hear the ponies," she said. She stood up. So did I.

"Come on," I said, reaching for her sleeve. "We'll find them." I started retracing our steps, but Ann pulled away.

I had no choice. I followed her. My flashlight picked up a boggy area. "Ann, wait. Let me lead. You'll sink again there."

For some reason, she let me get in front. I kept going the way she'd started, thinking I'd take us on a big curve back to the road. She followed me, muttering. I kept glancing back. She was definitely not well.

The rain picked up and slashed my face. The lightning flashes seemed brighter and became more frequent. It was almost impossible to stand upright in the wind. Branches tore away from trees and fell all around us. Then a large tree groaned and crashed to the ground. The shadows, the roar of the wind, the flashes of lightning had me on high alert.

I had a sudden sense of foreboding. Was she about to run? I turned toward Elise—just as she drove a knife into me.

I fell, clutching my side, suddenly unable to breathe. I thought, so this is how I die.

49

THE STREETS on Chincoteague had filled with water. There was nowhere for it to drain. "It's like the ocean's swallowing the island," Scott said.

"Yep. We could soon find ourselves in the belly of a whale," John said. His SUV plowed through the water, sending waves right and left, toward flooded parking lots and onto submerged sheds. All the stores and restaurants were closed, and they were the only ones on the street.

Scott's phone indicated an incoming text. "Here we go, here we go," he said. "Sunrise Beach Inn. You know where that is?"

"Sure! We're five minutes away," John said. He took a left, then a right, navigated around a circle, and continued down the road. Then he swung into a motel parking lot and came to a stop outside the office.

Scott jumped out. He glanced up and saw only one motel room window was lit. He tried to pull open the office door. Locked. He pounded on it.

John appeared beside him and peered through the door. He tried to use his phone. "Cell service is down again."

Scott turned and ran through the rain toward the lighted

window. The high winds buffeted him. He grabbed the sill and pulled himself up so he could see into the room. And he came face to face with an excited German shepherd, who pawed at the window, barking frantically.

"Luke!" Scott cried. He turned to John. "We've got to get in there!"

50

I think I passed out. Then I became aware of a searing pain in my side and an inability to breathe. I opened my eyes. I felt for the pain and found the knife. I knew right away it had punctured my lung.

Okay, stay calm. I squeezed my eyes shut again, fighting against the pain, fighting the panic. I counted to pace my breathing. My heart beat so fast.

Was she gone? I couldn't hear her. Maybe she'd run. I hoped so. I knew I couldn't defend myself if she came at me again. I pressed my hand as hard as I could on my wound, thinking maybe it would stop the bleeding or seal my lung. I didn't know what else to do.

Lying there in the mud, drenched by rain, trying desperately to breathe, I knew I was dying. In my mind, I saw Scott's face. I had run from him, run from Nate, run from everyone. Now, I was dying...alone...in a storm. I was getting what I deserved.

I'm sorry, God. I've run from you too. Please forgive me.

I think I passed out again for a while. Then I heard noises and sensed something near me. When I opened my eyes again, I saw ponies walking by me, splashing through water, all in a line, one following the other. They moved around me. One sniffed at me, its breath soft on my face.

I remembered. The ponies moved to high ground in a storm.

The storm. Flooding. My legs lay in water. I needed to move too.

I pressed my hand hard around the knife still stuck in my side. And then I inched my way uphill, dragging myself with my left arm, pushing with my legs, following the ponies, moving with the herd.

I didn't go far, just to where the ponies had stopped. They seemed so calm, so unafraid. As I moved near them, I heard one of them snort. Exhausted, I closed my eyes and focused on breathing.

Then something happened that I can't really explain or describe. A cloud, a mist of light, came over me. It felt comforting, like a blanket, or an embrace. I relaxed into it. I was no longer aware of the rain. My breathing, though shallow and painful, became easier. I felt warm all over, calm, cradled in a peace I'd never felt before. Above me I saw three lights, moving in a circle, energy flowing from one to the other, energy that I knew was Love, in a kind of dance.

And I knew in that moment that I was not alone and I would never be alone. All the time I had been running, I had been chased by the One who went before me and behind me and beside me, the One who had already decided the outcome of the race.

He was here now, surrounding me, enfolding me, and He was in me and I was in Him. I was safe. Safe with my Anchor, safe from this storm.

I closed my eyes.

51

THE MOTEL MANAGER emerged from the office. "What's going on?" he said, sliding into his coat.

"We need access to the room with the light," John said.

"It's the only one occupied. Everybody else left." The manager turned to retrieve a master key. "Door's in the back." He led Scott and John around the building.

"That's her car," Scott said, pointing to Jess's Jeep. His heart pounded. The manager fumbled with the lock. The door swung open, and in a rush of furious energy, Luke charged past all three men and took off.

"Catch him!" John cried out.

"Luke!" Scott yelled, but the dog kept running toward the woods.

John emerged from the motel room. "She's not here!"

Then Scott saw Luke put his nose down and move side to side, and he realized what the dog was doing.

"He's tracking her," he shouted and started running, running hard to keep up with Luke.

"I'm right behind you," John shouted.

Scott raced after the shepherd. The rain and wind sweeping

up the channel tried to blow him sideways. He pushed on. He would lose sight of Luke in the darkness, and then a burst of lightning would illuminate him again. His heart pumped hard. His legs worked, but it seemed like that bridge grew longer and longer.

Car lights appeared from behind him. Crockett's SUV. The vehicle helped light Scott's path, but he still couldn't see the dog. He started praying, asking God for help. He didn't know what else to do.

He ran around a gate. When he reached Assateague, he stopped. He'd lost sight of Jess's dog completely. Had he continued up the road? Run off into the woods?

"Luke! Luke!" he shouted.

"Did we lose him?" John Crockett ran up to him..

"Yeah." Scott leaned over, trying to catch his breath, trying to figure out what to do, trying to block the fear that surged like the tide inside of him. In his head, he silently screamed, *Jess! Jess!*

"Are you sure he wasn't just running away?"

"Absolutely. He's trained to find people. He loves Jess. He's tracking her. I'm sure of it."

The rain pounded down on them. "I'll see if Fish and Wildlife will open the gate so we can drive ahead."

Scott nodded.

"But where the road crosses the marsh," Crockett continued, "that's probably impassable. I don't think we'll get much mor'n half a mile further."

"I can run that."

"If the dog's run off into the woods, we may be stuck 'til dawn when we can do a proper search."

That sounded like Crockett was advising Scott to give up. *No, no way.* "Luke! Luke!" he called. "Look," Scott said, turning to Crockett, "I'm going to jog up as far as I can. Will you stay here and watch for the dog?"

"Sure, man, but—"

Before he finished his sentence, Luke emerged from the woods, raced up to Scott, planted his feet on his chest, and raced back into the woods again.

"Come on!" Scott yelled.

Where was the dog? Where was the dog? Scott ran into the woods in the direction Luke had headed. Forty feet in, he stepped into a bog and sunk halfway up to his knee. He pulled himself out.

"Let me lead!" Crockett said. "I've got a good light."

"Give it to me." He turned and grabbed it.

A couple of minutes later, Scott heard crashing ahead, and Luke came racing up and jumped on him, then ran away into the dark again. "He's found her," Scott shouted over the roar of the wind.

They had to wade through knee-deep water, push through brambles, and step over fallen trees, but then Scott reached a clearing. He stopped in his tracks.

In the beam of the flashlight, he saw a herd of ponies standing on a rise near the lighthouse. On the ground in the middle of them lay a crumpled figure. He knew right away it was Jess. *Jess!* She wasn't moving. Luke stood off to the side, panting, staying back as if aware he could spook the herd.

Scott turned to John. "We need an ambulance. Tell them to come in cold." No lights, no sirens.

Then Scott slowly made his way forward. He needed to get to her. He didn't want a panicked pony stepping on her. Rain dripped off his hair and down his neck and into his eyes. He stayed focused on her, focused on Jess.

"Whoa, mare, whoa," he said. "Easy now. Whoa, whoa." He forced himself to step slowly, steadily, though he wanted to race ahead, to touch her, to find out how hurt she was or if she...

He couldn't even think that. "Whoa, mare, whoa." Lightning flashed. A pony snorted, and slowly the ponies moved away from him, away from her, until finally—Yes!—she was clear. He ran the last few steps and dropped to his knees in the mud.

"Jess? Jess?"

52

I HEARD a familiar voice and opened my eyes. Scott. Scott! I opened my mouth but words wouldn't come.

"Oh, Jess...Jess! I've got you now. Help is on the way."

I glanced toward my side.

"I see the knife. Did Elise do this?"

I nodded slightly.

"Okay, I'll take over. I'll apply the pressure now. You can take your hand away."

It felt good to be able to move my hand. I flexed my fingers, then reached for Scott, found his jacket, and gripped it.

Was I alive? Was I really alive? I couldn't believe it.

"Luke brought me here, Jess. He saved you!"

I nodded and closed my eyes again. But I didn't let go of Scott.

———

LATER, Scott told me the whole story, about how John Crockett had helped him and how Luke had found me. And what a good idea it was to send those text messages so he could identify the motel, because that's how they found Luke and that's how Luke found me. He told me about riding with me in the ambulance through the flooded causeway, about hearing the water swishing as we went through, about seeing me, muddy, bloody, but alive and how he thanked God over and over.

Scott. Thanking God. That made me smile.

The closest hospital was almost an hour away. There, doctors sedated me, removed the knife, and patched my lung using tiny incisions and fiber-optic instruments. Impressive. They kept me in the hospital for four days to be sure I was okay. Scott stayed with me most of the time. I gave a statement to the police and so did he.

Meanwhile, the hurricane moved on, leaving behind fallen trees, washed-out roads, damaged homes and buildings, and a brilliant, impossibly blue sky.

Nate crossed over to the Eastern Shore as soon as they let him. He rescued Luke from the kennel that was his temporary housing. I know that dog was happy to get out of there. I stopped worrying about Luke once I knew Nate had him.

With the help of John Crockett and a local waterman, Nate actually did some water searches with Luke, poking around Assateague and in Tom's Cove, looking for Elise. That impressed me. He'd told me how much he hated boats. Still, he was out there, trying to help.

He found her. Luke found her. She'd drowned not far from where she'd assaulted me.

Nate broke that news to me gently at the hospital. "I'm sorry, Jess. You did your best."

I insisted on reading the medical examiner's report. Scott wasn't happy about that. He thought I should let it go and concentrate on my own recovery. But I wanted to know more. I just wasn't prepared for what I read.

Danville had identified her body. Elise had died of drowning, the report said. I read the usual details—the size of her heart, the weight of the liver, the absence of external trauma—and then I stopped short. On her right shoulder, the medical examiner had noted a heart-shaped birthmark.

I sat straight up in bed.

"What?" Scott said, alarmed.

I told him what the report said.

"And?"

"Miss Lottie's missing daughter!" I inhaled too sharply and started coughing. I grabbed my side, pressing against the pain.

He jumped up. "Calm down, calm down." He handed me my water and rubbed my back. When I stopped coughing, he said, "Elise was her daughter?"

"Oh my gosh, Scott! I can't believe it." I took another drink. "Elise told me she'd run away when she was a teenager. That her husband was older and she'd never been in contact with her parents again. I started to wonder if there was a connection, but she was telling her story and I didn't want her to stop."

"He isolated her. A classic abuser move."

"I've got to tell Miss Lottie!" I swung my legs over the side of the bed.

"Hold on! Hold on there." Scott stopped me. "What are you doing?"

"I've got to tell her!"

"Jess, wait!"

I glared at him.

He held out his hands and softened his voice. "Just wait." He took a deep breath. "Don't you think you should wait for DNA results?"

I could not argue with that.

Scott helped me get those results.

Then he drove me around after doctors released me, collecting my belongings from the motels. We stopped by Hope Ranch to say goodbye to Kate. After he'd gathered my stuff from the Chincoteague motel, I made him drive me over to Assateague, so I could say goodbye to the ponies.

The sky was a brilliant blue, cloudless, and the air hot, as it should be in early September. I watched cattle egrets and herons feeding and a couple of pony bands grazing in the marsh. They looked placid, peaceful, like they were where they were supposed to be, doing what God made them to do. In my mind, I thanked them. They'd led me to high ground. They'd helped me live.

We met Nate and Luke at a motel near Route 13. Nate had paid for adjoining rooms, one for the guys and one for me and Luke, for that night. He wanted to keep an eye on me. We'd drive home the next day.

Tears welled up in my eyes when I embraced my ecstatic dog. Scott was a little overprotective, watching me like a hawk, afraid Luke would plow into my wound and deflate my lung again. I narrowed my eyes at him.

"Don't try to get between me and my dog!"

He grinned, but I could tell he knew I was serious.

As close as I was growing to Scott, there was one story I hadn't told him. I asked if we could eat dinner in the motel room. I didn't want to admit it, but I was tired. Over a big salad for me and burgers and fries for the guys, I told them about the mist and the lights and knowing I wasn't alone. Nate stopped eating. And when I told them I realized I'd been running from God, but that He was one step ahead of me all the time, and yet with me every minute, Nate suddenly stood up. So did I, and we embraced.

Over his shoulder I saw Scott, looking like he didn't quite know what was going on. He will one day. I just know he will.

53

TWO DAYS LATER, I finally got to see Miss Lottie. Scott insisted on coming with me. I protested at first, but in the end, I was glad he was there.

Miss Lottie was barely conscious in ICU. She looked so tiny and pale. I took her hand and told her about Tamara/Elise/Ann, everything I knew. I showed her the picture of Elise, the one with her dark bob, on my cell phone. Tears escaped Miss Lottie's eyes, sliding down toward her pillow, and she squeezed my hand.

"The Lord knew you were the one to find her."

"But I found her too late!"

She patted my hand. "It's the Lord's timing, all of it. Now, I know," she said in a whisper. She motioned me closer. I put my ear near her mouth. "Thank you. Will you take care of Tiger for me?"

"Yes, of course," I said, and I kissed her cheek.

The next day, she died.

And I wept.

A MONTH LATER, I was called to the office of Rachelle Bennett, the woman I'd met once at Miss Lottie's. Turns out she was not only a member of Miss Lottie's church, but she was also a lawyer—and the executor of her will.

Miss Lottie, who lived poor, was actually pretty rich, the lawyer said. What's more, she'd left it all to me.

Me. Me, who'd resisted helping her. Me, who'd only known her for a short time. Me, who considered myself a failure for finding her daughter way too late to do any good.

Between Miss Lottie's investments and the sale of her house, I inherited over $500,000, a fortune, enough to let me stop working as a PI.

Amazing. A miracle.

But there were two jobs I needed to close out first.

———

COLTON DANVILLE. I had a lot of questions. Elise's story didn't match his reputation, so I did some digging. I confirmed that they were never legally married. Secondly, I found out that her Social Security number was wrong. It belonged to a woman who was born in 1926 and died in the 1950s.

Apparently, Danville had talked teenaged Tamara into running away with him. He soon tired of her, but as his business grew he realized he didn't know how to get out of the relationship without being implicated in identity theft, contributing to the delinquency of a minor, and other crimes. So he'd kept up the facade, while conducting a fifteen-year affair with his assistant. He'd blamed Elise for trapping him. In truth, he'd trapped himself.

Then there was Luke, sniffing around his backyard, lying down, giving me the signal that he'd detected the scent of human remains, a signal that I had ignored.

I took this information to Detective David O'Connor. We

couldn't get Danville on domestic abuse—the complainant was dead—and I wasn't sure about the other charges. But how about unauthorized burial of human remains?

All we had to go on was what Elise had told me and the testimony of a four-year-old German shepherd who could be bought with a steak. David connected me with the DA, we went to the judge, got a search warrant, and, while Danville glared at us from the back porch, we dug up what was left of a four-month, unborn baby.

He got probation, but he lost his reputation and his real estate license was suspended. That, at least, represented a certain level of justice.

———

Susan Larson.

State police detectives found numerous problems with the investigation, as I had suggested. So they went back to look at the death of Susan's second husband, Tyler Burns, who died of anaphylactic shock after exposure to shellfish. Susan had collected a cool $100,000 in life insurance on him. Finally, they tracked down her first husband, who, it turned out, had filed a restraining order against her after repeated domestic assaults.

"That woman, she ain't crazy," he told investigators, "she's just mean. She knows what she's doing."

Armed with the search warrant McCoy had initiated, investigators found a white Ford F-150 in her garage, and a black brush guard hidden behind it. The paint on the brush guard was a match to the black smudge on my old Jeep. Also in the garage? My old camera.

So, they had her on vehicular assault, attempted murder, theft, and trespassing. As the charges piled up, Susan Larson became enraged. When an examination of her computer turned up Google searches on "how to make a murder look like a _suicide," detectives had her. Soon she had implicated herself in Bob's death.

Justice for Bob Larson—and his brother Sam. And me.

Oh, and how'd Susan know the PIT maneuver? The investigators asked her! Between husbands she'd dated a cop. One snowy day, in an empty parking lot, he had showed her how to do it.

———

HAVING CLEARED MY PI CASES, I was now free to pursue other career options. In Northern Virginia. Near Scott.

I'd seen the power of fear in Elise's life, how, isolated from family and friends, she'd become unbalanced. Fear had overcome her, had driven her to panic, and ended her life.

My fear had controlled me long enough. In the middle of that storm, lying in the mud with a knife in my side, barely able to breathe, I'd tasted something different. Love. Perfect love. The kind that drives out fear.

I didn't want to run anymore. In fact, I was ready to dance.

ACKNOWLEDGMENTS

No author flies solo. I am so grateful for the many people who have generously provided engine tweaking, ground control, and routine maintenance (not to mention instrumentation when things got foggy) to help this book take off.

Kim Merida and my children grew up in church together. Now a busy pastor's wife and mom with five children of her own, Kim introduced me to Hope Reins and connected me with her Wake Forest book club. Anyone who thinks book clubs are sedate hasn't met Kim's group! Kim's graciousness has blessed me tremendously.

Kim's sister, Priscilla Arthur, is involved with Called to Peace, a ministry serving victims of domestic abuse. Through Priscilla I learned that abuse may be hard to identify, both as a victim and a bystander. The website, calledtopeace.org, is a good place to find information about this sad reality — and hope.

Retired FBI Special Agent Dru Wells not only shares her Bureau expertise with me, she uses her sharp analytical skills to catch many of my errors, grammatical, geographical, and logical. Thank you again, Dru!

Sharon Johnson and Jessica Burnside of Dogs East Search &

Rescue, have patiently taught me much about SAR. I so admire their dedication to serving the community. If I ever get lost, I hope Dogs East comes to find me!

Darcy Cole and her husband Steve (DSCphotography.net) are passionate about ponies, specifically, the Chincoteague ponies that live on Assateague Island off the Virginia coast. They willingly shared their extensive knowledge with me over lunch one rainy day on Chincoteague. To the delight of thousands of people they post pony pictures on their website and Facebook page. Watching stallions compete for mares and new foals arrive through the eye of Darcy's long lens is a great joy.

Kim Tschirret and Lory Schuler of Hope Reins opened up the world of equine therapy to me. I never knew the role horses could play in healing deep psychological wounds. The work they and their volunteers do at Hope Reins is a blessing to the horses they rescue, to the children they help, and to their families. Just reading the stories at hopereins.org will make you smile.

I appreciate Barbara Scott's careful editing and the support of my literary agent, Janet Grant of Books & Such.

My daughter Becky Chappell's sharp editing skills and diligent attention to detail chiseled the rough edges off of this manuscript several times. She's the one who took it from Word document to actual book. Becky, I appreciate you so much!

Soli Deo gloria

QUESTIONS FOR DISCUSSON

1. Why did Jess choose to move away from her friends? Could you identify with her decision? Would you have advised her to do that?
2. Have you ever had a close friend move away? How did that impact you?
3. In both "All That I Dread" and "The Fear That Chases Me," Jess and Nate Tanner are close friends. Have you ever had a close but platonic friend of the opposite sex? What was that like?'
4. Scott experiences a traumatic incident when he is forced to stop a shooter in a store. What part of that experience was hardest for him?
5. Seventy percent of adult Americans have experienced some kind of traumatic event in their lives—the death of someone close, a serious car accident, random violence, and so on. What did Scott do to process the shooting incident trauma that was good? What did he do that was not helpful?
6. Jess has found some healing in her relationship with Luke, her dog. Scott begins to process long-buried

grief when he starts interacting with a horse. Has an animal ever become emotionally meaningful to you? In what way?

7. Colton Danville appears to be a pillar of the community. A wealthy, successful businessman and philanthropist, he is hiding a dark secret. Would you have guessed he was an abusive husband?

8. Elise was an "invisible" woman trapped in a dysfunctional, abusive relationship. What could people in her community have done to help her? Anything?

9. Jess used self-protection to fence off not only romantic relationships, and also her relationship with Miss Lottie. How did Jess grow over the course of that friendship?

10. When did Jess's emotional protection begin to crack in her interactions with Scott? What made her start opening up to a relationship with him?

11. What happened to Jess in the marsh, when she was stabbed? What did she experience? Have you ever experienced anything like that?

12. Where do you think Jess's life is headed now?

ABOUT THE AUTHOR

Linda J. White is a former journalist and author of multiple mystery/suspense novels. Her books have won the HOLT Medallion and have been finalists for National Reader's Choice Awards. Her late husband was a video producer-director at the FBI Academy for decades. Mom of three, grandmother of five, Linda lives near Quantico, VA. A speaker and Bible study teacher, Linda also enjoys working with her Shetland sheepdog, Keira, and spending time with her grandkids, especially on Chincoteague.

Website: lindajwhite.net
Email: lindajwhitebooks@gmail.com
Facebook: LindaJWhiteBooks
Twitter: @rytn4hm

ALSO BY LINDA J. WHITE

Bloody Point

Battered Justice

Seeds of Evidence

Sniper!

Words of Conviction

The Tiger's Cage

All That I Dread

Made in the USA
Middletown, DE
20 August 2021

46499127R00198